*Dedicated to the memory
of Northwest Florida historian*

Marlene Womack

Author of:

*War Comes to Florida's Northern Gulf
  Coast
Anchor of the Bay
The Magic of Cape San Blas
Centennial Stories
The Bay Country
Moonshine Mayhem
Ghost Towns, Mysteries & Tombstone Tales*

Also by Sue Riddle Cronkite

LOUETTE'S WAKE

~ ~ ~

Copyright © 2020 by Sue Riddle Cronkite

ISBN - 13: 978-0-9724101-4-4
ISBN - 10: 0-9724101-4-7

For information contact:

Sue Riddle Cronkite
New Hope Press:
2715 St. Hwy. 85
Geneva, AL 36340

E-mail cronkitesue@gmail.com
Telephone (850) 653-6965.

4

White Sheets

A Wiregrass Series Novel

Blessings !

By

Sue Riddle Cronkite

Sue Riddle Cronkite

New Hope
Press

Cover design by Merri Rose Fink
merrifink@yahoo.com

The Wiregrass

. . . where the trees always murmur, where the
butterflies are enormous, where plants that
eat insects grow in moist places, where
alligators inhabit the slowly moving
waters of the rivers.
Laura Ingalls Wilder

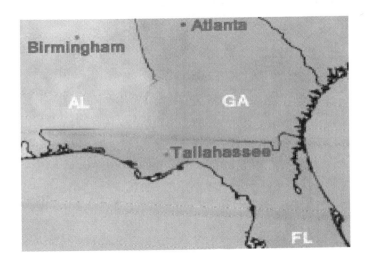

Words and expressions common in frontier times
reflected Wiregrass settlers' origins. Accents were
musical or guttural, high-pitched or low-pitched, slow or
fast.

My goal is to preserve the idiosyncrasies of a
vernacular still spoken in the Wiregrass area, as in much
of the South. The expressive language is an American
treasure.

Outcries Against an Unpopular War

Protesters against the Vietnam War moved across the United States in droves in the 1960s and 1970s. In large cities and in Washington, D.C. many groups held rallies, sit-ins, marches, and parades. Young men flung draft cards onto bonfires, and many fled to Canada and other countries.

They were called flower children and hippies, cursed for laziness and irresponsibility, and derided for the idea of free speech. Many students added their voices at colleges and universities and joined caravans crisscrossing the country to join those railing against the mounting death toll of American soldiers in the rice paddies of far-away Vietnam.

White Sheets tells of a group of protesters aiming toward a peace march in Atlanta, who take a wrong turn and find themselves in a sheltered community near the Choctawhatchee River in Northwest Florida. Many residents want the uninvited young people with slogans and peace signs, gone.

Others try to help them, offering food and compassion. Some have sons slogging through the trenches in Vietnam, and sons and daughters traveling and demonstrating with protesters.

White Sheets reflects how people in regular neighborhoods lived in the 1960s. The big news was in the trenches and at home in the protests. This is an effort to help readers see up close how ordinary people were touched and changed in interesting and sometimes unexpected ways.

Pidge

Chapter One

School bus tires slapped asphalt in a singsong that
went something like "Read that book. Write that report."
Wild horses couldn't divert Pidge's attention until the last
page. Words pulled her deep into the tangled world of
other people, other places, other lives.

Pidge's real name was Margaret, shortened to Peg,
then Pidge by her brother Luke at two years old. Now
poised on the edge of teen years, she was serious about
most things, with an active curiosity and imagination.

When the bus slowed and the brakes screeched at
the west end of the Choctawhatchee River bridge she
pushed a tendril of brown hair out of her face and
scrunched farther down in her seat.

If it hadn't been for voices yelling "Hippies go
home," and "flower children," Pidge wouldn't have
dragged her eyes from the printed page. She grasped the
back of the seat in front of her, still reading.

"Look, long-haired guys, and barefoot girls! Lots
of them." Her seat-mate Lena raised the window.

Mr. Bob, the bus driver, propped himself on the
top step at the door. "Wow! What a cool Volkswagen
bus."

"Maybe we'd better not watch," Lena whispered.
"My mom'd have a cow if I did something like that."

"What?" Pidge couldn't resist. She turned down
the page in *Little Women* where Amy destroyed her

sister's journal, put the book on the seat, and joined Lena at a window on the north side of the bus.

As she stared Pidge put her hands over her sister Julie's eyes. "You're too young for this," she whispered.

A girl standing beside a pickup truck switched her long, dark hair back and forth, then jerked on a pair of cut-off jeans under her red and yellow flowered skirt, dropped the skirt and stuffed it into a duffel bag.

"Whoo." Lena fanned her face. "She's changing clothes right there in front of God and everybody."

As Mr. Bob and the students watched, the girl pulled a tie-dyed tee-shirt over her head, shoved it into the duffel bag, then slipped on a tiny top that stopped just above her bellybutton, prompting whistles and catcalls from the students. She picked up the duffel bag and carried it into a nearby tent.

"Whoa! Turn your eyes away children." Mr. Bob called out. "Don't stare at that girl!" He plopped down in the driver's seat and pulled a blue handkerchief from his overall bib pocket. He swiped his red face and cranked the bus.

Pidge looked around, students had switched their eyes toward a converted school bus covered in peace signs, doves, hearts, flowers, and words: "Peace, not war," and "Love, not hate."

"Look at that skinny boy's Afro hair," said Lena. "It's as big around as a foot-tub."

"What does the round sign with a slash through it mean?" A thin middle-schooler called out in a high-pitched voice. "Or the swirly one with two sides, like spoons stuck together?"

"How should I know?" The bus driver shook his head. "This stuff is as new to me as it is to y'all."

Pidge leaned out the window and watched as more cars, trucks and vans pulled into the field beside the Choctawhatchee River, right in the same spot her parents

8

usually took her, brother Luke, and sister Julie fishing. She saw a young man on the bank with a trot line folded over his shoulder, like her dad used when he caught a mess of catfish for her mom to cook over an open fire.

"Who are those people?" called out one of the younger children.

"Peacenik's!" Mr. Bob answered.

"Looks like a revival. Without the benches." Pidge shook her head.

"Yeah, or a carnival," Lena rested a chin on Pidge's shoulder. "Without the elephants, or the hurly-burly music."

"Enough!" Mr. Bob called out. "Shut the windows." It was immediately quieter, and hotter. He put the big yellow bus into gear and pulled off the grass onto Highway 2.

"Don't go!" Roly Poly, the seventh-grade school bully called out. "I wanna see this."

"We're out of here. Sit down, Roland. All of you. Sit." The gears groaned and grunted as the school bus headed west.

Pidge ran to the back of the bus, leaned over the last seat and strained to see through the smeared back window. As she eased down, her eyes latched onto a girl about her age and a woman in the family way, standing at a campfire.

Pidge stared. Their eyes met. Frances? How could it be Frances? As far as Pidge knew, Frances had moved with her family to some 'desert' state a couple of years ago. Pidge watched the girl watching her as the bus crawled away.

"Lena," she called out.

But Lena was lost in her book again. "Hmmm?"

Pidge held her eyes on the girl until she no longer could see her or the camp. She shook her head. *Why on earth would Frances be with a bunch of hippies?*

"That was Frances." Pidge went forward and took her assigned seat, smoothed out the turn-down marking her place in *Little Women.*

"Frances?" Lena half leaned toward her.

Pidge jabbed her finger against Lena's shoulder. "Frances, the girl who moved away in fifth grade."

"Lived in the old Rocker house?"

"That one." Pidge shook her head, as if to straighten out her thoughts. "She moved off in 1968, it's now '70. What's she doing at a Vietnam War protester camp?"

Lena carefully closed her book, then looked up at Pidge. "You're not kidding! You saw Frances?"

"Yes."

"Or you saw somebody who looked just like her. Lanky, dirty-blonde hair, hollow-eyed."

"Her. It was her."

"How can you be sure?" Lena's eyes strayed toward the book in her lap.

"We recognized each other."

"Forget it. If it was Frances, she'll come down to Daylight Grocery to see you or come by my house." Lena started reading again.

"Yeah." Pidge slid down in the seat. What could she do? Should she go down to the river field to see if the girl was really Frances? She had a feeling, as if someone had walked across her grave. Like mama always said. "I don't know about this." She shrugged her shoulders.

"Me neither." Lena leaned forward. "We're almost home."

Pidge peered around the curve as Mr. Bob stopped and opened the door at Roly Poly's house. The seventh-grade bully sauntered past Pidge's seat, poked Pidge's ankle, then slapped a wad of chewed bubble-gum onto her shoulder.

10

"Ugh." Pidge scraped at the gooey stuff. Her hair had already attached itself to the gum.

"Here." Lena stood up and dug a dirty handkerchief from her pocket.

Next stop was for the Burns children, then Mills' and Taylors. Pidge swiped at the sticky mess on her shoulder. She could see the Daylight Grocery and the big white rock on the northeast corner, where Florida Highway 2 crossed the Geneva-Westville road.

The shoulder-tall white limestone rock shimmered, dust devils swirled in the dirt at the edge of the concrete. Pidge waited for the bus door to open, jumped out and ran into the store, yelling "Mom! Mom!"

Rose

Chapter Two

As the bus left Bethlehem school, Pidge's mother Rose, minding the store for the day, prepared to clean the butcher block. Swabbing the surface with a bleach-soaked rag, she glanced at the clock.

Near the dairy cooler a barefoot shopper shrieked "What is this?" The woman, wearing a man's dress shirt with the sleeves rolled up, held a round of butter.

The slow words of Linda, the preacher's wife, sort of rolled around the room. "It's butter, from a mold."

"It's got a shell carved on it."

Linda reached a long fingernail into the beehive bun of her bright blonde hair and scratched.

The customer made as if to put the butter back.

"No." Linda grabbed her by the arm and pulled her over to the bread counter. She opened a round loaf of homemade raisin bread, broke off a piece, smeared it with butter and stuck it up to the bewildered face. "There! Eat that!"

Rose swiped a chocolate-colored curl from her forehead and picked up an envelope from the desk in the corner. Another letter from the Department of Agriculture, Food Stamp Program:

> This is not a cease and desist letter, it is a warning. Do not sell toothpaste, soap, light bulbs, or toilet tissue for food stamps. The food stamp program is for FOOD ONLY.

She thumbtacked the letter to the bulletin board on the wall behind her.

"Them people again." It was a statement, not a question. Linda continued to scratch beneath her helmet of hair while the stranger gulped down the bread and butter.

Rose sighed. "They don't understand. These old people around here who need food stamps also need to take a bath, brush their teeth and wipe. The stamps should be for other necessities, besides just for food."

"I put some toilet tissue and soap in the Free Box, with other stuff. Good idea you had, Rose."

"I don't know what I'd do with bent cans if it wasn't for the Free Box. People can use the food in the bent cans, even if I can't sell it."

"I just want you to know, Rose, that you coming home to live, bringing Josh Reed and the children, was a good thing."

"Why thank you, Linda." Rose was surprised and pleased. "When Josh retired from the Army, it seemed only natural. Course he got back into the military by signing up to work at the National Guard Armory."

Linda wasn't through. "That Pidge is a delightful little tomboy and Luke is becoming a handsome young man. Sweet Julie might be my favorite though."

Rose looked at Linda. Commentary was not Linda's strongest trait. But the preacher's wife didn't look like she was up to anything. *Is she about to ask me to be on a committee at Church?*

Linda shook her head. "I don't know what this neighborhood would do without the Reed family." She pulled money from her purse. "Might as well pay you for the round of raisin bread and butter that starving girl is wolfing down."

"Be glad for you to." Rose smiled. "That's a good deed."

Linda shifted the purse strap on her shoulder. "I've got to go with Preacher Willy to make a call. My husband is a busy man, what with people being sick all the time."

The goat bell hanging over the door tinkled as Linda left.

We could use a prayer about the sudden influx of hippie young folks down at the River Field, thought Rose. She slid cardboard boxes of canned peaches over by her chair and opened them with a box cutter.

The bare-footed girl chewed slowly on her feast of bread and butter.

Rose heard the squeal of the school bus brakes. Aha! Her children! Rose was happiest when they were around. Their energy and enthusiasm recharged her batteries. She wondered if other mothers felt the way she did about her children. Surely, they must.

Rose heard a groan as the school bus door strained to open.

"Mom!" Rose watched through the window. Pidge ran around her brother, side-stepped her sister and ran toward the store.

"I'm here." Rose caught her at the door and hugged her. "What's that on your shoulder?"

"Just some gum."

"Gum?"

"That's not what I ran to tell you, Mom. I saw Frances at the river field."

"Our Frances? Your friend Frances?"

"Yep. She was standing beside a black-haired woman in the family way. The woman didn't look like her mother, though."

"Not many people look like Frances mama." Rose laughed. "Go change your blouse. Put this one in the freezer so we can peel the gum off when it's cold."

Luke and Julie were in the kitchen. "You want a tomato sandwich?" Luke slathered mayonnaise on slices of white bread.

"Sure. Be right back." Pidge changed her clothes and returned to stuff her shirt with gum on it into the freezer.

Julie munched on her peanut butter and jelly sandwich. "What were you excited about back there?"

"I saw Frances at the river field."

"She moved away." Luke handed her a sandwich, mayonnaise and tomatoes between two slices white bread.

"Why would Frances be with those people?" Julie munched as she opened the door to go into the store.

"That's what I'd like to know." Pidge took a bite and rolled her eyes. "Ummmm. Good."

"Tell Mom I'm at the pumps," Luke ran around the side of the building to the gas tanks in front of the grocery store.

Pidge finished her sandwich and returned. "Luke's at the pumps," she told her mother.

"What this about Frances?" Rose pulled another box to her and sliced it open.

"Yes," Julie chimed in as she placed cans on a shelf.

Pidge reached into the ice-filled cooler box for a Nehi drink, snicked it on the bottle opener on the side of the cooler and poured a packet of salted peanuts into the icy liquid, all while her mouth ran like a buzz saw.

"People were putting up tents and dragging in limbs from under oak trees. Cars and trucks and an old school bus raised up dust all over the place. Lots of people. I swear the girl I saw was Frances."

"I haven't heard from her folks since they moved away to California." Rose closed the box cutter and stretched up on her toes to place it on a high shelf. "I wrote them a couple of times but got no answers."

Pidge munched thoughtfully on a mouthful of peanuts and chased them down with the grape-flavored drink. "Oh, I froze my brain."

Rose pulled her daughter close and rubbed her temples. "Maybe the girl just looked like Frances."

Rose squatted to roll price stickers onto the tops of corned beef cans. "It's been two years since they moved. Frances may appear different from the last time we saw her. She was ten; now she'd be twelve. You, yourself are certainly larger and more grown-up than when you were ten."

Pidge shifted the labeled cans into the front of the grocery buggy. "I don't know. She did look bigger, but still looked like herself when she lived here. She was tall and lanky, with round eyes that stared me square in the face. Seemed like she recognized me."

As her mother emptied boxes and stamped on prices, Pidge moved cans to shelves where Julie worked, then flattened the boxes and piled them in the small storage room outside the back door.

"And she was skinny. She was so skinny she looked like a starving orphan, you know, like those children they show on television to get people to send money."

Anger flashed in Rose's eyes. "Nobody should have to go hungry these days."

"Could be Frances' folks couldn't buy groceries." Pidge chewed on a few left-behind peanuts from the Nehi bottle.

"Don't forget to put these bent cans in the Free Box. Some of those war protesters may be running out of food, and money." Rose said.

16

"Yep," said Pidge. "I wonder if Frances is related to the pretty girl she was standing beside." Pidge pushed the buggy with the bent cans toward the door.

"Your dad went to check on why there's a continuous stream of campers pulling into the river field. He hasn't told me what he learned." Rose stood up. "When the first one, Aaron, asked if he, his wife, and two other couples could camp by the river for a few days, I understood they'd be moving on to Georgia. I wouldn't have given my permission if I'd known such a flood of protesters were right behind them."

"Looked like more than a hundred people to me," said Pidge. "Lots of cars and trucks pulling in; a neat Volkswagen bus with all kinds of signs on it."

Rose thought about her husband Joshua's many years in the U. S. Army, and retirement was good here in the community where Rose had grown up. But when the big to-do over the United States getting involved in the Vietnam War started, he had joined the National Guard. Most of the time he was up in Geneva, the town just over the Florida-Alabama line, running the Armory, keeping records.

When Rose talked with Josh about "hippies," "peaceniks," and "flower children," he told her the labels were insulting and implied that young people didn't want to work, but wanted to walk around lazy, carrying flowers. "They're against this country sending soldiers, young people like them, to Vietnam. Their gatherings are anti-war protests."

Rose understood. She felt the same way and hadn't thought twice about telling the three couples they could stay at the river field while the pregnant wife rested. It hadn't come up that more hippies were following behind them to squat on the property beside the river.

The goat bell tinkled. Rose looked up.

"Could I help you?"

A tall young man with long brown hair, wearing one hoop earring, a red and orange tee shirt and patched, bell-bottom jeans, stood uncertainly just inside the door. "What is this place?" he asked. "This town?"

"New Hope." Rose straightened the stack of Ms. Leahs' homemade peanut brittle on the counter. "It's not a town; it's an unincorporated community."

"Oh." His eyes roamed around the room, lighted on the big stalk of bananas hanging from the center of the ceiling. "Never saw a stalk of bananas that long. Looks like clusters climbing up a tree limb."

"They're a nickel each, unless you eat one of the really, really ripe ones. They're free."

After carefully selecting an overripe banana, the young man sat on the tall stool near the banana stalk.

"I'm from Oklahoma. I've seen little towns, but this is more like a crossroads in the country."

"That's exactly what it is." Rose leaned against the counter.

"Bunches of people coming in down at the campground. Some from Stanford University, all the way across the country. That mournful sound I heard when I pulled in this morning, sort of like a cow bellowing; what is it?"

"It's the whistle at the cotton mill in Geneva; blows at six, two, and ten o'clock, calling people to work." She shifted and rested her elbows on the counter. "We have hoop cheese, all kinds of soft drinks, and moon pies if you're hungry. And Ms. Leah just brought in this world-class peanut brittle, made in her own kitchen."

"Oh," he scratched his chin, swung his head around. "Where's the ice cream?"

Rose walked from behind the counter and slid open a glass door to a freezer.

A smile spread across his face. He pulled a half-gallon container of strawberry ice cream out of the cooler.

"Far out! Is there a gallon?" He leaned down to peer inside.

Rose helped him look. "Only half-gallon cartons."

"All the way from home, I've been craving ice cream. I'm going to eat a whole carton." He licked his lips.

Rose selected a wooden paddle from a jar and handed it to him. "No, no." He pulled out a large Army-issue metal spoon from his back pocket. "I've got my own spoon. My old man kept it from his tour in Korea." He handed money to Rose. She gave him change and he stuffed it in his pocket. "Is it all right for me to sit on the magic rock?"

"Sure," Rose walked to the screen door. "It's a big chunk of limestone. Been there as long as I can remember. Why do you call it a magic rock?"

"I was looking at that thing when I drove up. It shimmers, sort of in waves of colors."

Rose and Pidge laughed.

"It's not hot enough yet, but it sounds like you may be having a heat stroke," Rose told him. "I've never noticed that rock shimmer."

He hugged the strawberry ice cream. "This should cure whatever ails me. I may be back for that carton of vanilla." He chuckled as he walked solemnly toward the massive limestone boulder.

Rose watched from the door as he settled on the rock and scooped ice cream into his mouth like a drowning man gulping air.

"Mom, back to Frances." Pidge walked behind the counter as Rose resumed stamping prices on cans.

Rose watched as Pidge took the last swig of soft drink and rolled it around in her mouth.

"I don't need you right now. Why don't you ride your bike down there and see if the girl is really Frances?"

Pidge sucked in her breath. "Sure, I could do that," she said casually. "Can I take her a moon pie?"

"I don't see why not and throw some of those potatoes in the bike basket. Add a can of corned beef." She pointed to a stack of unpriced canned goods. "Get a head of cabbage from the hamper by the door. And check out the Free Box. I don't think there's anything but green beans in it, maybe some magazines and newspapers. There'll be more bent cans when the rest of the boxes are unpacked."

Pidge filled a bag and rolled her bicycle to the big white rock.

The fellow shoveling melting ice cream into his mouth smiled and winked at Pidge.

Pidge

Chapter Three

At the highway, Pidge made a choice. There were two ways to the river. She could take the long way—the most sensible route—that ran south beside Limestone Creek, past Mt. Ida Methodist Church. The shorter way, although more dangerous, was a straight shot down Highway 2. The State kept bushes and trees cleaned off the right-of-way. The danger in taking the shorter route was that halfway along the two miles from the store to the river was Roly Poly Johnson's house. Could be this time the aggravating rascal wouldn't see her. She decided to take her chances.

Luck was not Pidge's friend on this day. Near the bully's house, sure enough, there he was.

"Where you going Pidgie Midjie? Oink, oink, whatcha got in your basket?" The meanest boy on the school bus was even worse in front of his own home. He shoved Pidge's handlebars, which was no surprise. She'd actually learned how to lower her injury rate by swinging the bike around when he did that.

"None of your business." Pidge aimed the bag of groceries at the side of his head and stomped his foot at the same time.

She jumped on her bike and plopped the bag into the basket. *Uh oh, smashed moon pie.*

"I'll get you for this," he called.

"I'm scaaareed." The wind whipped her words as she peddled toward the river.

"You'd better stay away from the hippie camp," his taunt trailed her as she turned down the dirt road her grandfather had built when he homesteaded the stretch of land along the Choctawhatchee River.

The field was spotted with tents. Pidge could see a faded school bus converted to a bunkhouse, and the Volkswagen bus decorated with peace signs and slogans. Young people dragged bundles, duffle bags, lanterns, hibachis, tents, and poles, from pickup trucks and vans, jostling one another in their haste. A profusion of sounds rolled like waves; voices called, motors revved, dogs barked, hammers clanged.

Pidge aimed her bike toward a tent near the pole barn and shed where her dad kept plows and tools. The bike bumped up and down as it struggled over last year's corn rows. A little boy flashed right in front of her, grabbed her leg and screamed like a banshee. By the time she stopped, he was gone. She pushed the bike after that to keep from hitting children, dogs, and barefoot people milling about. Both men and women were hard at work; some setting up tents, some digging holes for campfires.

A pretty girl wearing leather sandals which looked a lot like Mexican huaraches, thick brown hair kinked around her face, walked past carrying a large box.

"What do you call those?" Pidge pointed.

"Jesus sandals."

"Wow," said Pidge. "I want some, just like them."

"I found these at a little head shop in Napa Valley."

"Oh. Nice." *What the heck is a head shop?*

Pidge watched the girl put down the box and pick up another. A young guy hammered curved iron bars into the ground. Another one attached tent ropes. A blonde-haired girl, wearing a bright red headband, walked by with a baby strapped in front of her, its mouth attached to her nipple.

22

Pidge stared. *Lord a'mighty. Right out in front of people.* The girl smiled as she came near.

Pidge squeaked out, "So that's how you feed your baby."

"Only way," the girl said as she passed by.

Pidge climbed on an upturned wooden box and peered into the rusted old school bus. All seats had been removed, except two in front. Bunks took the place of seats on one side and the other side held a couch, an ice box, a stand with a hibachi on it, hanging rods for clothes. Every inch looked lived in.

As she stepped off the wooden box, she bumped into a boy she guessed to be about fourteen, her brother Luke's age. He had a shocking mop of red hair and friendly blue eyes.

"Sorry," she said. "Who are you?"

"I'm Arthur," he told her. "My folks joined the peace train last night. We're putting our tent over there," he pointed. "I'm about ready to crash. Where are you staying?"

"I'm Pidge. I'm not a camper." She remembered hearing parts of a song about a peace train. The words popped out. "Peace train bound for glory. . . Peace train. . . ."

Arthur picked up a line from the Cat Stevens song: "Dreaming about the world as one. . ."

Pidge reached out her hand. "Nice song."

They shook hands and laughed. "Glide on . . . peace train . . ."

"Nice to meet you," Arthur picked up a bucket, sloshing it as he walked toward the tent where his parents shifted boxes and unpacked cooking utensils.

"You too." Pidge watched as noisy vehicles rushed onto the field, gears meshing, motors growling. The crowd seemed to be increasing.

23

A large group swayed and snapped fingers as a young man with long hair and a beard slapped his guitar like he was mad at it. This music sounded familiar too, like the stuff her father switched the radio away from and the TV called "Beat."

Pidge aimed herself and her bike toward the tent where she'd seen the girl that looked like Frances. It was a little oasis of quiet in an otherwise noisy encampment. She called out "hello," and peeked in at camp cots and supplies spaced around like in a real home. Sketches of trees, flowers and sunsets hung on the center pole.

"Hello," a voice echoed hers and the girl expecting a baby came from behind a curtain in the rear of the tent. Straight black hair hung down her back and she stared at Pidge with startling blue eyes.

"Oh." She stopped. "Could I help you?"

"I was looking for a girl I saw from the school bus earlier today. She was with you outside this tent."

"She's not staying here." Seeing Pidge's expression of disappointment, she apologized, "I'm sorry. She was camped down near the spring yesterday. She carried water and ate supper with me."

The woman rubbed her bulging abdomen. "I haven't seen her since. I've been inside all day. What do you want with her?"

"I thought she might be Frances, a friend of mine who moved away. We were pen pals for a while, but we've lost touch."

"That's terrible. I'm Jasmine." The girl held out a pale hand. Her skin glowed white in the afternoon sun.

"I'm Pidge. Glad to meet you."

"Sorry about your friend."

"Aw, that's all right. Could be her dad wouldn't let her write me. He didn't like me much anyway. Said I was too mouthy." A chuckle bubbled up of its own accord.

Jasmine laughed. "You want me to walk with you to their tent?" She grabbed a tin bucket from a nail on a nearby persimmon tree. "I need water from the spring."

"Sure." Pidge leveled the bicycle kickstand. "Will my bike be all right here?"

"Put it in the tent, just in case," Jasmine told her.

Pidge gathered the bag with potatoes, cabbage, corned beef, green beans and the slightly squashed banana moon pie from the bicycle basket. "I brought these for Frances. If it's not her, maybe the other girl would want them. She looked like she could use a good meal."

"I wouldn't be surprised." Jasmine walked beside her. "Lots of hungry people coming in and most of them have been driving a long while. My husband Aaron and I, with two other couples, stopped here day before yesterday. These new ones just keep coming. We didn't invite them. I'm worried Aaron's uncle won't have room for all this many people in his field when we get there."

"Why are you going to his uncle's?"

"So we can be near Atlanta for the peace marches."

"Peace marches?"

"Yes. You *have* heard about the protest rallies against the Vietnam War?"

"Well, sort of." Pidge lifted her shoulders and let them drop. "But I thought it was all someplace far away, until I saw you guys from the school bus window."

"Oh." Jasmine breathed in deep and shook her head.

"Are you okay?" Pidge asked her.

"Just a little tired. But I can make it to the spring and back."

On the south side of the field an area had been cleared all the way to a cypress grove at the edge of the river. Farther north persimmon trees were scattered about the field.

25

Pidge and Jasmine walked beside the fence where blackberry plants bloomed. Briars grew all around the edge of the field and on the north side a row of blueberry bushes already had little blue and green heads hanging down.

As they passed the blackberry bushes, a bramble tangled in Jasmine's skirt. "Oh!"

Pidge knelt and pulled the edge of the flowered skirt away from the brambles. "At least the stickers didn't get to your legs."

"Those look scary." Jasmine moved onto higher ground.

They walked to the edge of the field, circling more tents. At the lean-to built from two-by-fours and wooden paneling, her dad's metal drums in which he kept fertilizer and pesticides had been removed and were stacked against the outside wall.

"My dad plows around the blackberries just like he does the blueberries. Says they taste better wild, but we could do without the thorns."

"Your dad!" Jasmine's arms flew up. She dropped the empty water bucket. "Then this is your family's field?"

"Actually, my mom inherited it from her parents."

"Tell them we won't be here long. My husband had our group stop here because I wasn't feeling well. He's gone now to look for a doctor."

"How long before the baby's due?"

"I'm not exactly sure."

Pidge picked up the water bucket and put the bag of groceries in it. "How can you not be sure? What did your doctor tell you?"

"I, uh, haven't been to a doctor. But I think I've still got a few weeks. A month, maybe . . . Closer to a couple of weeks."

Oh, Lord, thought Pidge. "My mom is a midwife. She could help you figure it out, but she always tells women to see a doctor, to be sure there's nothing wrong." This girl was pretty, but she sure sounded dumb about babies, and so near her time to have one.

"We ought not to be here more than a few days."

"I'm sure my folks will work out something about camping in the field," Pidge told her.

The troubled look left Jasmine's face and was replaced by a radiant smile.

Pidge got a sinking feeling in her stomach. Some of what she had been hearing about the protesters began to come together like pieces of a puzzle. Most people around the community were against the anti-war movement. They were angry that college students were holding sit-ins on campuses.

A path from the field to the spring had been cleared. A tent smaller than Jasmine's was tied down under a huge water oak dripping with grandfather moss. Buckets and shovels lay about. And even though Jasmine called out, nobody answered.

"They may be up where the guy is playing a guitar and singing" Pidge told her. "I looked for Frances but didn't hang around."

Glossy-leaved magnolias and oak trees draped with gray-green Spanish moss lined the path to the spring beside a huge cypress tree.

"This is such a beautiful place, so peaceful. Makes me sleepy to hear spring water bubbling." Jasmine crossed her arms over her bulging tummy. "Sounds like a song I can't quite catch. Guess you been here before?"

"Many times. My grandpa put the barrel staves around the spring flow. We call it Little Indian Spring. See how the water branches off toward the river? It's like magic. I played around it while my dad plowed the field."

"I love it," said Jasmine. "I'll sketch it so I can remember this spot."

"So you're the artist who drew those neat pictures in the tent," Pidge said.

"There are stories about Two Toe Tom, a big alligator from Sand Hammock Pond, coming around Little Indian Spring. I haven't seen him myself, but people claim they have. Some say old Two Toe thinks the Geneva Cotton Mill whistle is a female alligator giving a mating call, and he bellows right back," she laughed. "My dad said Two Toe is a myth, but people believe in him. He lost three toes on his right front leg to a trap. There are lots of sightings of his tracks along rivers and creeks, and right along in here."

Pidge handed the bag of groceries to Jasmine and cupped the bucket under the bubbling spring water.

"An alligator?" Jasmine looked around and stepped away from the spring.

"Aw, we're not afraid of alligators here," Pidge told her. "We just watch out for them. They won't bother you if you don't get too close."

Pidge carried the bucket of water and Jasmine carried the groceries as they searched for Frances.

"There are other things, like snakes, to be afraid of where we're from in Texas." Jasmine held to her skirt. "Suppose it's that way wherever a person goes."

They passed a group of men digging a hole beside the outhouse. "That's for trash and garbage," Jasmine explained. "My husband Aaron told them not to scatter stuff around."

"What did the girl standing beside you say her name was?" Pidge asked,

"She said the people she's with told her not to tell anyone her name."

"That's strange. Maybe she's Frances after all. Maybe she's been kidnapped or something."

"Could be, or maybe not," said Jasmine. "They say everybody's got a double."

They walked past a crowd gathered around a long-haired musician singing and picking a guitar. His song ended abruptly with a long wail . . . *Scary, like a panther's cry,* thought Pidge. She and Jasmine asked if anybody had seen the girl, but nobody had. They promised to tell Frances to contact Pidge at the crossroads store.

At the edge of the field they walked along the fence past more persimmon trees, wild plums, lowbush myrtle, sassafras, gallberry, and scrub oak. "She'd have plenty of places to hide," said Pidge. "Or, she could climb a tree. The magnolias and sweet gums have low limbs, and some of the live oaks just north of the spring have hollows deep enough for a person to hide in."

"I don't understand why she would want to stay out of sight from you. If she is Frances, wouldn't she have recognized you?"

"I thought so. She stared straight into my eyes."

Once they arrived back at Jasmine's tent, Pidge told her to keep the bag of groceries. "Maybe you could give them to her if you see her. If not, use them yourself. Frances looked like she could use a good meal."

"She came around in the afternoon yesterday and ate with me about dusk. I'll go ahead and wash these potatoes and cut up the cabbage. I'll cook corned beef and cabbage . . . I have bread from yesterday."

"This poor moon pie is a little smushed," Pidge apologized.

"It'll be perfect for dessert." Jasmine leaned to give her new friend a hug. "Thank you."

"I'd better get home." Pidge retrieved her bike and pushed it out of the tent. "Maybe I could come back tomorrow?"

"Sure." Jasmine nodded. "I'll tell the girl you're looking for her."

Pidge didn't think twice this time; the choice of which route to take home was simple. She wasn't going down the highway past Roly Poly's house, in a hurry or not. She followed the trail south of the highway, along Limestone Creek that led to a crabapple patch behind the Baptist church. She arrived in time to see the sun cast an orange glow as it dipped behind slash pine, hickory, and blackjack oaks.

When Pidge reached the corner, she could hear loud, angry voices coming from inside the grocery store.

She jumped off her bike and settled it beside where Luke pumped gas into a van decorated with peace symbols.

"I didn't find Frances, but what a sight! You can't imagine those people at the river field."

The van pulled away and Luke replaced the gas nozzle. "You're not going to believe what's going on in there." He jerked his head toward the storefront.

"Sounds like somebody's mad'ern torment." She realized she had whispered. "What?"

"They're having a meeting."

"Who?" Pidge leaned toward the store, trying to make out what was being said. "Sounds like a bunch."

"Mister Dauber, Mister Warell, Mr. Shipper, and them. . . you know . . ."

"The troublemakers. What's up their noses now? Did Miss Birdie hang up her bikini on the clothesline again?"

Luke shrugged. "They're mad about the peaceniks camped down by the river.

Pidge stepped closer to Luke. "Peaceniks? Another name. I thought they were war protesters who stopped by the river field on their way to someplace else."

He stuffed his hands in his pockets and nodded. "Me too. Somebody said the leader has an uncle over in Georgia who's got a field for them to camp in. Now they're a big topic of conversation. Most of them in the store want the whole bunch of squatters outta here. They're trying to organize a Ku Klux Klan posse to chase them away."

"That's terrible. We don't have Ku Kluxers around here."

"What I thought too. They're yelling most of the time. Sure heard march and Klan said a bunch. I think the only calm-sounding voices are Mom's and Dad's. The Reeds are being out-yelled."

"Did anybody invite Sheriff Clark?" Pidge walked to the big rock. It sort of glowed in the dusk. She rubbed it with the toe of her shoe.

"I don't know."

"Julie's in there?"

"No. She's doing homework with Mandy. Mom said you should go stay with her until the store closes."

Suddenly Pidge's stomach gave a loud growl. "On an empty stomach?" She rubbed it.

"Mom's got hotdogs on the stove. Make one and eat it on the way."

Yelling inside the store reached high pitch as Pidge went around the back way and headed toward the kitchen door of the rebuilt motel which was her family's home. Attached to the back of the store by a screened walkway, its ten rooms stretched east toward the river.

The old fellow who built the store and motel had put on a coat of pink-colored primer, but before he could finish painting, he died of a heart attack. By the time the Reed family bought the property, the sun had bleached the primer down to a peach color. Some of the primer had curled off to reveal the original dirt-colored concrete. The newer auto-parts building and garage had been painted white, which had peeled off in patches too.

Pidge came out of the kitchen door and through the screen-door of the walkway, which opened to the front yard. She got on her bicycle and crossed the two-lane highway. She steered with one hand as she ate her hotdog. She looked both ways, then crossed the two-lane highway and went down the road, passing the bait house on the creek. She passed the old school building that had been turned into a community center downstairs and a Masonic Lodge upstairs.

She wondered why the group hadn't met there, instead of the store. The rabble-rousers led by Mister Dauber were a strange bunch. When they got angry, the folks in New Hope community had better watch out. The voices coming from the grocery store sounded to Pidge like a nest-full of hornets.

Julie's friend Mandy lived in a building that had once been Branch's Store, across from where the old school house had been. Pidge scraped her feet on the thatch doormat.

Mandy's mom, Fiona, walked from the kitchen, wiping her hands on a towel. "Would you like a peanut butter cookie?" She pointed to a plate on the table.

"Would I?" Pidge answered. "All I've had is a hotdog with mustard. My stomach thinks my throat's been cut." She wanted to tell about the girl she thought was Frances but decided against it. She sat down to watch "I Dream of Jeannie" on television with Fiona while the girls finished their homework.

"I hardly turn on the news anymore," The tiny, dark-haired Fiona told her. "Seems everyone is so irritated at everybody else. I don't understand. Teenagers are usually rebellious. I like their long skirts and peasant blouses; don't seem too bad to me about them wearing their hair long or going barefooted. When I was growing up we only wore shoes to church and town, and got a haircut when somebody noticed our hair was long enough to sit on."

"My mom told me they're mostly mad about the war. They're trying to get President Nixon to stop sending soldiers to fight in Vietnam."

Fiona sighed. "I know about that, but I'd much rather watch Jeannie cross her arms and blink her eyes to make things happen than listen to people yell about what the government's doing or not doing." She leaned her lounge chair back.

Pidge

Chapter Four

Store lights were off when Pidge pedaled home, doubling with Julie on the back. "Guess the meeting's over," she said. Julie got her books from the basket. Pidge parked her bike under the overhang behind the store building.

Her parents looked less than happy when the girls came into the family room. The television was off. One lamp gave little light. Her father met her gaze with a stern, no-nonsense look.

"What were you doing at the hippie camp?" He used his military voice.

Pidge's spine stiffened. She shook her head. "I thought I saw Frances when the school bus passed the river field. You remember my friend Frances, the one who moved away? I went looking for her." Pidge's eyes aimed toward the door to her bedroom. How to get away? Julie and Luke sat on the couch practicing invisibility . . . no help from them.

Pidge's mother spoke up. "Don't be angry, Josh. I told Pidge it was all right for her to go down there and search for her friend. I don't see anything dangerous about a bunch of young people camping in the river field. Aaron told me they'd move on when his wife felt better. I understood they'd only be here a few days."

Pidge's father rubbed his hands over his cropped sandy hair and walked back and forth across the family room. "That was what he told me. He went for a doctor and couldn't find one in town that would see her or would come to the camp to check on her." His voice was softer now . . . more Dad, less military. "Guess that really shows how the people in this area feel about the flower children and their anti-war protests"

"Did Aaron ask at Dr. Collins' office?" Rose said. "Doc's not intolerant. Surely he would check her condition."

"I don't know." Pidge's dad reached out and touched her mother on the shoulder. "Don't worry. I'll ask him if he went by Doc's office."

Pidge saw a warm look pass between her parents. It made her feel good inside; safer somehow. She cleared her throat. "Her name's Jasmine. She helped me search for Frances. Looks like she's about to pop a kid any minute."

"Say 'expecting a child'," Rose quickly corrected. "A kid is a baby goat."

"Yeah," Luke spoke up. "I saw her from the bus too. Way her stomach's sticking out seems like that baby's pushing on everything, including the law of gravity, to get out of there. Looked like Frances standing beside her."

Rose shook her head. "A person in the family way ought not to be traveling around the country. I can't imagine her husband bringing her along. Some of these young protesters don't understand what the war's all about."

Pidge stood up. "Maybe we should go back and check on her."

Rose reached for her purse on the lampstand.

"You two stop it," Josh told them. "Pidge is a child. You're only a midwife under a doctor's charge."

I'm twelve years old. I'm no child.

"What if something happened tonight?" Rose reached for her husband's hand.

He put his arm around her shoulders. "Her husband Aaron said he'd send for us if they need us."

"Alright," Rose put the purse down and turned to Pidge. "Any clues on how to find Frances?"

"Jasmine said Frances told her she wasn't allowed to tell anyone her name." She took a deep breath. "Maybe I could go look again after school tomorrow?"

Her father issued a stern warning. "Don't push your luck, young lady. We don't know how many people are there. Aaron said he didn't know anybody but himself, Jasmine, and the two couples who came with them. New people are swarming in with no invitation. There's one bathroom, and it's an outhouse. He said they were digging a trash ditch. The spring should furnish enough water unless the crowd keeps growing. Your mom's getting more people in here shopping than she's got time to wait on." He frowned as he walked toward the door.

"The hippie camp is off limits to you, Pidge. I told Aaron his group could stay a few days while he gets a doctor to check his wife. Looks like a whole battalion of them have arrived since then. I'm going down there to see what I can figure out." He sounded determined.

Luke cleared his throat. "Need me to go with you?"

"I'd like that, but another time," said Pidge's father, then paused and glanced at the clock. He looked around the room. "All of you get to bed. Daytime will be here soon enough. There's work and school." He wiped his hand across his face. His shoulders slumped.

"Group hug." Rose reached an arm around her husband, then Pidge, pulling Luke and Julie inside the circle. "Bless us, Lord," she said prayerfully.

Josh sighed, stood tall, and smiled. "Love is in this room," he said, and let himself out the door.

Pidge

Chapter Five

Pidge's thoughts hung on to the edge of what should have been sleep. It didn't add up. She had seen a person at the hippie camp she thought was Frances. The girl looked hungry and even scared. Pidge rolled and tumbled until her legs were bound in twisted sheets. If the girl wasn't Frances, who was she? The look they had exchanged had felt like recognition. But what if the girl thought Pidge looked like someone *she* knew; someone she had been afraid of in another time and place?

By daylight she had convinced herself that the girl she had seen was Frances and that her friend had been kidnapped and was in imminent danger. When she heard the low, mournful call of the six o'clock Geneva Cotton Mill whistle, she dragged herself out of bed and tiptoed into the shower.

She rushed through breakfast. It was already hot outside. Still chewing on a piece of toast she settled beside the white rock. It was magic, according to the young man who loved ice cream. She stared for a long while, but couldn't see colors, or glittering; nothing but moldy white limestone. Could it help her find the truth in the mystery of Frances? She leaned against the big rock and dozed until she heard the other girls and boys yell that the big yellow school bus was rounding the bend.

"Cm'on." Lena poked her on the shoulder. "Wake up! The bus is here."

Pidge followed her friend up the steps and plopped down behind the driver.

"Mr. Bob, I need to sit up here so I can see the hippie camp from this side," she told him.

"What for?"

"I thought I saw Frances there yesterday. Remember? Could you please keep Roly Poly from pestering me long enough for me to see if I can locate her?"

The elderly bus driver turned toward her; his eyes crinkled when he smiled. "Frances moved away Pidge. It's been awhile now since your friend rode the school bus with you."

"I know it sounds crazy, but it appeared to be Frances out at the river field camp. She was standing at a tent next to a lady in the family way. She was wearing a green dress. It looked really shabby."

The bus driver closed the door, revved the motor, and raised his eyebrows. "Could it have been somebody who resembled Frances? She would have grown some. She was skinny then, but she was as tall as you." He circled the white rock and pulled the bus onto the highway.

"I know. I tried to allow for that." Pidge sighed. "I'm not real sure about anything anymore. Something tells me it's Frances. I can't imagine why she would be with a bunch of people traveling through here. That's why I want to look for her out the north window."

"Okay," Mr. Bob told her. "I'll drive slow and we'll try to spot Frances."

"Uh, oh," said Pidge. "Next stop's the devil."

"I'll see if I can't do something about that." The door slid open for Pidge's tormentor.

"Oink, oink," Roly Poly skipped up the steps. "Wha' 'cha doin' up front Porky Pidge? Wha' cha' being punished for scairdy, scairdy?"

The grey-haired bus driver leaned over and pinned the young man with his eyes. "Roland, sit and be quiet or I will be at your house about dark tonight to consult with your father on your rude behavior."

Roly Poly slunk down and went to his assigned seat. The others looked away, even Pidge. Everybody knew the lumpy fat boy's father beat him and his mother regularly. It was too embarrassing to even think about.

When she wasn't hornet-mad at Roly Poly, Pidge felt sorry for him, but not right now. Finding Frances was foremost in her mind.

"Pidge thinks she saw Frances at the hippie camp," the bus driver called out. "Those who wish may move to the north side of the bus and help her search." He slowed down, stopped, put on emergency flashers, and turned off the motor.

All of the girls and most of the boys, including Roly Poly, moved to the side of the bus facing the campground.

"I see someone wearing a green dress," called out a girl who sat behind Pidge in history class. "Uh, oh, it may be a boy. It's a long shirt. He's fatter than Frances."

"Wonder where all those people came from." Pidge's usual seatmate Lena hung out an open window. "They weren't there yesterday. Check out the decorated Volks bus. I'd like to take a ride in that."

"There's three girls banging on little bongo drums." Pidge's sister Julie, called out, waving her arms above her head, then doing drumbeats on the back of the bus seat.

"Look! Smokers. They look too young." Roly Poly spread his fingers against his lips.

"They sure do," echoed Luke. "Some don't look any older than me, and I'm going on fifteen."

Eyes peered at the river-field-turned-campground. "I see the tent you were talking about," said Julie's friend Mandy. "But I don't see anybody near it."

Pidge slumped down in her seat and stared until her eyeballs felt dry.

After a short interval, the driver spoke up. "Zero in on anybody who looks like Frances."

Pidge stood up. "Sorry," she told the others. "I don't see her anywhere. Maybe this afternoon, if Mr. Bob will let us, we can watch the hippies from the bus, but my dad told me not to come down here to search for her." Pidge felt her eyes tearing up. Not now, not in front of these people, she told herself. What she felt was real, hard-down fear for Frances.

The driver cranked the bus. "We can't stay any longer," he said. "I'm sorry Pidge, but we'll be late getting to school if we don't leave now."

"That's all right Mr. Bob," Pidge told him as she sat down beside Lena.

"We can search again this afternoon," he offered.

On the way to his assigned seat, Luke patted Pidge on the shoulder. "Don't forget," he told her. "Dad said YOU were forbidden to go to the river field. He didn't mention me."

"Thanks," Pidge told him. "I don't want you to get into trouble, Luke, but I sure am worried about Frances. She looked scared to me."

At third period as she walked to study hall, an idea hit Pidge. The school might know if Frances' family had moved back. She turned in at the office.

"You'll be late to class, Margaret," Ms. Wren used Pidge's actual name.

"It's study hall Ms. Wren," she blurted. "I saw a girl I thought was Frances at my dad's river field. If her family moved back, they'd have to register her at school, wouldn't they?"

40

"They would. I haven't seen anything of them, but I'll check the records." While Ms. Wren looked for a file, Pidge stood at the open office door and watched the students pass by. She didn't see anyone who looked just like Frances, but there were plenty of girls who seemed to resemble her in some way. Maybe she was wrong. Maybe it was a girl who reminded her of Frances.

With a tap, the school secretary neatened the pile of registration paperwork in her hands.

"If they're back, Frances has not been registered to attend this school," Ms. Wren told Pidge. "I'll let you know if they show up in this office."

"Thank you," Pidge told her.

As Rose turned the key in the back door, she heard Aaron knock at the front door of the Daylight Grocery.

"Sorry to bother you so early, Ms. Reed," Aaron stood on the top step, shifting from one foot to the other.

"It's all right." Rose patted him on the shoulder and walked around clicking light switches.

"It was nice of Mr. Josh to talk with us last night, but I was expecting he'd be back this morning." Aaron jiggled the change in his jeans pocket.

Pidge's mother was sympathetic to the pregnant woman's husband. "He had to make a quick trip to town for more hoop cheese, crackers and sardines," Rose told him.

"Oh." Aaron rubbed his forehead. "I was hoping I could catch a ride to town with him."

"He should be back soon. Is there any way I could help you?"

"I don't know, Ms. Reed. It seems like everything is hitting us at once. Jasmine sick and expecting any minute. I can't find a doctor to take a look at her. All those people moving into the camp without permission."

"Did you check with Dr. Collins?"

"I did. The receptionist said he didn't have an opening and that he wouldn't see my 'kind' anyway."

"What?" Rose jumped from her chair behind the counter and stood to her full height, which wasn't tall enough to look him in the face. "Dr. Collins said that?"

"He wasn't in. I talked to the woman at the desk. She looked at me like I had crawled out from under a rock."

"Oh." Rose plopped back down and slapped her hand on the counter. "Sounds like her." She shook her head.

Aaron leaned over to rest his arm on the top of the cash register. "It gets worse. We could head on to my uncle's now, but my truck's making growling noises and won't go out of first gear. I'd hoped to catch a ride to town to the auto parts shop. I can fix it myself if I get the parts."

Rose stood. "You're in luck this time. See that building?" She stepped to the door and pointed to a concrete block building with peeling white paint beside the grocery store, then picked a key off a rack by the door and handed it to him. "We used to sell a few auto parts. Had a mechanic too until he got drafted. Probably splashing around in a Vietnamese rice paddy by now. See if you can find what you need. Open up the big door and fix your truck in there if you want to."

"Thanks!" Aaron grabbed the key.

She watched as he rushed toward the building. The phone rang.

"Need anything not on the list?" her husband's voice asked.

"No, I think that was all." She told him about Aaron's truck troubles.

"Check and if we don't have what he wants, I'll go by the auto parts store."

Rose found Aaron with his torso folded into the truck's innards. "You had everything I need. I'm fixing it, Ms. Reed," he called out happily.

She hurried back into the store and picked up the receiver that lay on the counter. "Aaron said he's got what he needs. Hurry home."

It was quiet in the store for a few minutes. Rose wondered what, if anything, she could do to help Pidge find her friend Frances. With the way anger seemed to be building against the young people gathering at the river field, it could soon become too dangerous for Pidge to go there for any reason, including a search for her friend.

Strange she hadn't seen Fiona, her best friend in the community, so far this week. They had been like peas in a pod in grade school, then grown even closer as they grew older. Rose had married a military man and left to travel the world. Fiona married Richard from over near Bonnet Pond. They lived just down the Westville Road. Their daughter Mandy and Rose's daughter Julie were as close as Rose and Fiona had been. It was nice to be back home and it was really great to live near Fiona.

Rose was in the rear of the store putting up stock when the bell over the door jangled. She looked up and saw Fiona.

"Was just thinking about you!" The two met at the stool beside the hanging bananas. "Must have conjured you up. Where have you been?"

"At home, trying to keep Richard calmed down."

"Calmed down? I wondered why he wasn't at the community meeting. Is he sick?" Rose followed Fiona as she gathered boxes of grits, baking powder, and a gallon jug of milk.

Fiona looked apologetically at Rose. "I meant to call you. Richard has me worried." Her voice was soft, and low. "I'm frightened Rose. There's something scary about to happen."

43

"Here? In New Hope? At your house? What do you mean?"

Just then Fiona's husband finished pumping gas and entered the store, slamming back the door, almost popping off the goat bell. He looked red-faced and embarrassed.

"Pay for my gas," he told Fiona, and stalked back out to his pickup truck.

Fiona dug through her wallet. "Them guys led by Dauber are up to something evil," she whispered. "And now they've got my Richard sucked into it," Fiona counted out cash for Rose, the pennies dancing as she dropped them on the counter. "They're planning to drive out the hippies."

"What about Sarah Mae? His wife? Can't she stop him?"

"Went over to talk to her, but Joe wouldn't let me in the house, said she was busy. I told him to tell her I'd come back later."

"Do that. She's not a bad person. Let me know what she says."

"Okay." Fiona skittered out the door.

Pidge dreaded the ride home in the school bus. She had an uneasy feeling about Frances.

"We'll find her," Lena kept saying. "If we believe we'll find her, we will."

"Thank you for being positive, Lena," Pidge told her. "I'm hoping and praying you're right."

The bus moved slowly over the Choctawhatchee River Bridge. Mr. Bob called out "Students to the right. It's time to find Frances."

When the bus ground to a halt, Pidge saw the door of the bus open and Luke slip out. She hoped nobody noticed. If the others saw him and told their parents, it might get back to Josh and Rose, and there would be a big row, and she'd be blamed. They'd ground her for sure, and she would get no more privileges for the rest of her natural-born life.

Julie slipped up beside Pidge. "See that girl over by the Volkswagen bus?" she whispered. "Is that the one you saw?"

"That's her!" Pidge ran to the front of the bus. "See, Mr. Bob? That's her. That's Frances."

"Don't yell," he whispered to her. "Let Luke know."

He opened the bus door and Pidge leaned out. She saw Luke behind the gallberry bush at the end of the bridge and put two fingers in her mouth and a let out a low, fierce "help" whistle. He turned and Pidge pointed to Frances.

As Pidge and the others watched from the bus the scene became unreal. Pidge held her breath as Luke ran across the highway and into the camp, aiming straight at the girl who looked like Frances. As he got near to her, the girl saw him, turned and took off running, heading toward the river. Pidge wrung her hands as she watched Luke match Frances stride for stride.

"Run, Luke, run," Pidge whispered. Just before they reached the riverbank, Luke dived toward Frances in a swift tackle.

"Oh!" Pidge's fingers flew to her mouth. She watched, mesmerized, as the girl slipped out of Luke's grasp, ran the few feet to the river's edge, and with one swift lunge jumped into the foaming brown water and disappeared beneath it.

"Dive," yelled Pidge. And he did, right behind the girl. "Come on, come up," Pidge whispered. Her brother was under water for a long time, then she saw him stand, turning his head, uncertain which direction to follow.

Pidge and the others watched as he hesitated, waved toward the bus and ran up an old Indian path which crossed the branch of water from Little Indian Spring to the river. What if Frances drowned? If she swam underwater she'd probably be headed upstream, thought Pidge. If she didn't drown, she'd have to come up to get out of the river.

"Follow the Indian trail," Pidge yelled.

In a fast run, Luke disappeared around the bend in the river north of the cypress grove.

"Show's over," announced Mr. Bob as he turned the key in the ignition and drove slowly west. At the Daylight Grocery he stopped at the white rock and opened the door.

"I'm sorry, Pidge," he said. "That girl sure did look like Frances. It don't make sense she'd run. Hope Luke catches up with her and finds out what's going on."

Lena walked into the store with Pidge, and Mandy came in with Julie.

"Tuna salad in the refrigerator." Rose hunkered down at her desk with calculator and cash register tapes. "Make sandwiches for yourselves."

The others aimed toward the kitchen, but Pidge hung back. "Mom, you won't believe what happened."

Her mother looked up. "Not now, Pidge. I'm working on numbers."

Pidge gave a little grunt. She wanted to tell her parents about Luke chasing Frances, about the amazing escape, but they seemed so wrapped up in the store, the hippies. What about her? Wasn't she important? What about Frances?

Standing in the door to the kitchen walkway, she saw her dad and Aaron walking toward the store entrance. Lena put a plate in her hand.

"Tuna's good." Lena went back to the kitchen.

Pidge took a big bite of the sandwich and climbed onto the stool beside the banana stalk.

The goat bell tinkled as her dad and Aaron walked into the store.

"We now have a mechanic in the neighborhood." Josh had his arm around Aaron's shoulder. Pidge felt a tinge of envy. Since when had he put his arm around her?

"Wonderful." Rose beamed.

Pidge took another bite and rolled the food around in her mouth.

"Just 'till the doc says it's okay to travel, or until the baby comes and we know it and Jasmine are well and healthy." Aaron dipped his head.

Pidge's dad leaned down and kissed her mom on the cheek. "I talked with Doctor Collins and he said he'd examine Jasmine. Could you go with them to the see him at eleven in the morning?"

"Sure." Pidge's mom put rubber bands around the cash register receipts and went behind the counter.

"What about the store?" asked Aaron.

"Our neighborhood retiree Uncle Jim will be happy to tend the store," Pidge's mom assured him. "We want to be sure Jasmine's all right."

Aaron glanced between Josh and Rose. "I would like to have a doctor's approval for her to travel. I can't thank you people enough."

Pidge could hear Aaron's truck clattering as he drove off. Sounded like it still needed repairs. She slid off the stool and wiped her mouth with the napkin. "Good sandwich Mom."

"You're welcome." Her mom closed the counter drawer. "How was school?"

"School was all right." Pidge slumped against the banana stool. "We saw Frances. Luke chased her, but he couldn't catch her."

"Oh, I am so sorry. Why would she run away?"

Pidge walked to the door. No customers at the gas pumps. "I don't understand either. Could she be afraid of me? Of Luke?"

Her dad stood beside the cash register. "We need to stop any more hippies from coming to the river field." He touched her mom on the shoulder. "New Hope's trouble-makers are angry. They don't want the anti-war protesters in this neighborhood and are about ready to drive them out."

"But Frances isn't old enough to be a war protester." Pidge wrung her hands, almost in tears.

"I'll go down there to see if I can figure out something we can do." He put one hand on Pidge's shoulder and the other on her mom's.

"If you see Frances, tell her I'm worried about her," Pidge told him.

He turned his warning look upon her. "Remember what I told you, Pidge. That camp's no place for young girls especially you."

"I know." Pidge's face fell. Her dad didn't sound like much help would come from him. Maybe by now Luke had found Frances and would know some answers. All she could do was hope.

"Your dad will look around for Frances while he's there." Rose tried to cheer her up. "You know your father. He's stern, but he's fair. He'll tell us if he sees her."

"I know," Pidge repeated. But she didn't feel sure about anything anymore. What if something really bad happened to Frances? "I wish Dad would help. I don't understand about Frances, but I don't understand Dad either."

"Your dad's worried too. He's military, so he's been trained to follow the leader."

"I understand that." Pidge walked to the banana stalk and sat on the tall stool. "His leader is President Richard Nixon."

"People are angry all over the country because young men are dying in Vietnam. They blame the president. Those here are blaming the peace protesters."

Pidge got that gnawing feel in the pit of her stomach. She didn't understand grownups. The real world was a lot different from fights on the playground, where the teacher made them hug necks or shake hands and get back into the game.

"Two trucks from the hippie camp just drove up to the gas tanks." Her mother picked up the phone. "Luke wasn't on the bus?"

"I think he caught a ride." Pidge swallowed. It was not like her to fib. Had her mother forgotten that she told her about Luke chasing Frances? What if Frances HAD been kidnapped? But then her parents also could have hooked onto the peace train caravan and didn't want their friends in New Hope community to know they were anti-war protesters.

Keeping up with two gas pumps kept Pidge busy. More and more hippie cars and trucks pulled in. Just before dusk, Uncle Jim walked up to get gas for his lawn mower.

"Mom said she'll need you in the morning so she can go to the doctor with Aaron's wife, Jasmine," Pidge told him.

"She called me."

Sweat dripped off Pidge's chin. She swiped her arm across her face. The elderly man had been an accountant in his earlier life and looked like an office worker, even to the red bow tie underneath his chin.

"Seems like you're extra busy," he said. "Luke usually works the pumps. Where is he?"

Pidge acted as if she didn't hear. Dread made a sour lump in her stomach. If something bad happened to Luke, it would be her fault. She counted out change for a customer in a station wagon as a rusty old truck pulled in front of the tank.

"Why don't I work the pump on this tank and you go over to that one?" Uncle Jim hitched up his suspenders as if he meant business. "Where on earth did all these young people with long hair and dirty feet come from?"

"From all over the country, looks like." Pidge shrugged her shoulders.

"Let's fill their tanks fast so they'll head on off to somewheres else." The grey-haired gentleman straightened his bow tie and pulled on rubber bands to hold his sleeves above his wrists. "Some of them don't look too friendly and most don't smell very good."

Pidge tried to hand him her change apron. "I'll get another one."

"That's all right. I can use my pockets. If I run out, I'll buy change from you."

For a while it was touch and go for Pidge and Uncle Jim. Every sort of vehicle needed gas. A long-haired youth with a snake tattooed along his arm held a checkbook from a bank in California. Pidge had already pumped gas into his new model blue Maserati convertible.

"Cash only for gasoline," she told him. "Four dollars seventy-nine cents, to be exact." Pidge held out her palm.

"What if I don't have any money?" He grinned at her.

"You'll have to talk with my dad." Then she remembered her Dad had gone to the river field to check on the campers. It would be wonderful if he found Frances. "You mind pulling out, others are waiting."

The snake-decorated young man glanced at Uncle Jim. His meaning was clear. "That your dad?"

The kindly old man looked him square in the eye. "No," he said, "Just a neighbor."

Pidge didn't hesitate. She put two fingers in her mouth and out came the same low, mournful sound she had used to call Luke. It echoed like the sad cotton-mill whistle. Her mother's head popped out at the door.

"Regulars get put on a ticket, but what about these strangers?"

"Cash." Her mother's voice was firm. She stepped out, hands on her hips.

"This guy's trying to stiff me for gasoline." Pidge was tired. *What a crappy thing to do.* She felt older than her twelve years.

"I'll call the sheriff."

As her mom went inside, Arthur, the red-haired boy Pidge had met at the hippie camp, walked up.

"I'll loan him the money," Arthur told her. "His tent is next to ours. My dad can get it from him later."

"Thanks," Pidge told him.

"You're welcome," he said as he counted out the change.

"Hurry and tell my mom the gasoline's been paid for," Pidge told the barefoot serpent-decorated youth headed toward the store entrance.

"That was some signal," Arthur grinned. "Clue me in on how to do it?"

"Clue you in?" Pidge laughed.

"Teach it to me."

"Sure. I can show you now. Put your first two fingers in your mouth, leave a little space between them, then curve your hand toward your chin and blow, hard."

Arthur tried. "Weetwootweetpftt" Walking over by the white rock, he kept it up. Pidge rolled her eyes. Each time the burble sounded more like a real whistle.

"Remember, only in an emergency. It's a way to communicate with family or friends in a crowd."

"I'll get it perfect," Arthur told her. "If you hear me whistle, come running, there's real trouble."

"Sure. Right." Pidge turned to a customer who stood beside the red gas tank. "Could I help you? Or would you rather pump your own?"

Traffic slowed down at the gas tanks, but people going in and out of the store didn't seem to let up. Their arms held full bags as they stopped to poke around in the Free Box. Some took, some added.

Pidge worried about Luke. What if he had caught up with Frances? What if she drowned in the river? What if Luke drowned?

As if she could hear her thoughts, Rose stuck her head out the door. "Where's Luke?"

"I dunno." It wasn't *exactly* a lie. She didn't know where Luke was. But it stuck in her throat anyway. She swallowed.

The sun hung just above the trees. A light breeze whisked away some of the daytime heat. It would be dusk soon. Pidge stuck a fingernail between her teeth, then stopped. If she chewed her fingernails, her mom would see she was anxious and start asking more questions. She was doomed.

Uncle Jim let out a whoop! "I see your brother coming," he announced. "Maybe he'll spell us."

Pidge squared her shoulders. "He might be too tired."

"Think he walked all the way from school?"

"Looks like it." She hated to skirt the truth, especially to Uncle Jim, but she couldn't let her mouth get her into any more trouble than she was already in, or than what was absolutely necessary.

"I'm cashing in," Uncle Jim told her. "Soon's I fill my gas can. I still have time to cut my grass before dark."

Luke and Pidge

Chapter Six

Luke walked slowly around the white rock. For once, there were no vehicles at either of the two pumps. Pidge ran to meet him and before she could think about it she hugged him, tight.

"Am I glad to see you. I thought you had drowned. Did you find Frances?"

Luke shook his head. Steam rose from his wet clothes. He walked slowly toward the gas pumps.

"Whatever happened to you?" Uncle Jim picked up his filled gas can. "You look a mess."

"He jumped into the river chasing Frances," Pidge answered for Luke. "We saw her turn and run with him right behind her, then dive into the river."

Luke shook his head. "I still can't believe it." He leaned over and turned on the faucet, letting the water pour over his face and down his neck.

Pidge plunged in the window squeegee and swiped water over his shirt.

A smile started on Luke's face. "Wow! That feels good. I must smell like a skunk."

"You do." Uncle Jim turned. "Phew."

Pidge grabbed Luke's arm. "You didn't answer my question. What about Frances?" The knot tightened in her stomach as her brother shook his head.

"That girl should have been a racehorse. She'd flat out win the Kentucky Derby any day in the week." Luke turned off the water and shook his head, spraying droplets into the air.

"You didn't catch her?" Pidge blurted out. "I thought you could run faster than anybody."

"After she disappeared into the water, I lost her. I searched past Little Indian Spring, all the way up to Parrot's Creek. She must have gone downstream."

"Did you call her? Maybe she'd have stopped if she heard you call her name."

"I called out, yelled, screamed, did everything I could think of. Next time I'll take the trail south and look for her in that direction."

Pidge could see he was exhausted. His clothes were soaked with brown river water, his sneakers covered in mud. "Thank you for trying," she told him. "You look tired and hungry."

"Aw, I'll be all right. Just disappointed I didn't find out anything about Frances. Can't understand why she wouldn't talk to at least one of us."

"Me neither. Get something to eat and take a shower. I'll watch the pumps for you."

Luke looked down at his once-white shirt. "Don't know what I'll tell Mom about this. Hope she can get this dirt out. I'll wipe the mud off my shoes."

"That river was really muddy."

"Go clean up," Pidge told her brother.

"You don't have to tell me twice." Luke rounded the corner of the building at a trot.

Pidge went inside, popped the screened door, rattled the bell. She rolled up her change apron and reached under the counter for another one.

"Luke's back," she called out to her mother. "Looks like he walked home from school." She swallowed a lump in her throat. *Half-lying wasn't as bad as lying, was it?* Either way, it didn't feel right.

"You watch the outside while he eats a bite and changes clothes. We're still pricing cans. Take those bent ones to the Free Box," her mom pointed. Julie and Mandy were busy helping put price stickers on cans of green beans.

"We get to eat the overripe bananas when we're finished," Julie laughed. It was a standing joke about the bunches of bananas hanging on a large stalk ripening too fast, but they did taste sweeter with brown spots on the yellow skin.

"We can get my mom to make a banana pudding for us," added Mandy.

Pidge took her transistor radio out to the pumps. She was especially fond of Bob Dylan's "Blowin' in the Wind," especially when "Peter, Paul, and Mary" sang it, and Dylan's "Mr. Tambourine Man." She lowered the sound on Pete Seeger's "Turn! Turn! Turn!" Even if he did mention everything having its turn out of the Bible, there was something different, stirring, scary. *It's hard to tell which songs dad approves of.* He said there were too many about "aggression and dissidence" for his taste. Since he controlled the dial on the radio and the on-off button of the television set, both were often silent in the family room.

Pidge looked up and saw the blue Maserati turn off the highway. She sort of liked the scruffy-looking guy with the serpent-tattooed arm.

"Uh, oh," Pidge said aloud. "Here comes trouble."

He did a u-ie with the convertible into the store's parking area, barely missing the big limestone rock.

After he parked and slammed the car door, he walked slowly past Pidge, giving her a cautious eye, looking down at his bare feet.

She tried a gracious smile, but he didn't appear to notice.

His loud slam of the door and jingle of the goat bell echoed against the cedars across the road at the church cemetery.

Pidge scanned the highway. No other cars here and looked like none coming. She walked to the door as serpent-tattoo-man went into the store.

Rose turned from stamping prices on bean cans and went behind the counter. "May I help you?" she asked.

"I need a couple of six-packs of Miller's Lite." He smiled. "Don't worry, I have cash this time. It's not funny money either."

"Miller's Lite? I'm sorry, we don't sell beer."

"Beer? In the can? Or in the bottle?"

"We have soft drinks in cans and bottles, but no beer." A smile was blooming at the edge of Rose's eyes.

Watch out, boy, Pidge thought.

"You're kidding. Right?"

"'Fraid not," said Pidge's mom. "We don't sell alcoholic beverages, not even Mogen David wine."

"What do you drink for communion?" He pointed to the church on the other side of the four-way intersection.

"Grape juice," Pidge said from the door, a smile flickering around her lips. *This guy's not from around here; that's for sure.*

"I mean, really," he kept on doggedly, as if he thought there was a joke. "Where do you get beer then?"

"Nowhere in this neighborhood." Rose swiped a hand across her forehead. She looked at the corner where she had been putting price stickers on cans. Julie and Mandy carefully stacked beans, corn and tomato cans on shelves.

"You mean nobody around here drinks beer, wine, or hard liquor."

"I'm sure they must. But I don't know who, or where they buy what they drink." Rose turned and picked up a fly swatter. She spaced out her words. "There is a juke joint that used to be called The Pines, up near the Florida-Alabama line, but I don't know who in New Hope would patronize it. What I do know is that we don't sell alcohol."

"I wouldn't be trying to give you a check." He leaned against the counter and waved a handful of cash.

"Sorry, no alcohol. Not for love or money."

Pidge had to laugh. She glanced at the fuel tanks. Nobody waiting for gas. She was free for the time being.

"We've got hoop cheese, crackers, soft drinks, juice, orange and apple, just-right ripe bananas." Pidge pulled a fruit punch from the cooler beside the door. "Check it out. You might see something you'd rather have than alcohol."

He looked around, gave a disgusted grunt, and went outside.

Pidge followed him.

"Weird," he muttered, as he stomped to his shining light of a new car. "What kind of people don't drink beer?"

Pidge held out the dripping soft drink. "Try this. It's better than the other sodas. Or beer."

The hippie growled, shaking his head in disgust. The snazzy car gave a light burp as it scratched off.

"I'll take that." Luke reached for the cold drink, then slugged it down. He and Pidge stood beside the gas pumps.

"You know his name?" Pidge asked Luke.

"No." Luke grinned as he put the empty bottle in a rack beside the gas tank and pulled a rag from a rosin cup nailed to the post.

Fiona walked up, following the car with her eyes. "Sort of a cute boy, if it wasn't for that scary serpent tattoo."

Pidge rolled her eyes. "You can say that again, even if he is a hippie."

"Why did he scratch off toward town looking like he's mad?" She didn't wait for an answer. "I'm bringing Mandy's pajamas and a change of clothes for school."

"Good idea. I saw her books on the kitchen table with Julie's." Pidge gave Fiona an impulsive hug.

"Thanks." Fiona hugged her back. "I need to talk with your mom."

"She's in there and Julie and Mandy have overripe bananas for you to make a pudding."

A wide smile split Fiona's face. "Just what I need. Some normalcy in this place." She went inside.

"Wonder what Fiona meant by that," said Pidge.

"Normalcy? You haven't noticed? There's nothing normal around here right now." Luke swiped the wet rag to clean dust from the faded red gasoline pump.

"What are you talking about?" asked Pidge. "Trying to find Frances is sort of normal, isn't it? That is if she has been kidnapped, and if the person I saw is actually her."

"It's not about Frances." Luke hunkered down in the shade of the pump, wiping dust. "The men are rounding up for trouble. They mean to chase the hippies away from the river field."

"But it's our family's field where they're camped. Wouldn't Mom and Dad have something to say about that?"

"Not much from what I hear. They're out-voting Dad. They said his humanitarianism has gone too far, that for a military man helping out a bunch of protesters is treason."

"That's strange," answered Pidge. "Just because he's military doesn't mean he can't be kind to a woman with a baby on the way."

"I know," answered Luke. "But there's lots of other people there too, most of them not married, smoking pot and sitting around buck naked, right out in the open. My friends say their dads are angry and that trouble is ahead."

"Smoking pot?"

He held up two fingers. "You know, marijuana."

"Oh," said Pidge. *The language changes by the minute since the river field turned into a campground for anti-war protesters, and everybody is in on it but me.*

A couple pulled up in a pickup truck with a topper on the back. The man handed Luke a ten-dollar bill. "Put five in and give the change to my old lady to spend inside." He pulled out a lumpy tobacco bag and rolling papers.

Pidge slapped her hand over her mouth.

"Don't," Luke told him, bringing his face close to the open truck window.

"I ain't lightin', just rollin'."

Luke put five dollars worth of gas in the tank. He raised his eyebrows at Pidge and nodded toward the store.

"Don't think Mom could hear him from inside," Pidge whispered, but she followed as the couple walked through the door, then leaned over to straighten cans Julie and Mandy had dumped in the Free Box. Luke was right. She heard an angry voice and stuck her head in, holding the screen door with her elbows.

"Did you just call your wife your 'old lady?'" Rose exploded. She reached under the counter.

"She ain't my wife, ma'am," the man explained. "She jist belongs to me; she's my woman."

"She's not an old lady and she certainly does not belong to anyone but herself," Rose shouted.

The young woman's sagging shoulders shot up straight and as she shook her head; thick, brown hair sprang out in every direction. "Right on! You tell it like it is Ma'am. You just made my day."

Pidge ducked her head as Rose noticed her. "Come watch the counter," Rose called out, then turned to Fiona. "I want a cup of coffee, a cooling down, and you and I need to talk."

Several young women roamed around inside the store, poking and peering closely at fishing tackle, plows, hoes, bags of rice, flour, sugar sacks, as if they were in a museum.

"This local?" a young woman asked, as she held out a small chicken from the cooler.

"Sure is. We try to use things people raise on the farms around here as much as possible," Pidge told her. "The meal's ground at a mill right down the road, but the flour is shipped from somewhere else to the distributor out of Marianna." She pointed to the chicken. "We get our chickens, beef, and vegetables from the Cook family up the road. Always fresh."

"This will taste wonderful cooked over an open fire."

"Are you having fun on your trip?" Pidge asked her. "I hear you're going to Georgia to hold peace rallies in Atlanta. That's got to be exciting."

"It is. The idea is exciting but riding on a shaky truck all day is not that easy on the body. It'll be worth it when we stop the war."

"You think you can?" Did the young woman really believe that a bunch of hungry hippies in need of a bath could stop a war? It didn't make sense. Oh, well, Pidge thought. *I'm only twelve. What do I know?*

The girl raised her hand and gave her the peace sign.

"Don't forget to check the Free Box outside the door," Pidge called out. *Might be fun to go to a protest.*

Rose and Fiona came from the kitchen. "You could sweep up inside the store," Rose told Pidge. "I've got the girls cleaning up the kitchen."

"And I've got bananas and vanilla wafers for pudding." Fiona patted the paper bag. She looked less anxious than when she had arrived.

"Mom." Pidge wanted to tell her what Luke had said about the men being angry with her father.

"What?" The cheerful look on her mother's face stopped her. "Nothing Mom," she said.

"When somebody says 'nothing' it usually means something important." Rose held the doorknob and trained her gaze on Pidge.

"Tell you about it later." Pidge wiped the counter.

Rose

Chapter Seven

It was early when Rose, sorting bills, saw Aaron and Jasmine pull up in front of Daylight Grocery. Aaron parked his truck behind the auto repair shop. Jasmine walked into the store.

"You look nice," Rose told the young girl. "That pink blouse suits you."

"You don't think it clashes with the green leaves on the skirt?"

"Not at all." *Will Pidge or Julie look anything like Jasmine when they're eighteen?* Rose wondered.

Aaron stuck his head in the front door. "Thought I'd work awhile before we leave," he told Rose. "All right if Jasmine waits inside with you?"

"Sure," Rose told him. "The store's not really open yet, so we've got time for breakfast." She led Jasmine to the kitchen. "Pidge, Luke, and Julie just left for school and Josh for work in town. I'll fix some food."

"We had coffee at the tent," Jasmine told her. "Aaron ate cereal, but I didn't eat. My stomach feels queasy."

"Uh-oh, could be the baby's getting ready to come." Rose turned. "Mothers-to-be are usually ravenous,"

"I hope it's not about to arrive." Jasmine put a hand on her belly. "We thought we'd get to Georgia in plenty of time." A frown wrinkled her brow. "Nothing seems to be turning out the way we expected."

"What did your mother and dad think of this trip?" Rose tried to sound casual as she stirred grits into a pot of hot water.

Jasmine flinched. "They didn't much like the idea, but they agreed that a wife should go with her husband."

"To live in a tent?" Rose couldn't stop the question. It flew out of her mouth and hung in the air between them.

"We're supposed to live with Aaron's uncle and his wife in their farmhouse when we get to Georgia. The others will camp in the fields."

"He doesn't plant his fields?" Rose's curiosity seemed to get the best of her.

"The government pays him not to plant cotton and peanuts on his land, he told Aaron. That's where the war protesters would camp." Jasmine's chin trembled.

"You'd prefer not to go to Georgia?" Rose wished for words that would give comfort to Jasmine. *What if this was my own child far away from home and about to become a mother? Bereft is not even a big enough word to describe how Jasmine's parents must feel.*

"I want to go with Aaron, wherever he goes," Jasmine held back tears.

"But you really want your mother?"

Jasmine nodded and swiped at her eyes.

"I'm sorry. I didn't mean to upset you. My mouth gets in the way sometimes." Rose broke eggs into a skillet.

"That's all right, you hit on the truth. This is a mess and a half." Jasmine rubbed her nose with the back of her hand. "I miss my mother so bad. I don't know what I was thinking. I don't know if I can have a baby without my mother." She sat at the table and leaned her head on her arms.

"Have you called her?"

"No, I'm too embarrassed."

Rose put fried eggs and grits on two plates, added bacon. "The biscuits are in the oven beside you," she told Jasmine. "Get two. Let's eat, and then we'll call your family." At Jasmine's hesitation, Rose switched to her mother-style voice. "Sit down and eat. Now."

Jasmine sat. Rose poured her a large glass of milk and herself a cup of coffee.

Nothing more was said as they finished off a hefty breakfast. Rose eyed Jasmine's stomach.

"Probably a girl. Boys usually ride low. What are you planning to name it?"

"If it's a boy, we'll name it Royal Aaron, the first for my father and the middle for Aaron and call him Roy." She hugged herself.

"What if it's a girl?"

"We're thinking on that. I believe it'll be a boy." Jasmine laughed. Except for that bulge, she was so thin.

"Yeah. Right. That's probably a sign it'll be a girl. Did you bring baby clothes?"

"I have yellow and green things, blankets and onesies and such. We'll have to get more clothing when it gets here."

Rose nodded, once. "And you thought there would be plenty of time."

"I did." Jasmine grimaced. "I hope I'm not wrong."

"Me too," Rose stood and ran water in the dishpan. "The dishes can soak for now; we'd better go and check out some things with Doc Collins. He's a good doctor. I'm a midwife. I work with him and call him when he's needed at a birthing."

As they entered the store, Rose pointed toward the telephone. "First, call your mother." Her words sounded bossy, but her smile seemed to give Jasmine confidence.

Rose watched as Jasmine listened to the ring, then hung up.

Rose waved a hand in the air. "Dial again and let it ring a long time. I know your mother is praying every minute for word from you."

Jasmine took a deep breath, then let it out slowly. "Okay," she whispered. She redialed, then held the phone to her ear, staring at Rose.

"Still ringing," she reported. Finally, Jasmine put the phone back in its cradle and looked at Rose. Tears ran down her cheeks.

"You did right," Rose put her arm around Jasmine's shoulders. "Don't give up. Sit at that desk, reach into the bottom drawer on the left and take out an envelope and paper. Write a letter to them. Now. We'll put it in the mailbox outside before we leave."

After Jasmine addressed the envelope and wrote on a sheet of stationery, she pushed it across the table to Rose. Jasmine had written that she was fine, that a family at a country store was helping her and Aaron, that they would soon be on their way to Aaron's uncle's farm near Atlanta, Georgia, that she would keep calling their telephone.

Rose pushed the letter back to Jasmine. "Tell them to call you here." Rose gave her the number and Jasmine wrote it on the note.

She handed Jasmine a stamp. "Never sever ties with your family. No matter what. They are the ones who love you the most. Don't ever forget that."

The screen-door bell jingled as Uncle Jim walked up in his red bow tie and long-sleeved plaid shirt. "I'm here, Rose," he announced. "Ready to represent you. The store is in good hands."

"Young Lady," he turned toward Jasmine. "You shine like the sun, even the Florida sun, this morning. If

65

that baby isn't as pretty as you, or as handsome as your husband, it'll be a big surprise."

Walking to the auto shop building, Rose realized that Uncle Jim was right about the handsome couple. Both had thick black hair and fair skin. A shame that soon they'd get peeling noses from the relentless Florida sun.

At least a dozen vehicles were parked around the auto shop. Aaron listened while a young man with long hair plaited like musician Willie Nelson's gunned the motor.

Aaron grinned at Rose. "You think it would be all right if I stay here and work while you take Jasmine to the doctor? These vehicles need repairs and I need the money."

"I'm sure that will be fine; I can vouch for you with the doctor." Rose patted his arm. "Did Josh tell you how we run the auto repair?"

"He said I put the money for parts in the bank bag, then halve the rest with you. You pay the utilities and I keep the place clean."

"Good. That works out fair for both of us, don't you think?"

"I believe it is more than generous." Aaron looked relieved.

"By the way, were you a mechanic out in Texas?" He didn't appear sunburned enough to have been making a living repairing cars.

"I wasn't. I tinkered with old cars on the side. I was actually a third-year college student. Does that surprise you?"

"No. That's what I'd have guessed. What was your major?"

"History, like my dad. Must be why he didn't seem surprised when I wanted to get active in the war protests."

Rose squared her shoulders and walked to her car. "Ready Jasmine?" she called out. *These young people are making history all right, but how far will they go, and what good can possibly come of their efforts?*

Aaron and Jasmine exchanged an awkward hug. He wiped smidgens of tears from her cheeks.

"Could I bring my sketch pad, Rose?"

"Sure." Rose cranked the car. Maybe she'd get the history-major mechanic to check that groan it gave when she turned the key.

Rose

Chapter Eight

Rose looked sideways as Jasmine gazed at wildflowers along the highway; some had tiny blooms. It was exciting to Rose to see red clover inching out and bees buzzing around milkweed. Deceptive-looking yellow bitterweed unfolded tight buds.

"See the buds sticking out like tiny fingers?" Jasmine pulled pencils and sketch pad from her shoulder bag. "No, don't look. You're driving." She sucked the end of the pencil, waved it across the paper and a stalk appeared.

"I can look and drive at the same time." Rose pointed. "Nothing more beautiful than black-eyed Susans, or wild azalea and yellowbells edging that pond."

Jasmine sketched, dainty spring growth appeared, showing promise of flowers. She sighed and looked up, worry wrinkles across her forehead. "Do you think my mom will call me, Rose?"

"Sure, she will," Rose said, without skipping a beat.

Jasmine pressed fingers to her temples as if she had a headache. "It's hard to describe how angry they were when Aaron and I joined the anti-war protesters. I don't know if I would forgive me if I were her."

"You're not the first to be taken in by strong rhetoric over the fighting," Rose said. "Lots of folks around here support the war in Vietnam, even though they are against war in general. They believe our soldiers are fighting for a good cause; that the war will lead to peace."

"My parents were disappointed that I chose to follow Aaron and his anti-war, idealistic opinions." She picked up her sketchpad and drew peace and yin-yang symbols.

Rose drove and glanced sideways as Jasmine rested her head against the door and kept sketching. *That girl is a talented artist.*

Jasmine filled the page and turned over a sheet. "My dad told us sensible young people should stay in college, settle down, that the authorities know better than us what's good for the country."

"Aaron disagreed?" Rose glanced at her.

"He sure did." Jasmine wiped her face with the hem of her long floral-print skirt. "Aaron told my parents the elected officials were escalating the war and sending young people over there to die. My dad looked like he was having a heart attack when we left. My mom cried."

Rose peeked at Jasmine. "When I was expecting, I yearned for peace and quiet. My nesting seasons were not pleasant."

"I'll be glad when it's over. I'm looking forward to having a baby that's part me and part Aaron. I love him so much, but I am really worn out. I'd like to hang it all up, but I can't hang out a baby." Her head rested against the seat.

"You're okay, just exhausted from long hours on highways," Rose told her.

"It was tiring, riding from Austin all the way here." Jasmine shifted in the car seat. "But it was pleasant most of the time. Being with Aaron on a cross-country trip was comforting. But the radio blasted out speeches about marches, protests, the law, and against college students. Aaron argued with them, shouting louder than the newscasters. I was beginning to feel like I didn't know who to believe anymore."

"Yeah." Rose maneuvered the car around potholes in the crumbling highway. "When college students make speeches, law enforcement rushes in to crack down. There is an anger building up here that's frightening. Some people of the community feel kindly toward you all, while many more want the protesters gone."

Jasmine was quiet. She glanced at Rose. "What will you do if a showdown comes? You, and Josh, and your family?"

Rose hesitated. "That's a good question. Josh is military. He's lived his life sworn to uphold the decisions of his superiors. That's what the military does, even if he's only in the National Guard."

"I hope and pray your neighbors won't turn on us and make it bad for you."

Jasmine sat up as Rose drove over the levee. The first glimpse of Geneva was mostly roofs. "This is cool." She turned over a page on the sketch pad. They passed houses shaded by ancient trees and passed the squat red-brick cotton mill where most of the Wiregrass area's men and women worked.

After the cotton mill village, the oldest and most beautiful homes gave way to churches and a business district which included two grocery stores, two clothing stores, two banks, the *Geneva County Reaper* newspaper, and the Osceola Hotel. "These are great!" Jasmine sketched swiftly.

Doctor Ben Collins' office was down the street from the library. "Here we are," Rose announced. She opened the car door for Jasmine, who looked nervous as they walked from the parking lot and up the steps of the refurbished Victorian house. "Head high. Eyes forward." Rose said.

Inside the doctor's office Jasmine wrote her name on the appointment pad. Rose spoke to an elderly couple in the waiting room.

"How do," the ancient gentleman nodded his head, the skin of his face stretched dry and tight.

His wife reached out and clasped Rose's hand. "Oh, it's so nice to see you. How's that handsome husband of yours?"

"He's fine," Rose told her. "Working hard."

"I heard you have some of the war protesters camped down near your store. Are they as mean and belligerent as they look on television?"

"Not the ones I've met," Rose told her. "This young lady, Jasmine, is one of those traveling through."

Jasmine reached out her hand and the elderly woman grabbed it with both of hers.

"I'll be praying for you," she told Jasmine. "It must be hard riding in a vehicle with a little one growing inside."

"Brown!" the receptionist called out.

"That's us," the elderly woman helped her husband from the chair. "Take care of yourself, and your baby."

"Why are you hauling that sorry hippie to the doctor, Rose Reed?" a woman called out from beside the fake rubber tree.

"Why, Lucy," Rose replied. "Meet my friend Jasmine."

Jasmine reached out a hand.

The woman jumped up, pointed a sharp finger in Jasmine's face. "What are you doing running around making free love and showing off your pregnancy? I'd like to know why you don't go right on back where you came from. And what's your mother got to say about this?" Her face twisted as she spat out the hateful words.

Tears sprang to Jasmine's eyes. She dashed toward the nearest chair as Rose turned with a fury toward the woman.

"You have no right to say a word to this girl, Lucy Harrelson. Just because your own daughter dropped out of college and took to the road to protest the Vietnam war does not make it all right for you to attack Jasmine for doing the same."

Lucy's nasty expression set into a mask as she jumped to her feet. "Well, I never!" she huffed, and ran out the door.

Rose patted Jasmine's hand. "She has a daughter out there among the protesters, a blonde-haired girl named Jacklyn Harrelson, and Lucy hasn't heard from her for nearly a year."

"Oh." Jasmine put her fingers to her lips. "I am so sorry."

Doc Collins walked into the waiting room. "I see you just put a cork in Lucy's nervy mouth," he said with a chuckle. "Let's check out this young mother before she is ridden out of town on a rail for having an opinion."

"Thank you for letting us come in," Rose's temper flash cooled down. "Her husband Aaron said he was told you wouldn't see her under any circumstances, at the camp, or here."

"I'm afraid he got that information from someone who is now working out her notice before her replacement arrives." He nodded at the receptionist.

Rose looked at the receptionist. "You shouldn't fire her, Doctor Collins. Maybe she doesn't know any better."

"Don't speak up for me," the girl turned on Rose. "My husband is in Vietnam right now, doing his duty to his country. I am sick of those hippies coming in here wanting free health care. They're the ones stirring up the country about the war. Your husband should be over there too, like mine, instead of wet-nursing that bunch of National Guard wanna-be soldiers."

"I pray God will keep your husband safe." Rose touched the woman on the shoulder. A change had come over people she thought she knew. There was too much anger. Hate flew, looking for a place to land.

The atmosphere was much more congenial inside where a nurse weighed, measured and checked Jasmine from head to toe.

"Did you bring your records from your previous physician?" The nurse peered over her glasses.

"Uh, I haven't been to a doctor."

"Not at all?"

Jasmine clasped her hands and shook her head.

"Why not," asked the nurse.

"I don't know. It wasn't convenient?"

The nurse shook her head. "Do you know your due date?"

Rose listened. *That nurse is hanging on like a bulldog.*

"I think so. I know when I got pregnant."

The nurse looked up in amazement. "You do? How?"

"The first time I had sex with Aaron."

"Oh, so the first time you had sex?"

"No," said Jasmine. She rolled her eyes, as if explaining something to an idiot. "I had sex before Aaron." Jasmine fidgeted, running her fingers along the edge of her chair.

"And," the nurse looked up expectantly.

"It had been a year since I had sex with anyone before I had sex with Aaron."

"I'm sorry; then you did know. By your calculation when is your baby due?" The nurse took one last look at the sparsely filled intake form and put the pencil down. She looked Jasmine full in the face.

Jasmine paled. "I think it might be coming up in about two weeks, maybe?" She sucked in her breath.

The nurse jotted on her notepad as Doc Collins came into the examination room. "What do we have here? An exquisite young lady about to add to the population of the world." He sat down and read the nurse's notes.

He turned to Rose. "What do you think?"

"Her back hurts, but there's plenty of reasons for that with the weight she's carrying. She seems to tire too easily."

Doc Collins listened to Jasmine's heart, then moved the stethoscope to the baby. "Good strong heartbeat there." He shifted the stethoscope around. "Good shape. Might be about ready to turn to the birthing position."

Jasmine cuddled her stomach as if the wee one were already outside.

"What do you eat?" Dr. Collins asked Jasmine.

"Well, I drink lots of milk that Aaron brings me from Rose's grocery store, and one day her daughter brought me a meal of corned beef and cabbage."

"What else?"

"Dry cereal. Ramen Noodles. Mostly we eat a lot of peanut butter and jelly sandwiches. It's easy, you just put peanut butter on one side, jelly on the other and chew."

"Nothing wrong with PB&J. I ate lots of it going to medical school all those years ago." He touched her shoulder and grinned at her. "Raw carrots, apples, any fruit you can get. A general vitamin. Walk. Get out in the sun some each day. I know your mother warned you about the sun, but you're too pale." He turned to Rose. "Can you monitor her food intake?"

"I'll try," Rose said.

Jasmine's voice was just above a whisper. "Aaron doesn't have much money and it has to last us until we get to his relatives' farm in Georgia."

"His auto repair business ought to be able to take care of that." Rose stood up.

"He works on cars?" Doc Collins asked. "Maybe I should get him to listen to mine. It's got an extra little grunt when I crank it."

"Good idea," Rose told him. "When do you need to see Jasmine again?"

"A week ought to be about right. Keep watch and see that she eats the right foods, Rose. That'll get her strength back up. Sleeping well?"

"Not too much. I sleep on an Army-surplus cot in a tent." Jasmine blushed a deep pink.

"That could account for some of the backache." The doctor turned to Rose. "Could you put her up in one of your motel rooms?"

"Good idea. We'll do that," Rose assured him.

"I might take a ride down that way in a few days. Get Aaron to check my car." He turned to Jasmine and gave her a hug. "Tell your husband that you're just fine; might need a little more of the right kind of fuel."

"Thank you, Doctor Collins." Jasmine reached into a pocket and pulled out a wad of crumpled bills. "I hope I brought enough money."

"Old grouch out there takes care of that part," Doc Collins laughed. "Tell her your check-up is in trade for a check-up on my car. If she's nasty to you, Rose can handle her."

As they walked out of the examination room, Doc Collins patted Jasmine on the shoulder. "Young lady if that baby comes out as beautiful as you, it'll outshine the sun."

On the way back across the levee and south to New Hope, Jasmine thanked Rose.

"No problem," Rose told her. "We'll get you set up with a real bed. A good night's sleep might wipe out the exhaustion."

"I don't want to seem ungrateful, Rose, but I can't stay in the motel. I'd rather stay with Aaron in the tent."

Rose raised her eyebrows.

Jasmine paused, in thought. "He won't leave the campground at night. He's supposed to be their leader and he said he must be there to take care of any incidents."

"Incidents? Like what?"

"Like people getting drunk, or stoned, and causing trouble."

"That's easy. Put up a sign that says 'No Alcohol,' then appoint a committee to collect the beer and whiskey. I don't know what you'd do about the stuff they smoke, but there ought to be a way to ration it."

Jasmine sighed. "It would be nice if it were that simple. But more and more people are coming in every day. Hardly anyone leaves. Just keeping the newcomers contained on your land is hard. They're stretching over onto the Cook family's fields and Mr. Cook was there last night, yelling threats."

"I see," said Rose. "Do you have a ruling committee or something?"

"We do. Aaron named the men of the original three couples as the Camp Council. They meet every night. Mr. Cook was bad enough. You'd be shocked at the complaints they hear from the people coming in without permission."

"Has he asked Josh to help him?" Rose wondered. "Josh is military. He knows about organizing people. I imagine Sheriff Clark could help."

The color faded from Jasmine's face. "Please don't call the sheriff. He'd probably arrest everybody, because of the marijuana."

"I doubt that," Rose told her. "He's a good sheriff, and he's friendly. I don't know how he feels about the protesters being here. Maybe Josh can figure out what to do."

"I hope so." Jasmine looked relieved. "Although Aaron believes we have imposed on Mr. Josh and you about enough."

"Not so. We want you to be safe having this baby, which may come at any minute. Josh gets off work at five. Maybe he and Aaron can come up with some solutions."

"Look straight ahead, Rose." Jasmine held the sketch pad on top of her round stomach.

Uncle Jim met the women at the door of the Daylight Grocery. "I called the doctor's office but they said you'd already left," he said.

"Looks like you've been busy. What did you need?" Rose asked him.

Jasmine had stopped to look in the Free Box outside.

"I was going to ask you to get more rolling papers."

"Rolling papers? Whatever for?" Rose glanced at the shelf behind the counter. There were plenty of bags and cans of roll-your-own cigarette tobacco, but no papers.

"They're not rolling tobacco cigarettes, Rose, they're smoking marijuana," Uncle Jim told her. "We had lots of customers while you were gone and most of them were stoned out of their gourds."

"Out of their gourds?"

"I know it's a strange expression, but that's what the tattooed boy told me smoking marijuana does to people." Mr. Jim appeared to be a little frazzled. "All this new stuff the young people are coming up with is very disappointing to me, to say the least."

Jasmine came in with magazines from the Free Box. She looked from one to the other. "What did I miss?"

"Do you smoke marijuana?" Rose asked her.

"No," said Jasmine. "I can't, because of the baby."

"Did you smoke it before?" asked Uncle Jim.

"Sure, I smoked a little reefer. Not much. Aaron said it would relax me when I was uptight about a test," Jasmine looked surprised. "Most college students smoke it some."

"Reefer?" asked Rose.

"It's the same thing as marijuana, they just give it different names, like Mary Jane, pot, or smoking a joint. Whatever you call it, the smell's still the same, except it sometimes smells different because it's grown in different places."

"Phew," said Rose, and sat down on the stool beside the huge banana pod. "All this time I thought I had been smelling unwashed bodies."

Jasmine laughed out loud. "Well, that's mixed in too. Though most everybody's been bathing in the branch off the spring. That bubbling spring is wonderful."

"I believe we've been leading sheltered lives in this forgotten place," Uncle Jim told Rose. "We tried smoking pieces of hemp rope when I was a teenager, but it tasted terrible and smelled worse."

"Yeah." Rose shook her head and stood up. "We did too. Wasn't worth the trouble we got into for cutting off a piece of rope."

"No offense," Jasmine told them. "You guys are real cool, but you do seem a little backward around here."

"Backward from what?" Rose pulled an overripe banana from the pod and peeled it. "From smoking something that makes you feel calm and move slow, and stinks to boot? Maybe we're more like forward."

Rose turned to Uncle Jim. "Could you stay awhile longer?"

"Sure." Uncle Jim straightened his tie. "All I need's an R C Cola and a moon pie." He chuckled as he turned over a wooden crate and sat on it beside the drink box.

Rose turned on the outside lights. "Jasmine and I are going to plan menus for this underfed mother-to-be. Doc Collins said that all that's wrong with her is a sorry diet and sleeping on a camp cot."

Aaron came in the door, "I was afraid it was much worse, that she had some horrible disease, or was about to have the baby right away."

"We're not sure about the 'right away' part," Rose told him. "But we're about to fill her up with food."

Jasmine turned to Aaron. "Doc Collins said I should sleep on a real bed, and Rose said we could sleep in one of the motel rooms."

"I couldn't be away from the camp at night." Aaron ran a hand through his thick black hair. "It's scary enough with me there. I don't know what would happen if I'm not available when a squabble breaks out. I've been thinking about asking the sheriff to post a couple of deputies to keep down trouble."

"That's not a bad idea," Rose told him. "But Sheriff Clark might not like it. Some say he's anti-protesters from the word go, but you can't tell about him. He's like everybody's big brother, when it comes to straightening out a mess. But if you're nervous about the sheriff, get with Josh. He'll be in after five. The sheriff might be just what you need right now."

Aaron agreed that Jasmine should stay in the motel at night. "It would be quieter, and she doesn't need the aggravation of that crowd that we've got down there now."

"One of the rooms has two double beds in it," Rose told them. "You could take one down to the camp and put it in the tent."

Jasmine turned quickly to Aaron. "That way I could stay with you in the tent at night and come up here with you when you work on cars." She threw her arms around his neck.

"She might be right," Rose told Aaron. "Do you have enough business to spend the day at the auto shop?"

"I do," said Aaron. "There is an added benefit. The sooner I repair their vehicles, the more likely they are to go on to the camp site in Georgia. But that way we'd be using your motel room." He shoved his thumbs into his pockets. "How much will that cost us?"

"Since Jasmine would be here, she could help watch the store. That way I wouldn't charge for the room."

"Rose, you're doing enough already!"

"Jasmine could paint signs and sit behind the counter when I have to work on orders and bills, or go to the kitchen," Rose told them.

Jasmine leaned over, enclosing Rose in their hug. "Helping Rose would be wonderful. I am an artist. Remember?"

"Glad that's settled." Rose pulled an apron from beneath the counter.

Jasmine clapped her hands. "Me too!"

Like a young'un, thought Rose. *Like a nice, big teenager.*

"When the children get home from school, we can get a bed ready for you and Josh to take to the camp," Rose told Aaron. "Meanwhile, sweet Jasmine, let's see what we've got for sandwiches." She pulled ham slices out of the meat cooler and a couple more bananas off the stalk. In the kitchen she grinned at Jasmine. "Looks like we're fresh out of peanut butter."

Pidge

Chapter Nine

"We've got to find Frances. What if she drowned in the river?" Pidge told Lena as they left the school building in the afternoon. Her mouth was dry, and her throat hurt. *Could be a cold.* She was so worried about Frances it must be making her sick.

"Luke said he saw small shoe tracks at Little Indian Spring. She couldn't be making tracks if she was dead," Lena walked backwards. "Relax. We'll find her."

"I wish I was as positive as you," Pidge muttered as they climbed the steps of the bus waiting to take them home.

"This is the last time I can stop the bus on the route home, or coming to school, Pidge." Mr. Bob shook his head. "Some parents complained about the bus stopping at the campsite to search for Frances."

Pidge turned angry eyes on Roly Poly.

"Don't worry," Mr. Bob motioned for her to come on up the steps. "We'll slow down on the bridge and stop near the gallberry patch, but not for long." He raised his voice. "The students who wish to, may help look for Frances."

Pidge felt a little less scared, and more confident as Mr. Bob drove west toward the Choctawhatchee River.

When the bus stopped, Pidge and the other students gathered at the side with the best view of the camp. She stared as Luke jumped from the bus and made his way down the embankment toward the river. All the students watched him. There would be no way to keep his search for Frances from parents.

Pidge's eyes fastened on the tent where she had last seen her friend.

Lena called out, "Look to the left beside the Volkswagen bus. There's a girl."

"No," muttered Pidge. "Frances would be taller than that one, but there's another one in a green dress."

"That's not her," said Pidge's sister Julie. "I don't know why you're stuck on that green dress business. Surely she's got a change of clothes."

"Even if I saw her, I wouldn't tell you," Roly Poly snorted at Pidge.

"All right, Roland!" Mr. Bob told him. "Would you like to walk the rest of the way home?"

"Y'all ought to know, my dad's getting ready to chase the dirty hippies away."

"I understand," Mr. Bob told him. "But if Frances has been kidnapped, we'd be ashamed if we didn't search for her while we could."

"There's so many people, it's hard to pick out a single person." Kneeling on her seat, Mandy hung onto the top edge of the open window. "If we could walk around out there, we'd have a better chance of finding her."

Pidge chewed her fingernails. She knew Mr. Bob wouldn't disobey orders. Even if he wanted to. Letting Luke out was as far as he'd go today, and not that much tomorrow. Time was moving fast, and she felt that her friend was in grave danger. "What about the people she's with?" she asked. "Seems they'd know something."

"That young couple who've been hanging out at your parents' store—what about them?" Mr. Bob held to the steering wheel with one hand and waved the other.

"Jasmine said she hasn't seen Frances, nor the people she was with, for a couple of days. Aaron only saw her once."

"Well, there you have it!" Mr. Bob cranked the bus.

"There you have, what?" Pidge asked. *Whose side is he on?*

"They might know something about Frances but aren't telling. This hippie invasion is getting out of hand," he grumbled. "In addition to what may have happened to Frances."

Pidge pulled herself into her seat. She shook her head.

Mr. Bob jerked on the wheel as he turned in at the rock at the entrance to the Daylight Grocery store.

"I'll ask them some more questions," said Pidge as she got off the bus.

Mr. Bob leaned toward her. "You do that," he said. "We need to get to the bottom of what's happened to Frances, and these hippies aren't helping."

"I know." Pidge said. Lena, Mandy and the other students scattered toward their homes. She and Julie trudged toward the store.

Uncle Jim opened the door. "You look sad, Pidge. "Perk up. Things will get better."

"We didn't find Frances. Again," Pidge took the apron he handed her.

"Maybe next time. Don't lose hope." He went outside.

Pidge hugged her mother. "I don't feel well. I think I am coming down with something."

"You do seem fevered a bit." Rose felt her forehead. "Get a nice cold drink and sit behind the counter. Julie can straighten the shelves. I need you to watch the front for me."

Julie had already opened a fruit punch and held a Baby Ruth bar. "Sounds like a plan to me." She waved the cool, dripping drink bottle.

Pidge noticed Jasmine waiting at the kitchen door. "Hi! Did you learn anything more about Frances?"

"I didn't." Jasmine smoothed the fabric of her flowered skirt over her stomach. "Aaron went to the tent near the spring last night, but there was no one there."

"Come on," Rose touched Jasmine's arm. "Let's eat a sandwich and then we'll get clean sheets and fresh pillowcases for the single beds."

"I'm sorry, Pidge, I'll ask around again."

"Hey, Rose," Fiona called from the store's front door. "Where did the pink sheets in the Free Box come from?"

"Pink sheets?"

"Yeah. Who dyed sheets pink?"

Pidge spoke up. "The preacher's wife said she accidentally threw a tie-dyed shirt in the washing machine."

"Only Linda," said Fiona. They laughed. "You sure they're free?"

"They are," Rose told her. "She put them in the box herself, didn't she?"

"In that case I'll take 'em."

"Go ahead. You want to eat a sandwich and help us get a motel room bed ready for Jasmine?"

"Sure." Fiona stashed the pink sheets under the counter, and they headed for the kitchen.

Rose pulled mayonnaise and mustard from the refrigerator.

"Be right back," Jasmine told them. "I'm headed for the bathroom. Again. Seems that's what I do most of the time these days."

"Rose, maybe you or Josh ought to talk to my deluded husband. Richard's in tight with them rabble-

85

rousers planning to chase the protesters out if they can get enough men together." She looked at the bathroom door. "Jasmine and Aaron seem like such fine young people. I wish they weren't in with this bunch."

"Me too," Rose agreed.

Jasmine returned to the kitchen. "I'm itchy all over, Rose. Could that be a sign?"

Rose raised an eyebrow. "Probably a sign you need a nice, warm shower."

The women went toward the rear of the building. Pidge watched the road for Luke.

When he did appear, it was from the direction of the auto repair shop. He stomped in at the front of the store, snagged a drink from the cooler.

"I thought you got off the bus to look for Frances." Pidge came from behind the meat and cheese worktop.

"I did," Luke bumped his sister on the shoulder with the cold drink bottle. "Those people Frances is supposed to be living with are never at their tent, so I thought Aaron might get a handle on them. He said he'd look again tonight."

"Good." Pidge moved around the banana post and took her work position behind the counter.

As Luke walked to the kitchen, a barefoot young man wearing cutoffs and a "Repent!" shirt, sauntered in the store's front door.

From the cooler he pulled out an orange soda, clipping the cap off on the opener on the side, rolled back his head, then drank. "Phew," he said. "That ought to cool me off some."

"Could I help you?" Pidge asked.

"Another soft drink, peanut butter crackers, a couple bananas, and I ought to be fine for now." He put the crackers and bananas on the counter and pulled change from his pocket. "That enough?"

"Looks like it." Pidge shoved the coins around on the counter.

"Add a rasher of hoop cheese to that and some regular soda crackers. I'm hungry."

"We've got moon pies, too." Pidge pointed to a display near the canned goods.

The boy sat on an empty overturned crate. He chewed on the chunk of hoop cheese. The smell made Pidge hungry.

"Where is this place?" he asked.

"New Hope, Florida, which is almost Alabama. Why are you guys here, if you don't even know where you are?"

"I saw a big sign at an off-ramp that said those going to Georgia for the anti-war protests should turn off. I did. It was on Highway 81, I think. There's a couple guys with me. They're catching some z's at the camp site. I was too hungry to sleep. Besides that, it's hot'ern Hades, unless you can find a spot under an oak tree."

Pidge rested her elbows on the counter. "Muggy, not too comfortable, but we're still in spring up here," she agreed. "It's never as hot here as they say it gets in South Florida. Still, it's more steamy this close to the river."

He turned his sunbaked face toward Pidge. "I'll trade you a joint for a packet of rolling papers."

"A joint? I'm twelve."

"Whoa! Don't turn me in to the fuzz!" A smile started on one side, then moved across his wide jaw. "You fakin' me?"

"Name, rank, and serial number." Pidge pulled a yellow-lined pad toward her and picked up a pen.

"You don't want my address?" He gave her the wide grin again.

"I know where you are," she said. "I just need to know who you are. Driver's license is a good identification tool."

Up close, he looked Luke's age, Pidge thought. Leathery face and all.

He dumped the contents of his front pockets on the counter, including two large plastic bags filled with what looked like rabbit tobacco. From a back pocket he pulled out a driver's license. "Beau Smith," he said triumphantly and slapped the license on the counter.

"Beau Smith?"

"That's it." His grin had turned smug.

"We spell it B-O around here." Sounds bogus, thought Pidge. The age said 16. He'd probably lied about that. She took her time and wrote down his name, age, driver's license number and the address in Oklahoma, where it said he was from.

"All this to buy rolling papers?"

"No," she said with her most polite smile. "My dad said to get information on any young men who treated me inappropriately."

"How'd I do that?" he dropped the banana peel in the waste basket beside the cooler box. "I just bought a bunch of stuff to eat." He gave the lop-sided grin again and pulled the plastic wrap from the moon pie.

"Offering a 12-year-old marijuana is a felony in Florida actually, something like that. Lying on your driver's license, or using one that belongs to somebody else, might also be. Either way I got your number."

"Okay, okay. Be that way." The young man shook his head. "Damn!"

"I think swearing at a minor may be some sort of felony, too." *Listen at me.* Pidge couldn't keep the laughter back.

The two guffawed. *Funny, I like this guy.*

They stopped laughing. "I know it's serious, but it's hard to get a handle on just what's going on with the war protests." Pidge hoped she sounded more grown-up than she felt.

Beau munched on the moon pie. "This might sound crazy coming from me, but the whole thing about Vietnam is so complicated. All I hear is angry stuff about the war. Don't get me wrong, I don't think our soldiers ought to be there, but why are we so mad about it?"

"Don't ask me." Pidge shrugged. "You going to march in Atlanta?"

"Sure. I'm not just along for the ride." Beau grinned again. "But I will return, for more food," he said. "Without the mari-juana."

"Don't need no Mary guano." Pidge leaned against the cash register. She hoped he would come back. He was sort of fun.

Pidge helped Julie work along the wall of shelves, dusting and putting up cans. "Strange," she said. "No customers."

Julie stood up straight. "It's awfully quiet in here without at least one person muttering and grumbling because we aren't a big supermarket, like Piggly Wiggly."

"Be right back," Pidge walked out to the gas pumps as a customer drove up.

"Could I help you?" Luke stepped back as the car drove up to the pump. When he got the nozzle settled, he turned to Pidge and winked.

"Anything new on Frances?" she asked him.

"I think I have an idea where Frances might be."

"Where?"

"I saw footsteps on the trail south of the bridge. If they belong to Frances, she's probably staying down at Dead River with Granny Blue Sky and Jimmy John."

"That makes sense. How we gonna know for sure?"

"I'll go farther down the trail toward Dead River tomorrow."

"Yes!" Pidge jumped high and pumped her fist into the air, then hop-scotched back into the store.

Frances

Chapter Ten

At the river field campsite, Frances stood beside a decorated tent and watched the big yellow school bus rumbling down Highway 2. It was early. Pidge was surely on the bus. Hadn't they locked eyes before?

She aimed her gaze at the window and pushed lanky dishwater blonde hair from her forehead. There were two girls standing, one was Pidge. Was the other one Lena? Looked like it.

What if she took off after the bus at a trot? Wouldn't that be grand? If she ran to the road, would Mr. Bob stop and let her on?

She closed her eyes and wished, more than anything in the world that she could get onto that bus and ride to and from school, to talk homework with Pidge and Lena and watch Luke out of the corner of her eye, like she used to.

But life had turned scary after she and her parents left California in a caravan headed to Georgia and a protest march against the war in Vietnam.

Now she was back in her old neighborhood but was not allowed to speak to her friends. They weren't supposed to know she was here. It was like acting out a play. She had been told that if she followed orders, she stayed alive. If she notified anyone about her captors, she'd be killed. She looked at her arm where Sam had sealed his instructions with a lit cigarette, leaving a round,

festering wound. The red flesh and the memory of how
she had received it throbbed with pain.

Now Frances was caught in a trap. Back in
California it had sounded like a great adventure, as her
parents and their friends Sam and Betty talked about
joining a war-protest caravan,
"What about school?" she had asked.
Frances' dad had hugged her. "That's already
winding down. The rest of April, and May. I'll go over
and talk with the principal."
Some other friends of Frances' parents would stay
at their house while they were gone to Georgia. Choosing
what to take and what to leave had been the hardest part.
By the time everything was packed in her parents' truck
and Sam and Betty's car, it turned out her spot was in the
back seat of the car, behind Sam. She had a sinking
feeling as she burrowed out a place for herself, suitcase,
quilt, pillow, and books.
"I'd rather ride with you," she told her parents.
"I know. But there's not enough room in the cab
of the truck," her dad had said. "We can carry more stuff
this way."
"What if we get separated, or lost?" She was
trying hard not to cry.
"You'll be fine, Sweetie," her mother assured her.
"We'll follow behind the car and when it stops, we stop.
It'll be easier this way."
But it wasn't. Sam slid the driver's seat back so
there was hardly enough room for Frances behind him.
"Can you ease your seat up some, Sam?" she
asked, her knees square up against the back of the driver's
seat.
Sam didn't answer. He gunned the motor and
headed east on Highway 90, the Old Spanish Trail.

She held to her book *Rebecca of Sunnybrook Farm* and placed history, math, geography and English books on top of the suitcases beside her.

It wasn't too bad at first. It was so late at night when they checked into motels that they fell into bed and got up early to head out again at daylight.

Stopping at service stations to gas up and eating lunch under the trees at rest stops along the way were pleasant. It was plain that her dad and Sam were tired of driving. Frances helped her mom and Betty clean up and fill the water jugs.

Most of the time she dozed or read. Sunnybrook Farm was a magic place to Rebecca, even if it wasn't to the rest of her large family. Frances loved the young girl's positive outlook.

She was at the spot in the book where Rebecca asks Mr. Cobb if she can ride with him up front on the stagecoach.

"I can't see out the back window," Sam snapped and pulled the car off the road beside a litter barrel. He grabbed an armful of books, raised the lid, and dumped the books inside. "See? More room."

"Sam, don't throw those away," yelled Frances as she jumped out of the car and reached into the barrel. "These are my school books."

As she leaned in, Sam gave her a push, then pulled her from the barrel. "You don't need no books where you're going," he told her, then chuckled as if he had made a joke.

Frances swiped at tears as she put the history and geography books beneath under her feet, pushing against pencil box and notebooks filling the space under the driver's seat.

With her head on her jacked-up knees, Frances slept, dreaming of her parents and home. She awoke as Sam pulled up to service station gas pumps.

The truck! Her parents! Frances jumped from the car and ran across the parking lot.

"Mom," she called out. "Sam threw my school books into a trash barrel." Tears flowed as she buried her face against her mother's shoulder.

"There, there," her mother soothed her.

"What's happening?" her father pulled her into his arms.

Sam walked up. "There's not enough room for her in the car," he said. "I told you it would be a tight squeeze."

"I thought so too," Frances' dad agreed. "Maybe we can find room for her books in the truck."

"It's not just the books," she told them. "There's not enough room for me in that small space," she said. "My legs hurt."

Betty spoke up. "You've got as much room as I do."

"Don't be a whiner," Frances' mother told her. "Suck it up."

A lump of dread formed in Frances' stomach as she squeezed back into the tiny space. The triumphant look from Sam didn't help either.

She tried to sleep as they continued through big cities, small towns, miles and miles through deserts and ranches with cattle, horses, long fences. The two families usually stopped just before dusk, sometimes at cheap motels, mostly at a service station for food and bathroom visits, then hit the road again.

"I told you it'd be all right," her mother assured her. "As long as we stay on the Old Spanish Trail, we're going east. We won't get lost."

And then, what Frances had dreaded happened. She woke up as Sam pulled the car into a clearing filled with cars, trucks, buses, and tents. People milled around, claiming spaces. Sam ploughed through the crowds until he reached the edge of the clearing and stopped under a huge tree dripping with moss. He nosed the car in beside a shed, which had been claimed already.

"All right with you if we get in here?" Sam called out. The man mumbled and Sam parked.

"Where's the truck with my mom and dad?" Frances asked. "Is there room for them?" She stumbled in the dark as Sam turned off the lights and rummaged in the back seat for a lantern.

"I don't know and I don't care," Sam told her.

"Are we in Georgia?" Betty climbed out of the car, stretching. The place looked spooky in the lantern light.

"I don't know where we are," Sam told her. "I followed the sign. Let's catch some z's." He threw a quilt on the ground beside the car. Betty and Frances rolled up in quilts and got as near to the trunk of the big oak tree as they could.

The knot of fear in Frances' stomach eased some when the people parked under a pole barn not far from them got a fire going. The place was less scary. Maybe her parents would be along soon. She pulled her quilt over her ears and snuggled down.

The sun peeked over the treetops before Frances realized she was in the Reed family's river field. She jumped up. "I'm home! I'm home! This is New Hope!" She shook Betty. "This is where we moved from. My friend Pidge and her family run a grocery store here. I went to Bethlehem School. Over there is the Choctawhatchee River."

"What?" Sam stood, his eyes wide. "We're in Holmes County, Florida?"

"Yes. Yes." Frances hopped up and down. "Isn't it wonderful?"

"Hell! I said I'd never come back to Florida!" Sam shook his head. He grabbed Frances by the arm. "Don't tell anyone we're here!"

"Why?" Frances stopped jumping.

"Because I said so!" He pointed to Betty. "Neither of you give out your name. As for you Frances, you are to have no contact at all with the Reeds."

"Why not?" Betty looked him straight in the eye. "What is it, Sam? What's wrong?"

Sam didn't answer. His eyes flaming, he swung his right hand and slapped Betty across the face. She fell against Frances.

"Either of you get in contact with anyone here, or tell who I am, and I will knock you in the head, with. . ." He looked around for a weapon and picked up a hammer from beside his quilt. "This." He swung the hammer in the air.

"What about my parents," cried Frances. "Where are they?"

"I don't know. About half my stuff's on their truck. Guess we'll have to wait for them. Then, I'm splittin'." He paused, scratched his head. "Let's get the tent up."

They emptied the car. Suitcases, fold-up cots, mosquito netting, boxes of food, buckets and jugs, a hibachi, lighter fluid, cooking utensils, and tin plates.

"Make yourself useful," Sam told Betty, handing her a water bucket. "Follow that woman. She must be going to a spring, or the river."

Frances crept around looking for her dad's old truck. She pulled her cot in and settled it near the door flap, holding back tears.

On the trip Sam's manner toward her had been resigned, as if she were only a burden to endure. Now he stared at her, rubbing his chin reflectively. "If you tell anyone about me, I'll kill you and feed you to the alligators."

Frances didn't answer. She shook with fear. When she leaned to put her suitcase under the folding cot, Sam grabbed her.

"You got a cute hiney, little girl," he said.

"Sam!" Frances yelled.

"Sam!" Betty rushed into the tent. "Get away from Frances." She tumped the bucket of water onto his head.

"What's got into you?" she screamed. "You're not yourself. Not since we got here."

"No, I'm not," he answered. "And you'd better keep your mouth shut. While we're here, our last name is Smith." Water spattered on them as he shook himself like a wet dog, grabbed the bucket and ran toward the spring.

The woman and girl looked at one another. Betty held out her arms and Frances ran into them, sobbing. "I used to live here. There are people nearby that I know."

Betty wiped their faces with the hem of her long skirt. "It doesn't make sense. He hates this place, but I've never seen it before."

"I don't remember him from when I was little." Frances hiccupped. "My parents said he had been their friend for a long time."

"He must have done something awful and is wanted by the law." Betty rubbed her face where Sam's handprint glowed an ugly red. "I wouldn't sleep here if I were you. If he grabbed you in daylight, what might he do at night? I wonder if someone has room for you."

That's when Frances remembered the trees twined together, where she and Pidge had played house. "I think I know a place," she said.

"Don't tell me any more. You go." Betty stuffed food in a sack. "I won't watch you leave."

"I can put my book and pillow in my suitcase and carry the mosquito netting and food sack with one hand."

"Better take this." Betty wrapped a quilt around her shoulders. "Watch out for Sam."

"He won't ever see me again if I can help it," said Frances, and ran.

The hole formed by the twined trees had plenty of room. It didn't take long to clean out the leaves, and the mosquito netting fit over her just fine. Since the natural shelf was not wide enough for her suitcase, she tied it to a limb with a piece of twine. After eating a muffin from the bag Betty had handed her, she spent a restless night. In the morning, she'd put her suitcase and other stuff in the hollow of a nearby magnolia tree.

With the morning sunlight filtering through the trees, Frances felt less afraid. It didn't take long to stash her belongings in the hollow tree. She ate the donuts from the bag. All she had left was an apple and a package of soda crackers.

At Little Indian Spring she crept behind a palmetto bush. Surely someone who looked friendly would come for water. As she hunkered down, she saw a pregnant woman lean to fill her bucket and almost tump over into the spring.

Frances took the bucket and filled it. "I'll carry this for you."

The woman reached to rub her back. Her tummy stuck out like a ripe watermelon. "I'm not usually so clumsy." She reached out a hand. "My name's Jasmine."

Frances mumbled something and walked ahead. "I'm happy to help you." She said.

"Our tent is right over there." Jasmine pointed. The route took them past Sam and Betty's tent, but they weren't there. The car was gone.

"These people came in here last night."

"I heard them." Frances didn't tell Jasmine she had come to the camp with Sam and Betty. At Jasmine's tent, Frances looked around at the people, trucks, cars, and tents, but she saw no sign of her parents or Sam and Betty.

Jasmine poured the water into a drum beside the campfire.

"You need more water?" Frances asked her.

"Yes, thank you. I could use another bucket, if you don't mind."

"I would be happy to bring you more water," Frances assured Jasmine.

Frances looked for her parents as she circled behind a row of blueberry bushes to get to the spring and filled the bucket. As she neared Jasmine's tent, she saw Sam and Betty approaching in the car and turned north and then west to reach the tent from the other side. Her hands shook as she poured the water into the drum.

Jasmine led her to a cot. "Sit. You're white as a sheet."

"I'm okay," Frances told her. After a moment, she stood. "You wouldn't happen to have an empty container you'd loan me for water?"

"I have an empty milk jug." Jasmine held it out. "Why don't you go lie down in your tent and come back for supper with us."

"Us?"

"My husband Aaron. He'll be back soon."

"I'll do that." Frances was so excited about finding a friend, she ran right by Sam and Betty's tent.

Sam snagged her arm. "Whoa. Where you going?" He pulled her to him as Betty ran from the tent.

"Leave Frances alone," yelled Betty. She jerked at Sam. He held their arms together and picked up his lit cigarette. They screamed as he ground the fiery end into first Frances' arm and then Betty's.

"Now you are sisters." He laughed as he released them.

Frances ran back the way she had come, then circled to reach the spring and the twined trees. She sobbed as she lay in the natural cavity. "Mom. Dad. Where are you?" Finally, she napped.

Sunlight filtered through the trees on its westward slide. Frances awoke with a start. Jasmine had invited her to supper! Her stomach grumbled as if on cue. She circled north at the edge of the Cook farm and approached Jasmine's tent from the west.

Aaron hadn't returned, so Frances and Jasmine ate peanut butter and jelly sandwiches, followed by milk in tin cups.

"That was the best sandwich I ever tasted," Frances told Jasmine.

"Come back tomorrow and we'll find something different," Jasmine told her. "Food is always better when there's someone to eat with."

For the first time, Frances felt hope. Late in the night she thought she heard Sam's voice at Little Indian Spring and the fear jumped into full gear, but it didn't last long. She felt secure in her hidy-hole.

The next day she stood beside Jasmine's decorated tent and watched the bus roll across the bridge. As it reached the campsite, she saw Pidge, looking toward her. She stared back. She didn't dare wave. She touched the angry sore where Sam had held his burning cigarette.

The next day she awoke early and searched over the camp for her parents. There were so many people. Several trucks looked like her dad's. Her hopes dropped. At the sight of Sam or Betty she fled to her hiding place.

She watched for the school bus. She couldn't help herself. It drew her, like a magnet. In the afternoon she stood beside a cypress tree at the edge of the field and watched the bus amble across the Choctawhatchee River bridge. With a longing mixed with fear, she wondered how it would be to get on the bus and ride to the crossroads, to be with her friends, to go home with them and use their phones to search for her parents.

If she ran across the field to the bus would the driver open the door? If it was still Mr. Bob, she was sure he would. But what if the bus had a different driver? Would her friends protect her from Sam? She couldn't chance it. She held no doubt that Sam would harm her, and the Reed family.

In spite of her misgivings, Frances put out a foot to run toward the bus. She saw Luke jump to attention and race toward her. She couldn't be the cause of injury to those she cared about. She turned and ran, not toward Luke, but away, heading for the river. She ached to turn and embrace Luke, but her feet kept moving away from him.

The dash of water revived her as she jumped into the river, then dived into what she remembered as a deep hole hollowed out by the main current. *Let the hole still be in its same spot.* Her arms and legs flailed. Her fingers connected with roots flapping. She kept going. The edge. It should be about here. Her head popped above the water line. She had rounded the curve. She couldn't see Luke. He might be under water. She left the river and sprinted into a cluster of cypress trees edging the branch as it flowed from Little Indian Spring. If she could make it to the twined trees, Luke might not think to look there.

With an overhanded jump she landed in the bowl formed by the twined trees, she landed right on top of her quilt. That wouldn't do. She heard Luke crashing through the underbrush, calling her name. Climbing upward as Luke barreled toward the clearing, she sought a wide limb and lay along it, holding tight, hoping water wouldn't drop on his head if he peered over the edge of her sanctuary.

Frances watched as Luke searched around the twining trees. She held her breath as he walked among cypress knees and backed up to the hollow magnolia tree where she had stashed her belongings. After Luke turned and walked toward the spring, Frances let out her breath. He was growing up handsome. When she was little she had told Pidge she intended to marry Luke someday. Her gut wrenched when she thought of seeing Pidge on the bus, of being afraid to speak to her friend.

When she could no longer hear Luke calling her name, or thrashing about the edge of the river, Frances crept down and ran to the hollow in the magnolia tree for a sliver of soap Jasmine had given her. She didn't dare bathe in the branch flowing from Little Indian Spring. What if Sam walked up? She pulled out a clean shirt, underwear, and jeans, and ran north along the river to Parrots Creek.

Her bath used up the sliver of soap, and though sloe bush leaves made suds, that didn't help wash the mud out of her dress. She did the best she could, put on the wet dress and sat in the sun for awhile. Then she walked to the edge of the campground the farthest away from Sam and Betty's tent. A girl with bushy red hair hanging to her waist sat beside a two-person tent, knotting twine to make a macrame bag.

"Wow." Frances stooped beside her. The girl smiled and slowed her looping and knotting so that Frances could watch. The twine looked like that on window blinds and the intricate design resembled a purse her mother bought that had come from India.

The girl looked up. "I'm Bubu," she said. "You want to know how to do this?"

Frances squatted beside the girl. "It looks easy."

"It is, weave the different colors, twisting knots about a half inch apart."

101

Frances soon had a colorful twisted-string macrame bracelet. She tried it on her arm, then handed it to her new friend.

"You made it. You keep it," Bubu told her.

"Thanks." Frances pushed the bracelet up to her elbow as she had seen others do. *I can't wait to show Pidge how to make one of these.*

"How long have you been here?" Bubu asked,

"Not long. I'm waiting for my parents." Frances swiped at unwelcome tears.

"I left mine crying. Now I miss them something awful." Bubu began packing her string and ties into the large bag.

"You didn't come with them?"

"No. I'm with my boyfriend. We are going to march in Atlanta. That is, if we ever get there." Bubu flipped her hair. "I wanted to look around this place. I've been to the spring, but I'd like to see more of the river. Is it all right to go under the bridge?" She pointed.

"I don't know," Frances stuttered. A memory hit her square between the eyes. "Bye. See you later," she called out as she ran around tents and buses, headed south.

Pidge's dad built a bench for us on the old Indian trail so we could see the sandbar and the river.

Undergrowth and new pines formed a dense barrier at the edge of the field as Frances ran through the cypress brake and pine forest. Granny Blue Sky and Jimmy John lived farther south, near Dead River.

Heavy pine straw covered the trail but it didn't take long for Frances to find the bench. She brushed off the pine straw, lay down and hugged the bleached cypress planks. It was eerily quiet. She could hear no sounds coming from the campground. A few bird calls and that was it. "I could stay here," she said aloud. Her words echoed against the cypress barrier, beyond which she could see the sun reflecting off the sandbar and the river.

Frances took a circuitous route back to the twining trees, retrieved her things, put them in her suitcase with pillow and book, rolled up her quilt and mosquito netting, and headed back to the Indian trail.

She stashed her belongings under the wooden bench, then ate the apple, some peanut butter with the crackers and yeast bread that the hippie woman had given her. When she finished, she put the peanut butter jar in the bag with the leftover bread and a spoon the woman had made from a gallberry twig.

The wooden bench wasn't as comfortable as the hollow of the twined trees, but the quilt served as a mattress, and the mosquito netting fit over her fine. She listened for footsteps or other evidence of people or varmints. Hearing nothing except nightbirds shifting and protesting and owl hunting calls, she fell asleep.

Josh

Chapter Eleven

Josh wiped his hand across his forehead. The
crowds of people overflowing the river field campground
were not only a worry to him, but his daughter was a
worry also. He saw how upset Pidge was about her
missing friend, and he wanted to help. At the same time
the men of the community were hell bent for leather to get
the hippies out of New Hope. Now, if not sooner.

However, Josh appreciated that his family's little
country grocery store was busy: bread, milk, locally-
grown chickens, cabbage, onions, Irish potatoes, cans of
everything from tuna to Vienna sausage, potted meat, soft
drinks, ice cream, you name it, were being sold as fast as
they could be put on the shelves.

He stood in front of the Daylight Grocery,
watching the colors dance on the white rock. Sounds
swirled around him: Voices of people, a truck backfired,
off in the distance a donkey brayed, followed by the bark
of a dog.

Josh went inside the auto shop mechanic's work
area. "Hallo," he called and knelt beside a bright orange
station wagon to get an eye-to-eye view. Rolling out on a
creeper, Aaron collided with Josh's Army brogans. How
young this boy is, thought Josh.

"Sorry." Aaron wiped his face with a rag as he
stood up, then dipped the rag in the wash-up sink and
wrapped it around his forehead.

"Now you look like a hippie." *Wouldn't be long before Luke would be as tall.*

Aaron scrubbed the oil from his hands. "With the big fan going, it's almost comfortable in here, but not under a station wagon. They're big. A person can put lots of gear in one of those things."

"Sure can." Josh rubbed his hands together. "Most of these protester's vehicles are crammed full."

Aaron took in a deep breath. "Smells good though, doesn't it?"

"Yeah. Smells just like oil, rust, radiator coolant, mildew." Josh pushed a pile of tools with his shoe. "How old is this coffee?"

"I made it this morning." Aaron looked at the clock. They busied themselves around the coffee pot on a hotplate, then perched on the desk and a stool.

"Ugh. This stuff's strong enough to peel the hide off an alligator. What'd you put in it?"

Aaron laughed. "That's how we make coffee in Texas. We got cast iron stomachs."

Josh rolled his eyes. "I believe you."

They sipped coffee in companionable silence.

"I can't think what to do about these people pouring in here like water under a bridge."

Aaron put their empty cups in the sink. "Two days ago it was a few. Now it looks like hundreds."

"We could put numbers on surveyor's stakes in front of the tents. Like addresses in a town. That'd give us a guesstimate on how many tents and shelters." Josh rubbed his chin.

As they walked in front of the huge fan, their spoken words took on a fluid and wavy quality.

Aaron wiped his hands on his cutoffs. "The field's full. People are crammed under the pole barn, and tents are spread out almost to the spring. No more room underneath the big trees. The toilet and sewage ditch take up lots of space."

"I'll go up the road to my friend Tony's house. He's a surveyor," Josh looked around. "He may come to the meeting with us this evening. If each living space has a number, then we can get information on who's there and check them in and maybe check some out. We can figure out how many stakes then."

"Sounds good." Aaron sat down on the creeper and leaned back in order to roll under the station wagon. "I can be ready when you get back. This station wagon and two trucks are all I have left and I had to order parts for one. That'll take a few days to get here. What about numbers for the stakes?"

"We have black paint on a shelf by the back door, and a paint brush I think will fit," Josh told him. "We'll need to paint the numbers on the stakes."

"Jasmine can do that," Aaron said. "She was an art major before we dropped out of the university."

Driving west on Highway 2, Josh wondered what Tony thought about the happenings in the community, about the swarm of hippies beside the river. Was he one of the neighbors fuming about the antiwar protesters?

Tony waved. Josh turned in at a wide gate and drove into the barnyard where piles of building materials and fencing covered the ground under a large shed.

"Hear you got lots of company down by the river," Tony called out. "Been meaning to go take a gander."

"We've got to do something about these outsiders, Tony. More and more are arriving every day."

"Maybe we can figure out some way to stop the flood."

They threw a pile of surveyor stakes into the back of Josh's truck. Tony checked the toolbox on his old truck and pulled out a clipboard and notebook. "Plenty of saws, hammers and axes to work with, if we need them. You want to ride with me?"

"Let's go separate," Josh told him. "You might need to leave sooner."

Tony looked at Josh's truck. "How come your truck's neatern' mine?"

"Because I don't drive down every dirt road and walk miles of woods with that hound dog of yours every day."

"It's the military in you. I dare you to spit and polish my truck like you do yours. Everybody around would ask me what I was doing driving Josh's truck."

Josh stopped with his foot on the running board. "We been friends a long time, haven't we?"

"Ever since Rose dragged you down here and said she was marrying a soldier from the Tennessee hills. What's on your mind, old buddy?"

"I need to talk to you serious about this sudden influx of war protesters. About half of the community hates us for allowing them on the river field, and even more hate the activists. I keep feeling like an explosion is about to happen."

"What about Sheriff Clark?"

"I don't know why he's not here now, helping divert the swarm of young people some other direction. I called him, and he said he'd be here in a few days, that he'd send deputies over to check it out. He said since I'm military I ought to be able to handle these people up here, that he's got his hands full in other parts of the county and no empty cells at the jail."

"Strange attitude for a law man." Tony shrugged. "Sounds like some of that uneasiness infecting the rest of the country is seeping into our neck of the woods."

"Sheriff Clark's a good guy. If he thought it was an emergency, he'd be up here waving his arms and straightening out everybody, including us."

"I just can't seem to wrap my mind around these hippies." Tony scooted up to a fence post and scratched his back. "Before they showed up here, I didn't know any war protesters, so to me they were just other folks, from somewhere else."

Josh nodded. "Now that we've got them up close and personal, I'm beginning to see them as more or less misguided young people, not too different from our young 'uns around here. I imagine some of the long-hairs are rabble rousers and hangers on but seems to me the majority of them believe it's their duty to speak out against the war."

"I know what you mean. I'm trying real hard not to fall in with my neighbors making harsh decisions and talking hate." Tony rubbed the side of his nose, a nervous habit. "I believe in following the leaders of our country, but you've got to admit, the protesters make sense some of the time." He climbed into his truck. "I guess we just have to take this anti-war uprising a day at a time, old Buddy."

Tony followed Josh's truck to the auto repair shop where Aaron was introduced. They shook hands, eyeing each other gravely. Tony pulled his truck up beside the white rock and waited as Aaron hung a "Closed" sign in the auto shop front window, locked the door, and climbed in beside Josh.

"Well." Aaron stuck his arm out the window and cupped his hand. "Air," he said. "Not cool. But air."

Josh smiled. Aaron was still a youngster, enjoying the feel of freedom with the wind pushing against his hand.

The noise from the campground swelled as they drew closer. Voices rose, motors revved and gunned, hammers hit tent poles, children laughed, dogs barked. Even so, it was coming into the time of day when everything slows down and people start to settle for the evening.

The men parked the trucks beside the highway and walked together through the campground, aiming for Aaron and Jasmine's tent.

"Thank God, it's not as noisy as it was this morning." Aaron scanned the area. "Seems like even more people, though."

They carried clipboards, tablets, notebooks, pens, and serious expressions on their faces as they sidetracked around the former school bus covered in peace symbols, yin and yang designs, anti-war slogans and graffiti. Over all hung a thin veil of smoke from campfires, mixed with the pungent odor of marijuana.

Paying little attention to the newcomers, couples talked, tamped down campfires and washed up skillets and dishes. Children played catch, and tag, and a few dogs barked. Somebody coughed. A guitar tuned up. The plaintive chords of a protest song echoed from the shabby Volkswagen bus. "Give. . . peace a chance. . ." Sounded almost like John Lennon.

Tony raised a skinny arm, counting vehicles and tents. "No such thing as two to a car here, looks like more people than seats to ride."

Hippies started gathering at Aaron's tent as they arrived. "Meeting at six-thirty," Aaron told them. "Spread the word."

It wasn't long before the other two original campers and their wives arrived. One carried a sign: "Georgia bound! Meeting here 6:30 p.m.," which they posted in front of the tent.

Aaron touched the arm of a young man in a dashiki shirt and rope sandals, flowing brown hair held in a ponytail. "This tall drink of water is David, Mr. Josh. He's our lawyer."

"A lawyer? You have a lawyer?" Josh reached out his hand, which David enfolded with his own.

"Not yet," David told him. "I dropped out of law school to join the peace movement."

Josh leaned back to look up at him, immediately liking the young man "I'll bet they're glad to have you along. Seven feet?"

"Close," David laughed. "Six-ten. Most people ask me if it's cold up here." He turned to the others. "This is Jeremiah, his wife Cindy, and my wife Doris. You know Jasmine. We are the original group. Sorry to take over your field. We'll be out of here soon and you can plow it all up for a spring crop."

Josh was pleased. He could see why Rose had trusted these people. "I'm just trying to help you guys along. I'm not into politics, but there are those around here who want you all gone as soon as possible. And I don't want any problems we can't handle."

"I don't understand why they want us gone," Doris spoke up. "Us squatting for a few days shouldn't bother the locals." She swung her long brown hair. "Everybody should be protesting the deaths of our country's young men in the rice paddies of Vietnam. What's to get mad with us about?"

Josh shook his head. *David's wife is no wilting violet. Strong men attract strong women.* "I agree with you," he told her. "The problem doesn't seem to be the original group, but the hundreds of others rolling in like a flood."

"There *are* too many." Doris waved her arm. "What can we do?"

"That's why we called the meeting." Josh handed a notebook and pencil to her. "Jot down ideas. Get the women involved."

Doris smiled. "C'mon Cindy, let's make notes."

Tony walked around the tent, pulling at guy wires. "You sure know how to set up camp," he told Jeremiah.

Josh looked around at the gathering crowd. David seemed already acquainted with many of them. He shook hands and chucked some of them on the shoulder. His head with its shock of a ponytail seemed too big for his skinny body.

"Your buddy reminds me somehow of Abraham Lincoln," Josh told Aaron.

"He does me too," Aaron agreed. "But I couldn't fit in his shoes. In the words of my father when we told him we were leaving: 'At least David might be able to keep the rest of you out of trouble'."

Josh watched as every description of young male and female, some singles, many couples, positioned themselves in front of the tent. Some had little children who ran around playing chase.

Fresh faces, thought Josh. Probably most had been college students. Some looked naturally tanned, and many had blistered noses. They were dressed in colorful headbands, bell-bottomed jeans, cutoff shorts and tee shirts (many tie-dyed). The young girls and women wore short print dresses, or peasant blouses and flowered long skirts.

Slogans and peace symbols decorated clothing, vehicles and tents. Many of the men were naked above their waists. The Florida sun hadn't yet cooked the bare skin of some late arrivals, but it would before long.

The sweet smell of marijuana smoke hung over the campsite. Many held a short hand-rolled joint fatter than a cigarette between stained fingers. Some wore an indolent look, as if they weren't all there in the wide-awake department. Most looked laid back and easy-going.

"We're here to sort out problems and see what we can do about congestion." Aaron stood on an upturned barrel at the front of the tent. "Raise hands, just like children on a camping trip."

"Man, it's laughable, but for all these brothers and sisters, there is only one toilet," a voice called out, followed by a ripple of agreement which swirled around the gathering.

"Yeah, I don't mind going behind one of these big trees, but it's not very private given the number of people camped here. And more coming in every day." The speaker wore sunglasses and tugged on a straggly beard.

"We've put up a sign: Women use the outhouse and Men the garbage ditch." Aaron held up his hand. "All we've got is a piece of canvas draped in front of the ditch," he said. "What we need are port-o-lets."

Josh looked at Aaron and raised his eyebrows. *Freeloaders can't be choosers*. He felt uneasy. It didn't sound like these people were planning to leave in the next few days. It appeared more likely they were here for the long haul.

Aaron cleared his throat and called out, louder. "What we need are fewer people. This is not a campground. It's a field, where crops are to be planted when we leave."

"We do have too many here," council member Jeremiah spoke up. "It would help if some of us would go on to the planned camp site in Georgia."

"I don't have a map. Could you tell us how to get there?" one young rebel asked. "We've been following signs along the Old Spanish Trail. That's what got us here."

"I can draw a map," Aaron said.

"I'll get copies made at the newspaper in town," Josh told them. "Those who want a map, raise your hand. I'll bring as many as are needed."

While Doris counted hands and jotted down a number, Tony walked around the circle, adding up tents.

112

Cindy, Jeremiah's wife, raised her hand. "We could use a curfew."

Voices rose in agreement.

"Waking up's fine, but it'd be more comfortable if some of you people would go to sleep at night," retorted a guy holding a joint in one hand, the other hand pushing long, blond hair out of his face.

"Talking awhile's not too bad but getting drunk and singing Ninety-nine Bottles of Beer over and over until daylight won't crack it," called out a female voice.

Josh pulled up a bucket, turned it over, stood on it and looked out over the crowd. He raised his voice and tried to put authority into it. "The folks around here are becoming upset at this many people squatting in a field. It would be best if you all kept as low a profile as possible. As for myself, I believe the original three couples who stopped here should stay until Aaron's wife either has a baby or gets better. Those with problems that are keeping them from moving on, speak up. We'll do what we can."

A voice came from those near the tent. "Why should we listen to you, man? It's obvious you ain't one of us." The young hippie, tugging at the bib of his cutoff overalls, walked up to Josh,

"My family owns the land where you are camped, where you are now living free. And according to my neighbor to the north, that one," Josh pointed, "with the peace sign tattooed on his right cheek, was seen stealing two of Mr. Cook's laying hens night before last."

"What would I do with a stolen chicken?" The guy waved his arms.

Josh shook his head. "You tell me."

The tattooed chicken thief slunk behind a larger sun-burned city boy and slipped away.

A hand raised from the crowd. "Could I come closer?"

"Yes," answered Aaron.

As the small auburn-haired youth reached the tent, he pulled off a red neckerchief and wiped his face. "My woman and I would split right now, but my car won't start. I don't have money to get it fixed, nor enough money for gas."

"When you wake up in the morning find me, here or at the shop beside Daylight Grocery," Aaron promised him. "I'll see about repairing your car."

"Why don't we take up a collection now for gas?" David raised his voice. "I'll start it with five dollars."

Aaron grabbed a water bucket from a persimmon tree limb beside the tent and held it up. "All in favor of David holding the gas money say 'aye'." He was answered with an enthusiastic roar.

Aaron clapped his hands. "That ought to make a difference," he said. "Anyone with extra bread jangling in their pockets, give it to David and he can dole it out to those in need of traveling dough."

"Or eating bills?" a voice called out.

"That too," answered David, shaking the bucket.

A barefoot young man, wearing a yellow shirt emblazoned with a peace sign, stepped up on a box near Aaron. "Check the Free Box at the Daylight Grocery," he yelled. "Newspapers, magazines, bent cans, potatoes, cabbages, and overripe bananas."

The crowd laughed. "I did that yesterday," one called out. "Found a Sears & Roebuck catalog from the 1940s." He pointed toward the outhouse area. "Thought I'd won the lottery."

Josh

Chapter Twelve

Laughter exploded from the protesters. Josh called out, "Most of the people of this community are trying to help you survive and move on. They understand your goal and whether they support you or not, many of them respect your right to your opinion.

"But," he said, looking straight out at the crowd. "There are some who want all of you gone. Right now. They are holding meetings on how to force all of you to leave." He took a deep breath to continue but was interrupted by a youth wearing a bright purple tie-dyed shirt, with an even brighter purple headband.

"What we are doing is waging a non-violent protest against the war in Vietnam. Our goal is to stop the slaughter of young men who are where they shouldn't be at the whim of military leaders." He stopped. "Not that a bunch of country hick rednecks would understand."

Josh clenched his jaw. Aaron reached out, took Josh's hand and raised their locked hands high.

"This military man is our friend," he said. "He, and many others here, are trying to help us as much as they can. We don't want to demoralize this small community. I say we work with them to get ourselves to our destination near Atlanta where we can achieve our vow to protest against the Vietnam War in an orderly and peaceful manner."

"Amen," yelled David. He, Aaron, Jeremiah, Josh and Tony joined hands and raised them in the air. "Those who agree, join us in a voice of appreciation."

The roar echoed throughout the field, and up and down the river.

Before the sound of the cheers quieted down, a young woman ran from the spring trail. She jerked at David's arm. "There's a fire-breathing dragon at the spring. I had to grab my water bucket out of its mouth." She hugged the bucket in fright. "Billy's right behind me." She pointed.

A young man wearing a cutoff tee shirt with his sunburned belly sticking out, loped up in long steps. He leaned over with his hands on his knees. "She's right," he said, catching his breath in huge gulps. "Biggest damned creature I ever saw."

The others looked puzzled. "An alligator?" asked Josh.

"I don't know. Long head and tail. It's big, and scary."

"Where you from?" A chuckle was building in Aaron. He gulped it down.

"New Jersey by way of Stanford. What's that got to do with anything?" The youth looked into his empty bucket and shook it.

"Not much. But you are in Florida," explained Josh. Several stifled grins. "We have alligators."

"Alligators? Plural? You mean there's more?"

"Probably not, if you saw only one," Tony, the surveyor, told him. "They won't bother you if you leave them alone."

"I swung my bucket at him. He's probably plenty mad. Think he's still there? I do need water."

"I'll go with you," Tony told him and reached out a hand to the girl. "You want to come with us?"

"No! I want to go home, or at least go on up to Georgia. I ain't staying around no alligators. When I left home, my dad cussed me and said I was nothing but alligator bait."

A young man, hunkered down and sitting on his heels, jumped up. "I know what to do with an alligator," he said. "You shoot 'em. Stay here while I get my gun."

"Wait." Josh grabbed him by the arm. "Don't shoot this alligator. Look at his tracks. If he's missing a toe, he may be Two-Toe Tom. He's an area pet, sort of."

"This is Florida. They have pet alligators down here," called out another voice. "I'll get my pistol."

"Whoa, there were to be no weapons on this trip." David grabbed the young man by his overall strap. "That's the rule." He stepped up on an overturned barrel.

"Listen up," roared David. "The law of this campground is, and has been, no weapons. Bring all guns to this tent. Now!"

"What do you have?" Josh asked the youth he held by the arm.

"Only a little ol' 22. Just enough to scare somebody, or maybe to do a little hunting if we need to live off the land."

"Bring all guns, that means pistols too," David called out. "To this tent. I give you 10 minutes to put your weapon in this barrel or you'll answer to the sheriff."

Looking at him, Josh, and the others, had no doubt that he meant what he said.

"All weapons!" David shouted again.

"What about pen knives?" asked a young man.

"You can keep pen knives, but not switch-blades. Bring them here; the weapon will be recorded under your name and when you leave the camp to go on to Georgia, you can take your weapon. But you can't have them here on this property. DO YOU HEAR ME?" His loud roar echoed off the trees and bounced back.

Yesses came from every direction. A few young protesters came forward. "I have a permit for mine," said one, holding a pistol.

"We'll record that." Aaron held a yellow legal pad. David held a clipboard.

"You write down the information and I'll tag 'em," Josh told him.

"You brought tags?"

"Don't know why; my hand picked up a box when we left the store." Josh pulled out a pen and wrote names as Aaron called them out.

"Is this all?" Tony asked. The line was short, only four people so far.

Josh did a double-take. Before him stood a youth in cutoff overalls, long hair sprouting on his head and face.

"Wilbur! Is that you?"

"It's me, Mr. Josh. I joined up with 'em." He put a .22 in the barrel.

"Why? You live right down the road. You're in 12th grade." Josh sputtered.

"I'm goin' with 'em to the big protests."

"But you got no dog in this fight." Josh aimed the pen at Wilbur's chest.

"I do, Mr. Josh. I found me a girl." He pointed to a smiling teenager in a red dress which reached almost to her knotty little knees.

"One squirrel gun." Josh rolled his eyes as he wrote Wilbur Fowler on the list.

"We now have two .22 hunting rifles, an antique German Luger, one switch-blade and a BB gun in the barrel." Josh stifled a grin. "These young folks aren't even near to being armed and dangerous."

Most of the crowd had dispersed, laughing and talking about how to handle an alligator. "A 'gator can't see very well. Just stand still and he'll go away," one cautioned.

"Like hell I'm standing still. Me and my crew will burn rubber getting otta here tonight," called out a tall red-haired youth with a sun blister on his nose. "Have you got enough cash for gas?"

"I think so." David reached for the bucket. "Sure getting low," he said, as he counted out bills to the youth.

The young man with the serpent tattooed on his arm stepped forward. "I can put some more in the bucket," he said. "My dad's not speaking to me, but I learned at the bank yesterday that he opened an account in my name and put a pile of cash in it. He hates my long hair and is all for war of any kind. But, since his bank fell in love with compound interest, he's taking in a boatload of dough." He pulled handfuls of bills from his pockets and put them into the bucket.

"Right on! Would you be on my committee for gas and food money?" David asked him.

The boy shook David's hand. "Sure," he said. "My name's Grant."

"Maybe truck fixin' too," a voice called out.

Grant looked around. "We'll see," he said.

"Hey, David," Aaron called out. "We've got the measly few weapons documented: What do we do with them now?"

"Don't ask me. My tent is open to everybody," David told him.

"There's a metal filing cabinet in the auto shop. We could store them in there, if Josh doesn't mind and has a key for it."

"My wife has a key for everything," Josh told him. "That's not many weapons and I'm not sure we have a right to take them."

"Maybe we should ask Sheriff Clark about it," Tony butted in.

"Wouldn't hurt," David was suddenly serious. "My law degree, if I had it yet, would be from California, not Florida."

"Aaron and I'll store the weapons, even if there aren't many, and Tony can contact the sheriff," Josh told him.

"Hey!" A voice rang out. "You gonna' hand them piddling little guns to the cops?" A phalanx formed at the front of the crowd. Two hippies moved toward the barrel. "You ain't gonna' give them things to no law."

David stepped up and clasped the shoulder of each man. Tight. "They'll only be with the fuzz until they are checked out legally. You own your gun, you got a permit, you have no problem." He tightened his hold on the shoulders. "Do you understand?"

"Yes, Sir." The men stepped back. One rolled his eyes. "What do I know? I'm a flower child against guns and war."

Josh stepped back onto the upturned barrel. "As to the matter of the one toilet. I know a guy down Highway 2 who owns a construction company in town," Josh told them. "Maybe he'll loan us a few port-o-lets."

"Check with him tonight?"

"Tomorrow morning. I promise." Josh laughed and a few joined him.

One of the protesters chucked Josh on the shoulder. "You're a regular cool dude to let us squat on your land," he said. "Want to smoke a joint with me?" He held out a marijuana cigarette.

"You're kidding," Josh laughed. "Boy, would that make the rounds at the National Guard Armory. Besides I get enough second-hand smoke around here. I'm likely to go in to work with my eyes crossed tomorrow—if not from pot smoke, from exhaustion."

The sun hung just over the western line of loblolly pines and oak trees when they left the campgrounds. "Not enough artillery to hardly notice." Aaron picked up the barrel and put it in the front of Josh's truck.

"I'll come with Aaron to be a witness that you have that stuff." David laughed. "I told you guys these people are nonviolent protesters. They don't want war, in Vietnam, or anywhere else."

"Yep." Josh shook his head in disbelief. "That's what the signs say: Love not War."

"Don't forget to ask the sheriff about the legality of our weapons confiscation that fizzled." David bumped shoulders with Josh.

"I promise, and I'll find out about getting some portable toilets, too."

David handed the collection bucket to Grant. "I hereby dub you the High Poobah Treasurer-in-Chief of the uninvited squatters."

Aaron reminded the fellow who needed his car repaired as soon as possible, to bring it to the concrete building with peeling white paint, beside the Daylight Grocery store.

Josh whistled as he cranked his truck. *Maybe it will work out all right after all.* The three vehicles headed for the crossroads.

"I still don't understand how you guys wound up here when you were headed to Georgia."

Aaron held the barrel as Josh unlocked the auto repair building. "There was a sign on Highway 90. It said for those going to the Georgia farm to turn right on Highway 2 to get to 431."

"That doesn't make sense." Tony clanged shut a drawer in the file cabinet. "Highway 2 doesn't go to U. S. 431."

"Who wants to go with me to find that sign?" Josh handed the clipboard to Aaron.

"I need to get home," Tony told them.

"Bring me back to the campground?" David asked.

"Sure. Aaron can lock up here."

"They used to call this road the Hog and Hominy." Josh speeded up, going west on Highway 2. "When it rained, the road was a muddy mess. Folks said it was where the hogs ate the hominy. It was unpaved for many years, before a law passed that made it illegal for stock to range free. Then farmers and stockmen built fences and the county paved the road."

"Some tale." David chuckled. "You know what I miss most about the city? Street lights. It's black here. Wonderful canopy of stars, but hard to see at night."

"Yeah. When there was no moon, my grandma used to say it was 'dark as cats afightin'.'"

Josh turned left on Highway 81 and soon reached Highway 90, the Old Spanish Trail. Several hundred yards west they saw the back of the offending sign on the right-of-way. He passed it, backed up, and turned around.

The big piece of plywood was nailed on a two-by-four with crude lettering painted on it:

"GEORGIA PROTEST FIELD turn right Highway 52, then U. S. 431 to Columbus and Atlanta."

"There it is!" Josh jumped to the ground.

"The 5 is so small you can hardly see it!" David reached up and swiped at the sign. "We could fix that with a magic marker. You got one?"

"No. Left the pens at the auto shop." Josh stood beside him. "We could burn the end of one of these stakes and write in charcoal."

As they shook their heads a loaded pickup pulled to the roadside beside them.

"You puttin' up a sign, or taking it down?" the man called out.

"We need to change it. The directions are wrong."
Josh turned.

"You got a permanent marker or a cigarette lighter?" David called out.

The man got out of the truck and eased the door shut. "Keep our voices down, she's asleep," he said of the girl with her face turned toward the back of the truck seat. "I got a lighter if you got a joint."

"Nothing to write with?" David rubbed at the small 5. "No spray paint?"

"No. Whatcha gonna' write?"

David showed him. "We want to make the five as large as the two. That's the directions to the Georgia protest farm."

Josh reached into the back of his truck, pulled out a surveyor's stake, and shaved it on the end with his pocket knife. "Here." He held it out. "Set this afire."

The three watched, mesmerized, as the end of the stake caught, and burned. The small pile of ashes on the ground was scooped up by David. He spit on his fingers and dipped them into the soot, then stood tall and fashioned a large 5 beside the 2 already there.

"What do you think?" He stepped back.

"Fantastic!" Josh started to clap his hands, then glanced at the sleeping girl in the pickup.

"Keep going," David explained to the long-haired young man. "That's the way to Highway 52."

"It will take you to Alabama, to Samson, then Geneva, and on to Dothan, where you get on 431 to Phenix City, then Columbus, Georgia, and on to Atlanta," Josh added.

"No Mary Jane?"

"Not a shred." David laughed. "Head off that way."

When the mutter of the truck's engine pulled it over a low hill and the lights disappeared, Josh and David jumped and yelled into the dark night. "Hallelujah!"

They stood for a moment beside the sign and watched as a truck built from a sawed-off car slowed down, pointed headlights at the sign, then slowly drove north toward Highway 52.

"We have stopped the hemorrhage of the peace train bound for the Choctawhatchee River field campground," said Josh. He wiped his face with his hands and looked upward at the field of stars blinking in the sky. "Thank you, God," he said. "Thank you."

"Maybe we ought to sit here and make sure the next ones get on the right road," David offered.

"Not a bad idea. We can savor our victory." Josh stretched his hands out as if holding to something solid.

"You're right," David agreed.

A wood-paneled station-wagon pulled up. "This the way to the Georgia Protest Field?"

"You got it!" David yelled.

"Keep goin' thataway!" Josh brushed his hands together and stood up. "What a relief," he said. "Maybe now these squatters will leave and I can concentrate on helping Pidge find out what happened to her friend Frances."

Pidge

Chapter Thirteen

Pidge helped customers in the store as her mother, Jasmine, and Fiona, prepared the motel room for Jasmine's use and got the single bed and bedclothes ready to be taken to the camp site.

"Time to close?" she called out the back door, but nobody answered from the kitchen.

Rose had ordered extra rounds of hoop cheese. As Pidge cut it into wedges, trying to keep them even, she realized there was no way to stay ahead of the demand. She marked on a list each time she finished cutting a round and soon put three empty wooden cheese boxes in the Free Box outside.

A young hippie girl walked in the door with one of the cheese boxes in her arms. "These are cool to store food in."

"That's what they tell me. I get tired of cutting cheese, though." Pidge walked behind the counter as the girl piled soup cans and crackers beside her chunk of cheese.

"I'm Pidge," she told the hippie.

"I'm Elsa," the girl told her. "Headed for the peace protests, as soon as my man gets his car fixed."

"That's really a nice headband," Pidge told Elsa. "It looks like lace."

"It's a special kind of lace, called tatting. My aunt makes them." She took the delicately tatted headband off and handed it to Pidge.

"Oh, I couldn't take that," Pidge told her.

"Sure, you can. My aunt will send more when I get to Georgia."

Pidge tried it on and walked around to look at her reflection in the glass door of the drink cooler. "I might get by wearing this lacy-looking headband to church, but I sure wouldn't be able to show off a regular one."

"Can't ever tell." Elsa handed bills to Pidge, who gave her change. "I thought my ma would die when I first put one on. Then she got to like them and now wears a headband herself. She calls it her 'badge of courage.'"

"Not bad." Pidge kept the headband on as she walked Elsa to the door. She liked talking to the war protesters. She asked where they were from. Some sounded homesick. "How long have you been away from home?" was frequently answered by females with an eye roll and a quick "Too long." Most males sneered, referred to their fathers, and said they were glad to be on the road and out of "rage range."

When the rush slacked at the gas tanks, Luke came into the store. He hooked his fingers around a cold drink bottle and pulled it out of the cooler box full of more water than ice.

"Whew, what a day," he said as he wiped his face with the towel hanging on a post for that purpose.

"What about Frances?"

Before Luke could answer the big front door flew open and Fiona's husband Richard burst into the store.

"Is my wife here?" he asked, looking around at shelves and display counters as if she might be hiding.

"She's in the back with mom," Pidge told him.

Richard stormed through the back door and down the walkway to the kitchen.

"Frances," she reminded Luke.

They heard raised voices coming from the living quarters.

"No customers in here, nobody but us," Luke told her. "Tiptoe." They slipped in at the kitchen door.

"Never heard of you renting out a motel room before, now you're inviting them hippies to live here?" yelled Richard.

Rose's voice rose, but it was calm and controlled. "I can invite whomever I want into my home. It is none of your business."

Fiona held Mandy close as they stood in the living room, eyes wide with astonishment. Jasmine stood behind them, crying softly.

"It is my business when you welcome a band of gypsies into my community." His voice kept rising decibels. He stomped around the living room in circles. "This is no place for them thieving hippies. I don't want my family cavorting with them."

"Nobody's cavorting with anyone." Rose stood her ground. "I'd suggest you lower your voice."

"I ain't lowering nothing. Come on Fiona and Mandy. None of us won't be visiting this lowlife place again."

Pidge and Luke slipped back into the store.

Richard was right behind them. He aimed angry scowls at Pidge and Luke as he ran past them, straight outside, slamming the door hard enough to shake the big front window.

"Phew," said Luke. "Richard is mad'ern a wet settin' hen!"

Pidge ran to the living room. Rose had her arms around Jasmine. Fiona held Mandy, and Julie stood to the side, hugging her favorite doll, Esther.

"What on earth's going on?" she asked.

"I see a couple of gas customers," Luke ran out, jingling the goat bell on the store's front door.

"You want me to close the store?" Pidge asked her mother, who shook her head no.

"We'll be all right," Rose told her. "Watch the front for me until we cool down in here."

"Could I help you," a breathless Pidge asked as she ran into the store.

The tall man with a beard, a long, sleek black plait of hair hanging down his back, plunked a half-full croaker sack on the counter.

"Give these to your ma," the man said. "Told her I'd bring her some frog legs. Biggest I've seen."

Pidge ran around the counter and hugged the tall man around the middle. He wore a bright red plaid shirt and blue jeans.

"Jimmy John! You came out of the swamp!" She pulled back. "I didn't think Indians had beards. You look like a bear."

"You know I'm not full blooded," the husky young recluse hugged her back. "Don't think there are many full-blooded Indians anymore. How you doin' on fishing poles?"

Pidge turned. "Only two left. One of these days you're gonna show me how you cut bamboo, hang it from oak tree limbs where it magically becomes fishing poles. Right!"

"When school's out for the summer. Who bought all those poles?"

"Luke's teaching the hippie boys how to fish."

"Ha!" Jimmy John exploded with laughter. "What do they use for bait?"

"Luke takes them to the garden for crickets and grasshoppers and shows them how to snore earthworms out of the ground with two sticks." Pidge followed Jimmy John to his truck and helped him carry in bright, lacquered fishing poles.

"I'd like to watch them city boys grunting up earthworms. That'd be a sight." Jimmy John and Pidge put price tags on the poles and positioned them in the rack.

"They learned quick how to work trotlines," Pidge told him. "My dad showed the first bunch the best places to tie up the lines and bait the hooks."

"Hope somebody showed them how to fry up the fish." Jimmy John appeared ready to go teach the hippies.

"Guess somebody did. We're doing a land-office business selling fine ground corn meal, which most of them never heard of before they came here."

They laughed. Pidge hugged her Indian friend again.

"Go on in the kitchen," Pidge told him. "They'll want to see you."

"I better get on back. Too much commotion in the settlement. I like the quiet better, down on Dead River. I can hear the hippies in the river field, but it's a way-off sound."

"I'm really worried, Jimmy John. I saw a friend that had moved away standing in front of a tent down there, but she's hiding from us. Luke chased her one time, but she outran him. It's really weird. I think the hippies she's with have kidnapped her."

"Did you call Sheriff Clark?"

"No. The woman I saw her with said he'd put the hippies in jail for smoking weed, if I did that."

"Wouldn't worry about that," Jimmy John laughed. "His jail's not big enough for that bunch. Call Sheriff Clark." He gathered up leftover price tags and put them in the box.

Pidge pulled open the cash drawer. "How much for the frog legs, Jimmy John?"

"Don't want no money for 'em," he told her. "I could use some sardines and crackers, can of cooking oil, maybe a wedge of hoop cheese—"

"And a box of moon pies," Pidge broke in.

"You got it, and a couple of Baby Ruths. That ought to cover the frog legs."

Pidge put a box on the counter and plunked in items. "Tell Granny Blue Sky hello. I'm putting in a couple of cans of her brand of snuff. I'm sure the frog legs are worth a lot. They cost a mint in town."

"This ain't town," Jimmy John turned his brilliant smile on her. "This is home. And there are frogs around every mud pond. You could get them yourself with a gig."

"I know, but don't tell the town people."

"Right. And they'll keep buying my frog legs."

"Jimmy John, you do remember my friend Frances? Lived in the big house on the hill?"

"I do remember Frances," He poked around, looking at labels. "Nice girl."

"Have you seen her?"

Jimmy John seemed not to hear. "You think she'd go to Dead River?"

He's not answering my questions.

Pidge got the fishing pole money envelope from the desk and handed it to him.

"Take six Coca Colas, five dollars worth of gas, and a five-gallon can of kerosene out of this," Jimmy John said.

"Okay."

He stuffed the rest of the money into his jeans pocket, then patted the bundle he had put on the counter.

"These frog legs are the tastiest thing in the woods, and Rose knows how to cook them perfect. Learned from my ma back when we were in eighth grade."

"I know. I like it when they jump around in the skillet after they hit the hot grease."

"That Rose is a jewel. Your dad is lucky. Tell 'em for me."

"I will Jimmy John. Wish you'd stay."

"Gotta go. Gimme another hug and be a good girl. I'll be back soon. Shave off this beard, just so you'll recognize me, I promise. When I get around to it."

Holding his box of groceries in one hand Jimmy John picked up the full kerosene can with the other. Pidge followed, held the door open and walked with him to his truck. "If you do see Frances around Dead River, tell her I'm worried about her. Okay?"

Jimmy John didn't answer her. "What's Richard doing walking circles in front of the big white rock?" he asked.

"Waiting for Fiona and Mandy," Pidge answered. "Don't look like they're coming, though."

"Bunch of hippie lovers," muttered Richard as he kicked at the limestone rock. "I told them to come on, and look what I got, a wife and daughter who won't even go home with me."

Jimmy John stepped to where the angry man stood.

"Hello Richard," he held out his hand.

Richard turned his back. Jimmy John shrugged.

"First they take up with the peaceniks, now they're consorting with Indians," Richard muttered.

Pidge stifled a retort. The Indian was not a stranger. He grew up in the same community, even if Dead River could be considered on the edge. Went to the same school. Umpired on the same baseball team.

Jimmy John smiled down at Pidge. "Swallow the words I see trying to bust out of your mouth. Remember, Richard's all right most of the time. He's just a little fractious sometimes."

Pidge hugged Jimmy John and went back in the store and put the bundle of frog legs in the meat cooler. Her mother could cook them any time. Right now it was too hot in the kitchen. The Indian had evaded her question. Did he know where Frances was hiding?

131

Uncle Jim came in. "Forgot my lunch cooler," he said, found it and went right back out. "Good night."

It was quiet for a change. Looked like people had turned in early.

"Think you'll get any more gas customers?" she called out the door to Luke, who stood beside a gas tank.

"Doubt it," he answered. "Over at the auto shop, Dad, Aaron, and David look busy, and we still got Richard muttering at the limestone rock."

"I'll ask Mom if we can close. It's time." Within minutes she was back. "Mom says turn over the sign to closed."

"What's Mom and them doing back there?"

"They're about through getting a room ready for Jasmine and a single bed that Dad and Aaron are to take to the campground." She peered out the door. "What do we do about Richard?"

"I'll ask him." Luke leaned out the front door. "Richard, Mom said for us to close up the store," Luke called out. "You want to come inside?"

"No. Tell Fiona I'm waiting for her and Mandy beside this infernal rock. I stubbed my toe on an oyster shell sticking out from it. And it's close to our bedtime."

Pidge

Chapter Fourteen

It was hard for Pidge to wake up. She stretched and hit the doze button on the clock. She could hear the others stirring. She rubbed her eyes with the edge of the sheet, stretched out her legs and counted out her father's "get-up" chant: "One, sit up; two, feet on the floor; three, stand up. One, two, three." It wasn't easy, but she did it.

Then the realization hit her. Luke had said earlier that Frances "might" be with Granny Blue Sky and Jimmy John on Dead River. But Jimmy John hadn't answered her questions. She splashed water on her face and ran to the kitchen where the rest of the family, plus Jasmine, milled around, getting breakfast.

"One egg or two?" Rose asked.

"One." Pidge turned to Luke. "You didn't tell me what you learned about Frances."

"With all the excitement, I forgot." Luke yawned and stretched. "There was a nest of leaves and a quilt in the hollow of the twined oak limbs and some candy wrappers. There were plenty of tracks around the tree and on the trail, but I couldn't pick out any that looked like hers."

"You told me you saw her tracks."

"It looked like her tracks were south on the way to Dead River. They were about the size your feet would make. Did you go south on the Indian trail?"

"No." Pidge held her breath.

"I'll check it today." Luke reached over and took a plate. At an angry glance from Pidge, he nodded his head. "I will. Today. Honest."

Rose handed Pidge a plate filled with a once-over fried egg, grits, and bacon. "Grab a biscuit. We're all running late."

"Where's Fiona and Mandy? Did they spend the night?"

"They went on home with Richard after they all cooled off." Rose cracked another egg and dropped it in the hot grease.

"Jimmy John brought frog legs," Pidge told her. "I put 'em in the cooler."

"Wonderful! We'll have them for supper tonight. How's Granny Blue Sky?"

"Jimmy John said she's fine. He said tell Dad he's a lucky man."

"Tell him for me, that I know how lucky I am." Josh reached out and gave his wife a noogie on the head with his knuckles.

Rose ducked and blushed. "I like Jimmy John. He's a good person."

Pidge swallowed. "You don't have to explain him to us, Mom. We all like Jimmy John and his mama. We're lucky. Not everyone has genuine Indians living close by."

"Listen up, folks." Josh cleared his throat. "I have important news for you."

"Yeah, yeah, the protesters left last night." Rose handed him a full breakfast plate.

"Not that, but almost as good."

"What then?" Rose turned and cracked another egg in the hot grease.

"David and I found the reason for the influx of war protesters," he said. "The 5 on the sign wasn't large enough. All the hippies could see was the 2. The 5 is now larger, so they can follow Highway 52, the correct

134

directions to the farm in Georgia. Hopefully, we won't get any more rag-tag travelers."

Pidge, Luke, Julie and Jasmine held loaded breakfast plates. Their mouths dropped open.

"So, the directions were wrong." Jasmine took a bite of bacon. "The puzzle is solved."

"What a relief," Rose reached out a biscuit, plopped it on her plate. "Maybe we can help them move on out of here."

At a puzzled look from Jasmine, Rose laughed. "Not you, young lady. You have a baby to think about." She turned to Josh. "What can we do?"

"You're doing all that's possible. I thought I'd take the week off to help around here and see what I can do to clean out the river field. Now that the sign's fixed, the glut of war protesters will leave."

"I hope so. Maybe we can manage to get them out of here and on their way to Atlanta," Rose told him. "It's getting crazier and crazier."

"Did you sleep all right?" Josh asked Jasmine.

"Much better than I expected," she said. "The bed was perfect. But I missed Aaron." She looked at the clock. "He should be here soon."

"He has a car to repair." Josh patted her shoulder. "I'm running up to Bradley's to see if he's got portable toilets we can put at the river field. Let 'em go to the bathroom before they leave."

"We could skip a week of school and help you," Luke told his father.

"No. End of discussion." Josh looked askance at his son. "School comes first. Besides it'll be out in a couple of months. Better learn what you can. You're going to need all that stuff someday."

"Yeah, that's what you tell us." Pidge rinsed her plate and put it in the dishpan. "I sure could do without math."

"You say that now." Josh hugged her around the shoulders. "But when the time comes that you need math, it will already be right there, in your little round noggin'." He tapped her lightly on the head.

"Yeah, yeah, you always make things sound better." Pidge ran to the parking lot to join the others waiting for the school bus at the big white rock.

On the way to school, dependable Mr. Bob pulled the bus to the shoulder of the road across from the campground at the river field. "Look for Frances." He turned a stern eye on Roly Poly as students moved to the north side of the bus.

"I'm looking," Roly Poly assured Mr. Bob. "I'd know Frances. She sat in front of me in English before she moved away."

Pidge scanned the scene. Reds, blues, purple, tie-dyed shirts, bell-bottoms, cut-off low-slung jeans with belly buttons showing. Trucks and heavily loaded cars cranked up. Calls of "goodbye, man" and "splittin' for Georgia" and "keep a truckin'" echoed over the campgrounds.

"See the girl by the big stump?" said a voice from the back of the bus.

Pidge watched Luke slip out the door.

"It appears that many of the campers are leaving," one of the bigger boys in the back of the bus called out.

"I don't think she's there anymore." Lena turned to Pidge. "I think those people murdered her and she's buried under the hollow oaks."

"The oak trees are not exactly hollow and it'd be impossible to dig under trees that big." Pidge wanted to tell Lena that Frances might be living with the Indians but had been warned not to say anything until Luke could find out for sure. "It's two trees twined around each other that make the big hollow."

136

"Girls, girls." Mr. Bob's voice was low, solemn. "Let's not get morbid. We're looking for Frances, alive, who needs to be on her way to school, like the rest of us."

"That double tree is not an oak, it's an el-em, or two of 'em," announced Roland in a normal-sounding voice.

He sounds much better than in that Roly Poly voice, thought Pidge.

"Could be elm trees." Mr. Bob's well-modulated voice cut in. "Though they mostly grow up east. Likely red oaks."

Pidge watched Luke climb the steps into the bus. Mr. Bob cranked up and students settled back in their seats. Lena moved over and Luke squeezed in beside them.

"I didn't see any more tracks of feet small enough for Frances," he told his sister.

Pidge was frustrated. She wanted to see for herself where Frances had gone, to talk to her and find out why she ran away.

At lunch in the school cafeteria, Pidge eased her food tray down beside Lena. Maybe Roly Poly would leave her alone. He'd sounded so grownup on the bus. No such luck.

"Hi, Midji Pidji," came a voice from behind her as she put down her food and sat on the bench attached to the side of the table. "Oink, oink."

Pidge didn't take time to think. She'd had it. Frances missing, maybe dead and all this jerk could do was torment her. She picked up the container of fruit floating in red Jello, balled up her fist and aimed straight for Roly Poly's jeering face, with all the power her skinny arm could muster.

There was a squishing sound and a scream. "I'm rebortin' you to the brincibal." Roly Poly grabbed at his nose and ran, bawling.

Pidge shook the Jello from her hand and swiped it with her napkin. "Uh, oh," she told Lena. "I forgot to put down my spoon."

"Looked like you may have punctured his eye." Nobody else sat at their table as the two girls finished their lunchroom food.

"Rubber meatball," said Lena. "Wonder where they get this stuff. The toy store, or the dump?"

Fighting was serious business and the girls knew there'd be hell to pay later, but they both looked up at the same time and erupted in laughter. "Looked like pieces of peach and those pale grapes sticking out of his nose," said Pidge. "I couldn't have done better if I had planned it."

Lena held her side with one hand and leaned over the table, pounding on it with her fist. "Remind me never to make you mad."

"Humph," said a voice. They turned. Principal Andrew Whittle. Holding a basketball. He reached out a hand and crooked his first finger, then pointed toward the front office.

"Me too?" whispered Lena. She sat primly on the bench, trying hard to look innocent.

Another crooked finger.

"But I didn't do anything. Pidge was just getting even with Roly Poly, uh, I mean Roland. He rags on her all the time."

With no change of expression, Whittle, all tanned muscle and curly blond hair, walked sedately to the principal's office without breaking his stride. The girls followed meekly. He went into the office and seated himself. "Explanation number one." He pointed his finger at Pidge.

"She didn't do anything. Roly Poly always terrorizes her."

Whittle held up his hand. "It's not your turn, Lena. Yet."

Pidge sat still, and quiet. What she did at home when she faced trouble. She wondered if it'd work with Whittle.

"Why did you sucker punch Roland?"

"What's a sucker punch, Mr. Whittle?" Pidge had fixed her gaze on his Adam's apple and it held there, like her eyes were stuck. She barely spoke above a whisper.

"It's a punch made without warning, allowing the adversary no time to prepare for defense. It is unfair and unethical. In a boxing match it's illegal." He rolled the basketball back and forth. And waited.

Pidge noticed he had cut himself while shaving and a piece of sticky paper clung to the underside of his chin.

"Pidge? Answer my question."

"It's time she took up for herself," said Lena hotly. "That boy picks on her all the time."

Whittle turned his sky-blue eyes full on Lena. "You are superfluous to this conversation, Lena. Why don't you go to whatever class you'd be having this period?" He pointed in the general direction of classrooms.

"You don't have to tell me twice," murmured Lena. "Sorry Pidge." She took off right on the bare edge of running, her flip-flops slapping the vinyl floor.

"Now." Whittle swiveled his chair. "Please give me your full attention, Pidge, and tell me what happened in the lunchroom."

"I don't know what made me come unglued, Mr. Whittle, honest. I've been so upset lately. I thought I saw Frances at the hippie camp in the river field and my brother's been helping me look for her. She may be

139

murdered or something. She ran from both me and Luke. I can't imagine why."

"Frances, our best forward in beginners basketball? I thought she moved away."

"She did, two years ago. But I saw her standing beside a tent where the hippies are camping at the river field. When I went to find her, nobody knew where she was. The people are never at the tent where she's supposed to be living."

"Don't talk so fast, Pidge. You're leaving out some important things, like the part where you punched Roly Poly."

"I am?"

"Yes. What does this have to do with Roland? And why did you hit him?"

"It doesn't have anything to do with Roly Poly, uh Roland. He's just a hateful, mean boy who torments me. His dad beats him, so in a way it's not his fault. He calls me oink, oink and teases me, all the time."

"Why didn't you choose a time and place and fight him fair and square?"

Shock showed on Pidge's face. "I usually do fight fair and square, Mr. Whittle. I do. I didn't plan on fighting him. It wasn't all about him being mean. Leave Roland out of it." Pidge stopped.

"Are you saying there was another reason why you smacked him right in the face, and probably broke his nose?"

"Broke his nose? I thought the spoon punctured his eye. Oh, I am so sorry. I didn't mean to really hurt him bad, Mr. Whittle. Honest I didn't. His dad will have a fit if Roly Poly gets licked."

Whittle pushed back his chair and stood. "We'll find out soon if he's injured beyond repair, Pidge. Now, let's get back to Frances. Did your folks call Sheriff Clark about Frances?"

"What with all those people camped down at the river field, and one of them, Jasmine, expecting a baby, they've got their hands full, Mr. Whittle. We thought Frances might be sleeping in the hollow oaks just above Little Indian Spring. But my dad won't let me go to the campground to search."

"Tell your parents tonight, Pidge, to call the sheriff. Worse things than kidnapping have happened at some of those hippie camps. Frances could be in grave danger."

"I know that, Mr. Whittle. And I promise to get them to call Sheriff Clark. He won't put me in jail if Roly Poly's nose is broken, will he?"

"No, since you attacked him in the lunchroom, the school has jurisdiction. We'd turn you over to the law only if we decide you committed a crime. If his nose is broken, we might rethink the punishment." Whittle was not only the principal, he was the school counselor, and the basketball coach.

"I hope it's not. Tell him I'm sorry."

"Not me. You'll have that chore. Write him an apology letter. Deliver it to him. You can tell me how it all comes out." The principal looked down at Pidge, rubbed his chin. "In addition, write 100 times: I promise to keep my temper under control, but if I have to defend myself, I will always fight fair. Do it now."

"But. . . I have a class."

"You should have thought about that before you sucker-punched Roland." He pointed to his desk. "Sit. Write. Turn in the neatly written pages to Ms. Wren. She'll give them to me. Let me know if you find Frances. We need her on the girls' basketball team. She's fast."

Pidge

Chapter Fifteen

Pidge pulled out her notebook and numbered the lines up to 100. Anger and frustration fought for expression. Mr. Whittle was said to be fair, but he could have taken into account all the harassment she had endured from Roly Poly. She peered around Mr. Whittle's office. The wooden paddle with holes in it was not hanging on the wall where it was rumored to stay at the ready. Untold numbers of boys had bragged about being whupped with that paddle. *I'd better get back to the assignment,* she told herself. *I don't want to know about a big paddle.* She wrote a few lines. *It's spooky in this office.*

Ms. Wren called out from the front counter. "Hurry and finish, Pidge, I have a picture of Frances I got from the yearbook photographer. It's two years old, but she may still look like it. We could get the newspaper to print up the picture for a poster or flyer."

Pidge jumped up and ran to the counter. "Am I glad to see you. I thought I was writing in a tomb or something." She grabbed the picture. "Ms. Wren, you always come up with answers."

Pidge hovered over the school secretary as she typed a flyer with the words: Looking for Frances / if you see her / contact Daylight Grocery 856-2222. They marked a space for the picture at the top.

"I have to go by the newspaper office this afternoon. If they will print the picture at the top of the page, we can use the mimeograph machine to put the type on for a flyer."

"Uh, oh," said Pidge. "They'd charge money to print the picture, wouldn't they?"

"Not too much if all they print is the picture."

"Mom might pay for that. We'll mimeograph the words at the store."

"I'll go to the newspaper on my lunch hour and call your mom. Bring me a ream of yellow paper and we'll call it even for the school. I'll find out if it's okay to put them up around here. There are students who might have seen her."

"Mr. Whittle. . . ," Pidge began.

"I know about the punishment. If the principal asks why you're not in his office, tell him I gave you permission to write the sentences and bring them to me in the morning."

Pidge hugged Ms. Wren and ran out the door.

Lena waited inside the door of study hall. "What happened?"

"Ms. Wren is taking a picture of Frances to get printed at the newspaper." She pulled the draft for the text from an envelope. "We'll ditto this part. Anybody can read it."

"I didn't mean about Frances. What happened about you clobbering Roly Poly?"

"I'm still alive," Pidge told her with a solemn look. "But maybe not for long."

Just before the school day ended Ms. Wren brought Pidge a bag of yellow sheets with Frances' picture at the top.

"Thank you. Thank you, Ms. Wren." She turned to Lena and waved the sheets in the air. "This will make a difference."

Mr. Bob stopped the school bus and Luke got out at the patch of gallberry bushes near the end of the bridge. Pidge's tormenter wasn't on the bus.

"Thank goodness you got rid of Roly Poly," Lena told her.

"Yeah," answered Pidge. She was eager to get the flyers copied and posted. Several young women looked a little bit like Frances, but not one dead ringer in the bunch.

"Maybe Luke will have better luck this time," whispered Lena. "Maybe he'll learn what's happened to Frances."

Chaos reigned at the Daylight Grocery.

"Uncle Jim's in the store," Rose told Pidge when she dumped her books on the kitchen table.

"I'll need to watch the gas pumps."

"No, you stay inside and tell Uncle Jim to watch the pumps. I'll speak to Luke when he gets home. He can't stay at school, working on projects. We need him here."

"Who?" Josh walked in, his hands filled with copies of maps with directions on how to find the farm in Georgia where the war protesters were to stay.

"Luke. He could hand out maps, but he's still at school. Julie can help me in here." Rose stood in the door to the family room, folding a sheet.

"Where's Mandy?" she asked Julie.

"She went straight home." Julie grabbed a cold biscuit, poked it with her finger to make a hole and poured in cane syrup. "Guess her dad's still mad."

"I've got a flyer on Frances to copy." Pidge pulled out the bundle of yellow paper with the picture of Frances printed at the top. "Ms. Wren helped me make this up. She said we could pay her back with a ream of yellow paper."

"I can run the mimeograph machine." Jasmine stretched as she walked into the kitchen.

"Good idea." Rose looked at the printed picture. "This is well done. She was a cute little squirt. I miss her."

"Mom! Don't say 'was'. Frances is still alive. We'll find her." Tears appeared in Pidge's eyes.

"Whoa, don't start crying." Rose folded Pidge in her arms. "We've got to stay clear-headed with all that's going on around here."

Josh waved his clipboard. "Send Luke with a handful. Tell him to blanket the river field. I'm passing out maps on how to find the farm in Georgia. Tony's down there now, setting up portable toilets. Aaron and David are repairing everything from fancy cars to jalopies out at the auto shop."

"Some of the protesters have left already." Pidge stuffed a sausage in a biscuit and headed for the door to the grocery store. "It looked less populated today than yesterday."

"If Sheriff Clark comes by and I'm not still here, send him to Aaron and David at the auto shop," Josh told them as he went out the door.

Pidge's heart flopped down to her stomach. *Sheriff Clark is coming for me*, she told herself. *Mr. Whittle lied. I'll get arrested.* She took a deep breath. *Stay calm. Be optimistic.*

"Why's he expecting the sheriff?" Jasmine asked. "Did something bad happen at the campground?"

"Not anything you can help with." Rose patted her on the shoulder. "You print up flyers. Pidge can sell groceries."

Jasmine finished moving the surveyor's stakes with freshly painted numbers outside along the wall of the storage room.

"Need any help?" Pidge asked.

"No, I'm through." Jasmine's tummy moved ahead of the rest of her as she waddled about. "I'll help you with the flyers."

Pidge prepared the mimeograph machine. "This is a picture of Frances from the school yearbook for two years ago."

Jasmine examined the print. "She still looks like that, only taller. I haven't seen her since that day at the camp."

Jasmine turned the mimeograph handle and soon a pile of flyers lay on the desk.

Pidge showed shoppers the flyer and then put one in each grocery bag. "I'm really worried about her."

Each person promised to let her know if they saw Frances.

Pidge walked to the front and taped a flyer to the door. Uncle Jim didn't have any gas customers. She saw her dad's, Aaron's, and David's trucks parked behind the auto shop. A barefoot boy in cutoff jeans, about Luke's age, walked around to the front and entered the store.

"Working with them at the shop?" asked Pidge. He was about a foot taller than her, with brown eyes and hair.

"I tried to; they wouldn't let me. Said I could help if I came back tomorrow."

"Where you from?"

"Oklahoma." He pulled a cold Nehi out of the drink box. "I'm probably the luckiest guy in the world. Got pulled out of eighth grade to go on the grand tour to stop the war. Now I'm stuck down by the river with a bunch of stoned adults, mine included."

"I thought most of the people down there were young people."

"There are some children. Not many, but some." He plunked down a dollar bill.

146

"What's your name?" Pidge put the bill in the cash register and counted out change.

"Orion."

"Just that? No last name?"

"Well, Smith. Not much of a last name. But I like the first."

"Wow." Pidge grinned. "Did your parents actually name you after a constellation?"

"Why not?"

"If they were going to do that, they could have named you Big Dipper, then your friends could tease you and call you the Big Bopper."

"Yeah. They didn't. They named me Rufus. I changed it to Orion."

"I see your point. My name's Pidge."

"Ha," the boy laughed. "You have the same kind of parents I do."

"I don't know about that. They don't get stoned. Do you know a red-headed guy named Arthur? About my brother's age; taller than me."

"You know Arthur? He taught me how to whistle if you're in trouble."

Before Pidge could stop him, he stuck his fingers in his mouth and gave the low, mournful "in trouble" signal he'd learned from Arthur.

In seconds Rose, Julie, Josh, Aaron, David, and Uncle Jim, ran to the store. "What's wrong?" everybody yelled at once.

Rose looked around. Orion had scooted under the counter.

"Nothing. Calm down. It was a mistake. I was practicing."

"Yeah," muttered Josh. "Something's fishy. When did you need to practice?"

"I'm sorry," Pidge told them. "I'm just nervous. Frances knows the signal. Maybe I thought she'd come running in if I whistled."

"Don't do that, young lady." Rose stomped out, followed by Julie. As the others went out the front door, Jasmine came in from the kitchen, rubbing her back.

"What happened? When I asked Rose, she just humphed."

Orion crawled from under the desk. "I gave the danger whistle and a crowd of people came running in."

"Hook up with Aaron and David. They'll put you to work, keep you out of mischief," Jasmine told him.

Pidge put a hand over her mouth to stifle the grin. Orion saw her.

"You people got something going with that whistle," he said. "Arthur was right."

"It won't work if you teach it to everybody at camp," Jasmine told him as she handed him a flyer.

"I could have gotten into real trouble." Orion shook his head. "Glad Pidge was here to cover for me."

Uncle Jim walked inside, pulled off his change apron and tucked it under the cash register. "Somebody can cover for me," he said. "I'm not cut out for all this excitement."

"I'll be at the pumps." Luke stuck his head in at the door from the kitchen. "Soon's I find a snack."

"Try these new potato chips," Orion told him. "They're cool."

"Oh, no." Luke shook his head. "Mom won't let us eat junk food."

"You sure sell a lot of it."

"I know. Other people eat it, but not us." Luke skipped back to the kitchen.

Orion looked at Pidge and raised his eyebrows. "You people sell junk food, but don't eat it? What do you eat?"

"Mostly meat and potatoes, vegetables and fruits, stuff people grow around here. I'll be glad when watermelon comes in. That's my favorite."

Uncle Jim stuck his head in the door. "Jasmine, there's a suitcase somebody put beside the Free Box. Looks pretty good. You might want it."

Pidge, Jasmine, and Orion walked outside and looked at the suitcase. It was mid-sized, blue leather, kind of old looking, but sturdy. They opened it. Not much inside. Some shorts and tee shirts.

"Think your mom might like this?" Jasmine asked Orion.

"It looks too little for her. Might fit Arthur's mom though. I'll ask her." He saw Josh getting into his truck. "Catch you later," he called out as he ran to hitch a ride.

"Okay," Pidge thrust a flyer in Luke's face. "Did you find Frances?"

"No." He backed up, munching a peanut butter and jelly sandwich. "I did find the people she came to the river field with." He took a big bite out of the sandwich.

"And?"

"They say they haven't seen her since she ate with Jasmine and Aaron. The woman seemed sort of spaced out. She seemed really worried about Frances."

"What do *they* think happened to her?"

"That Two Toe Tom ate her."

"What?"

"They told me a big alligator was seen the day she disappeared." Luke stuffed in the last of his sandwich and wiped his mouth with the back of his hand in an effort to stifle a guffaw. "Their names are Sam and Betty and they are friends of Frances' parents. They planned to shoot the alligator, but Dad, Aaron, and David, confiscated their artillery, a .22 rifle."

"Boy, are you a muddy puddle of information. What about Frances?"

"Sam and Betty said they brought her along because her parents were going to Georgia too and there was more room for her in their car. Now they are afraid they'll be blamed for her disappearance and have been searching everywhere."

"Did they look in the woods? Maybe she is holed up in the double-oak tree."

"I looked there and found a macramé bracelet," Luke told her. "Sam and Betty said it's not theirs."

Pidge sighed. "Might be her bracelet."

"You want it? You can give it to her when she's found."

Pidge took the bracelet and tried it on her wrist. "Too big," she said.

Luke pushed the bracelet up to Pidge's arm muscle. "There's where the hippies wear them." He grinned.

"Shoot. I wouldn't dare." Pidge put the bracelet in her pocket. She sighed. "I wish Dad hadn't forbidden me to go to the camp. I have a feeling I could find her."

"Dad's right about that," Luke told her. "You shouldn't go down there. There are all sorts of things going on. When I was looking for Frances, I saw a couple having sex in the woods."

"You mean, uh, doing it?" Pidge was shocked.

"Yeah. It."

"What was it like?"

"Ridiculous. Naked human bodies all wrapped around each other. Remember that time we saw the moccasins at the edge of the creek, all wound together in a big ball?"

"Gross. People, like snakes?"

"That's what it looked like, only two humans."

Pidge

Chapter Sixteen

On the way to school the bus stopped at Roland's house, but his mother came out and waved it away. "I wondered if he'd make it today," Mr. Bob muttered.

Pidge slouched down as low as she could and stayed in her seat. "I'm sure going to get it at school today," she whispered to Lena.

"I think I'd jump off the bus and head for the swamps if I were you," Lena whispered back.

It had rained the night before, just enough to turn the campground into a muddy mess. "I wouldn't want to slog around in that," Pidge told Luke.

"Could make it easy to see Frances' tracks." Luke seemed determined to help find his sister's friend.

"Looks like a commune of wet rats. You sure you want to go out there?" Mr. Bob asked Luke.

"I told my dad I'd hand out flyers." Luke stood poised in the stairwell.

Before Mr. Bob opened the door for Luke, he stood up. "I want to tell you students something." His tone was solemn. His voice stern.

"It's Friday. We are looking for Frances again. Pidge and the rest of you, look. We won't stop searching for her until we find out what happened. Luke may have figured out where she is, but we don't know for sure. What we do know is that when we start out to do something, we finish it. We may not find Frances, but we will not give up." He sat back down and eased the door handle for Luke to go out, his hands filled with flyers.

Pidge pulled in a deep breath. There's the weekend, the flyers, and the adults. It seemed they looked and waited longer than usual. They could all see Luke moving about the field, handing out flyers, speaking with people. Most nodded their heads.

"I see her," called out Julie. Then, "Naaah, guess not."

Mandy started to cry. Pidge hugged her close. "What's wrong?"

"That could be me, lost out there," Mandy sobbed.

"C'mon," Pidge told her. "If it was, we'd be turning over every huckleberry bush."

"Shush, eyeball that place the best you can," Julie told her friend. "We're all upset. Let's not go sniveling about it. They'll think we're little ten-year-old babies."

"And in the fifth grade." Mandy shifted and sat up, straighter and taller.

Pidge watched the people moving about the camp. With all her being, she wanted to go out there among them to ask questions about Frances. She'd be back. Even if she had to slip out at night. Whoa, she told herself. *Now you're really falling over the edge. Watch out for the fire and brimstone.* Nobody defied the adults in the Reed household. Even if she did want to, that was out of the question.

It did look like there were fewer tents, but a big Greyhound bus with music notes painted on it had parked near the road. A band. Pidge couldn't see a name on the bus. Those who had left were afraid of Two Toe Tom. Let them be afraid. Getting eaten by an alligator, even if only a legend, was likely not half as bad as what she'd face when she got to school.

Ms. Wren stood with Pidge before the principal's desk.

"No dungeon today, Pidge." Mr. Whittle seemed to be in a good humor. "It's Friday. Relax. Hand out the flyers. By the way that's a good likeness of Frances, Ms. Wren. Give me some of those. I'll put them in the dugout and around the basketball court. Hand me that stapler."

Pidge's knees were liquid fire. "But. . . Roland? How bad was he hurt?" She reached for the edge of the desk.

Mr. Whittle gave Pidge a stern look. "I understand that Roland's nose was not broken. He may lose a couple of teeth. Have you written your apology letter to the injured boy?"

"Not yet," squeaked Pidge. "But I will, Mr. Whittle, I promise."

Mr. Whittle waved the flyers at Pidge. "Be sure you do, young lady. Be assured you won't get off Scot-free. There will be repercussions." He turned and walked down the hall.

His footsteps faded. "Phew, am I relieved," Ms. Wren said. "I thought sure he'd kill you, or something just as bad. He didn't even suspend you."

"Not yet." Pidge straightened up, let out a long breath. She clasped Ms. Wren's hand. "I sounded like air escaping from a tire."

Ms. Wren looked shaky too, but she followed Pidge with a roll of plastic tape as they put a flyer on each door in the halls.

Her history class was almost over when Pidge slipped into the classroom. She handed the teacher a flyer. He motioned her to her desk.

"Alright boys," Josh said, watching the sheriff's car turn in to park at the auto shop. "Here comes the law."

153

Josh met Sheriff Clark at his official car and led the way into the shop. He stopped in front of the open drawer of the filing cabinet.

"Whatcha got here?" The sheriff scratched his head and looked at the meager pile.

David towered over him. "Weapons we confiscated at the protest camp."

The sheriff reached out to shake David's hand. "Tall drink of water."

"And this is the leader of the original pack," Josh introduced Aaron.

Sheriff Clark straightened his gun belt. "You having trouble down there at the river?"

"We thought we were," David told him. "A guy started waving a rifle and we lined them up and took these weapons."

Josh pointed to the file drawer's contents. "In the heat of the moment, it seemed the right thing to do."

A rumble started low in Sheriff Clark's throat and turned into a deep belly laugh. "Not enough firearms here to shoot up a mess of squirrels. I wouldn't of bothered."

"What should we do?" David asked. "We don't want to break the law."

Sheriff Clark cleared his throat. "You should've thought about that, before you gathered up these here." He patted the pistol at his side. "A man might need to own his weapon."

David leaned against the fender of a car. "Not if he threatens to use it."

"What if it's to kill food for his family and to protect them from wild varmints, human varmints, and rattlesnakes? Somebody threaten you all? Point him out. I'll arrest him." Sheriff Clark pulled out a walkie-talkie.

"To tell the truth, it wasn't us." Josh looked the sheriff in the eye. "He was going to shoot Two Toe Tom."

It appeared that Sheriff Clark would lapse into laughter again, but he didn't. He pulled a red bandanna from his pocket and wiped his face. "That's right thoughty of you boys, protecting an alligator that doesn't even exist." He pushed back his hat and scratched his head.

"It wasn't just Two Toe Tom, Sheriff, they'd have been shooting each other next. Not to mention us." Uneasy, David looked around for confirmation.

"I will have to give you authority to hold these, uh, weapons. When the rightful owners head for Georgia, they can collect their belongings from you." The sheriff was trying hard to maintain a somber expression. He clicked on the walkie-talkie. "Just checking in," he said.

Rose heard the crackle of the police radio and came running. "What's going on here?"

Josh put a hand on her arm. "Not much. Sheriff Clark says we're to keep the weapons and give them back when those guys head for Georgia."

Rose turned on the sheriff. "Are you harassing those young people? They think they can stop the war. That don't make them criminals. Lots of adults would like to see our young men come home from Vietnam too."

"Wait, Rose. I'm on your side." Sheriff Clark tapped her shoulder. "I don't think these young people are mean, either. Maybe a little dumb around the edges. You have to admit most of 'em look like they could use a good scalding and scraping."

Rose puckered up her face as if she would cry. Josh put his arm around her. "They do look kinda funny with all that long hair and running around barefoot," he said. "But, they have a right to their opinion. And we have the right to let them camp on our land."

"A lot coming from a military man," David told him.

"I'm a human first." Josh turned to David. "My mind tells me that the government should decide what's best for the country. My heart tells me to be kind to these young people. Misguided or not, they have a right to speak up for what they believe."

David reached out and took his hand. "I'm proud to call you friend," he said.

"Ya'll are getting sentimental," Sheriff Clark shook hands with Josh, David, Aaron, and Tony. He turned to Rose.

"You're a good woman, Rose, but you can't adopt a tribe of war protesters. Let us handle this."

Rose sighed and walked back to the grocery store.

"The numbers on those stobs dry?" Rose asked Jasmine. "Don't know if Josh will want to put them out now that some of the campers are moving on."

"They're ready for use, either way." Jasmine rose. "Do you need me?"

"Not now. Go lie down and take a rest. They'll get a bed moved to your tent, hopefully this afternoon."

As Jasmine went out of the door to the kitchen a handsome man, with a smooth tan, muscles stretching the sleeves of his cotton shirt and a big smile on his face, stepped through the front door. Reverend Willis, Willy for short.

"Lord, where have you been when we needed you?" Rose called out.

"I'm not the Lord, Rose, I'm just one little old preacher man. What's wrong?"

"While you've been gone, our neighborhood has been invaded by a horde of war protesters claiming they are headed for Georgia."

"I saw that crowd down at the river field on my way in. Linda said it's a bunch of hippies."

156

"Call them what you want, but the leader stopped here because his wife, a lovely young woman named Jasmine, is expecting a baby. Doc Collins said we should keep her here for awhile. She's tired and mostly rundown. I've been feeding her the best I know how."

Rev. Willy took the soft drink Rose handed him. "Don't see anything wrong with that. What can I do?" Sweat from the icy drink dripped off his hand.

"I don't know. Go ask Josh. You just being here helps me. I'm getting scattered in my head with all this activity. I thought I had moved home to a quiet, friendly little community. Now there's too much going on. I can't keep it straight."

Fiona pushed open the door. "Rose," she called out, then saw the minister.

"Oh, hi, Rev. Willy. I see you're back." She held an envelope in her hand.

"Glad to be back, Fiona. What you got there?"

A deep blush colored Fiona's face. "It's a letter to Josh. Richard would have brought it, but he's ashamed of how he behaved a few days ago. Said he's not showing his face in this place ever again."

A loud guffaw broke out of Rev. Willy. "He'll get over it, Fiona. He may lose direction sometimes, but underneath all that, he's a good man."

"I know he is." Fiona fingered the envelope. "But sometimes he gets too full of the Irish."

Rev. Willy laughed again. "Even the best of us swing back to our roots, at moments we least expect."

"What's in the letter?" Rose asked.

"An order to attend a meeting of the neighborhood men tomorrow night at the main room on the bottom floor of the old school building. It's from Mr. Dauber. He's too chicken to deliver it himself."

"Did you talk to Sarah Mae?"

Fiona fanned herself with the letter. "I don't see what good that'd do. That stuck up girl never was friendly to me."

"Sarah Mae's shy, not outgoing." Rose walked behind the counter.

"We weren't friends in school, that's all. She's probably got plenty of friends where she works at the shirt factory. I did go over there, like you told me to, but Joe said she was gone. As I drove away I saw her in the backyard garden. She waved her hoe at me and shrugged her shoulders."

"I've got a bad feeling about this, Fiona."

"Me too, Rose. She looked more like scared than like someone working her garden. When I got home Richard gave me this letter."

Rev. Willy rubbed his chin. "To compare the two men. Underneath Richard's cockamamie swagger, there's a good person. Underneath Joe's tough shell, is pure unadulterated evil."

Rose shook her head. "Josh is at the auto shop," she told Fiona. "Why don't you take the letter out there? Come back by here to talk about delivering a baby. I'll need your help, as usual."

Before Fiona could answer, Rev. Willy took her arm. "I'll go with you, Fe. You don't have to be embarrassed."

"It's helpful to have you back, Rev. Somebody needs to talk sense into our men. The protesters said they'd be gone as soon as they can get out of here. Isn't that enough?"

"They're angry, Fiona. Sometimes nothing's enough when people get boiling mad."

"I just wish I could get Richard to stay out of it. These boys and girls want to stop the war in Vietnam." Fiona fingered the envelope as if it burned her hand. "Shouldn't they be allowed to try?"

"You got me there, Fe." Rev. Willy held open the door to the auto repair shop. "Smarter people than myself are arguing in every direction."

Sheriff Clark met them at the door, shook the hand of Rev. Willy and hugged Fiona.

"What's this?"

"Notice of a meeting tomorrow night about chasing off the war protesters." Fiona handed over the envelope.

"Glad it's not tonight," said Josh after he had read the notice. "We're passing out maps and putting up tent markers this evening. You want to help us, Rev. Willy?"

"I am back, ready to do anything I can. I will certainly be at the meeting tomorrow night. You guys may need a few prayers."

Sheriff Clark rumbled out a laugh. "I'll be there too, with my chief deputy, in case the prayers need a little help." He gave Rev. Willy a friendly punch on the shoulder.

As the men brought Rev. Willy up to date on the community, Fiona turned back to the grocery store to face Rose.

"I can't help you with Jasmine's birthing." Fiona's voice trembled. "Richard has forbidden it."

Anger flashed across Rose's face. I'd like to wring that reprobate's neck, she thought. She took a deep breath. "Since when have you started kowtowing to Richard, like a sniveling ninny? I thought you were pretty good at standing up to him."

"You don't understand, Rose. This is different. Joe Dauber, Jim Warell, and Claude Shipper are leading the men. They aim to drive the war protesters out of the county."

"They'll leave, Fe. We're helping them get to moving on. Aaron's repairing their vehicles and the others

159

are helping with gas money. They're leaving as fast as they can. There are lots of young people. We can't just shove them out all at once." Rose said.

"Mr. Dauber says the White Sheets can get them out of here. In a New York second, he said. Richard's joined up with them. They plan a big to-do tomorrow night and I don't see how anybody can stop them."

"But, what about Jasmine? We've got to help her, Fe. We always have helped around here when we could."

"I know that. But you're the midwife. I'm just the aide. You can get by without me. Get Granny Blue Sky. She used to help you, before I moved back."

"Yeah." Rose rubbed her forehead. "That was awhile ago. She's on up in years now. May be close to a hundred. Her mouth looked like a prune last time I saw her."

"She'd be fine," Fiona told her. "You don't forget how to hand towels and pads and tie off the umbilical cord. She could do it, or maybe one of the girls."

"I suppose you're right. Pidge is too young and Granny Blue Sky is too old. I was counting on you Fiona." Rose turned briskly and picked up paperwork from the desk. "Guess we'll have to make do without you."

"I'm sorry," Fiona murmured. "Goodbye."

Rose, cool as a cucumber, turned back to her work. "Nice to see you Fiona."

Whatever happened to kindness and decency? Doesn't anyone care about these misguided youths? Where are their parents? I don't get it. We're supposed to love our neighbors as ourselves. Aren't these young people protesting the war in Vietnam our neighbors too?

Josh came in from the kitchen. "Rose," he called out, then saw her at the desk. Tears dripped onto the papers in her hand.

"The young people are being threatened with the White Sheets, Josh." Rose shook her head back and forth, and swiped at the tears.

"I sincerely hope it hasn't gone that far." Josh gathered her tenderly in his arms.

"They started on a mission to stop the war; now they are scattered over the country like branches broken from a tree by a wild wind."

"Rose, the strong wind is their own will driving them."

"Toward what?" Rose asked.

"Only the Lord knows." Josh kissed the top of her head. "It'll be alright. They'll be gone soon, and life here will keep moving along at its old dull, boring pace." He held her close, rubbing her shoulders.

"Promise?" She leaned into his chest.

"Promise."

Pidge

Chapter Seventeen

Pidge spent almost all of study hall composing an apology to Roland. "I'm sorry I hit you," she wrote. *But, I am not sorry. I've been needing to stop Roly Poly's mouth for a long time. Besides I don't even know how bad he's hurt. I didn't hear a sound like a crunch. Wouldn't it have sounded like it if I had broken his nose?*

Lena sat at the next desk, reading. She had long ago finished her homework and was now engrossed in *To Kill a Mockingbird.*

"Lena, how bad did I hurt Roly Poly?"

"Huh?"

"I've got to write a letter of apology. I don't know what to put."

"Geez Pidge." Lena closed the book, marking the place with her finger. "You just say 'I'm sorry.' Don't matter how bad he's hurt."

Lena turned back to her book. Pidge took off for the school office.

"I'm trying to write an apology to Roland and I don't even know how bad he's hurt," she told Ms. Wren.

"I don't know either, Pidge. Mr. Whittle might, but he's out."

"Did I hear my name?" the principal entered the office.

"I'm trying to write Roly, uh Roland, an apology letter and I don't know how bad he's hurt," said Pidge.

The principal placed his basketball on the desk and sat down. "His nose is not broken, just gashed up by the end of a spoon. He should be all right and ready to come back to school by Monday, with proper bandaging, of course."

Ms. Wren hovered. "Sit here and write your letter," she told Pidge. "I'll be back in a few minutes."

Dear Roland,

I'm sorry I injured your nose."

Since Frances has gone missing, I have been very upset. I didn't mean to take it out on you.

I hope we can be friends and that you will stop picking on me. At least until we find Frances.

Sincerely,

Pidge Reed.

She showed it to Ms. Wren when she returned. "I don't know, dear," Ms. Wren told her. "Is it necessary to mention that he picks on you?"

Whittle read the letter. "Looks fine to me. He should stop pestering you. I'll tell him that Monday."

"Thank you, Mr. Whittle, but I *could* leave out the part about picking on me, since his dad might whop him about it?"

"Pidge. Don't worry. Somebody needs to tell that man to keep his mitts off his wife and son. Give the nose time to heal and I might just have a word with Roland's father myself."

Pidge went back to study hall and rewrote the letter, leaving out the words about Roland picking on her and about Frances.

On the way home from school, Luke suggested to Mr. Bob that the bus go on without stopping at the campground. At the bridge Pidge asked if she could get out at Roland's house to deliver the apology letter.

"Won't your parents object?" Mr. Bob slowed down the bus.

"They don't even know I clobbered Roland," Pidge told him. "Luke can tell them I stopped at his house about homework or something."

"I'm not supposed to let any students off the bus, unless in an emergency, until we arrive at their designated waiting spot. And your waiting place is Daylight Grocery."

"I know, but you let Luke look for Frances. And I hit Roland because I was worried about Frances. Doesn't that count?"

"Oh, well, it is Friday. There may be a glimmer of reason in what you're saying. But you go on home as soon as you hand that boy the letter." He braked to a stop and Pidge jumped to the ground.

She waved as the bus droned off to the west, then pulled from her book bag the letter she had so carefully prepared. She stood still. It wasn't far to the river field. If she hurried, she could deliver the letter then head for the double tree and see for herself if Frances was there or had been.

With excitement building up, Pidge dreaded taking the necessary steps across the yard. At his door, she gave a tentative knock, then knocked again, louder.

"Hello." Roland peeked out. A round piece of gauze with tape running out like spokes on a wheel covered his nose. There were bruises on his arms and a knot stood out on his hand.

"I'm sorry . . . "

"Don't be. You didn't do that to my arm, or hand." Roland held to the doorknob.

"Here's my apology letter." Pidge thrust the envelope at him and turned and ran, back toward the protester's camp.

"Don't go there," Roland called. But Pidge was running too fast to hear.

The campground was busy. Pidge passed the musicians' bus parked on the road right-of-way, the Volkswagen bus, and the renovated school bus covered in peace slogans. She headed for Aaron's tent, then pulled up short.

People were lined up at Aaron and Jasmine's tent. Her dad held a legal pad, checking off names.

Pidge jumped behind the bus-bunkhouse, then ran to the musicians' bus. She'd have to circle the campground and go across Mr. Cook's field to get to the double tree. She hoped her dad hadn't seen her. *I should turn around and head home.* Instead she leaned over and ran in a zig-zag pattern to the fence row where briars, huckleberry, and poke plants reached toward the bottom limbs of wild plum and persimmon trees.

She scuttled behind the fence row, trying to watch her feet, her books slipping around in her arms. She didn't dare stand up or look around.

A zap hit across her knee and she fell. *I've been shot!* Then she saw the electric fence Mr. Cook had put at the edge of his field. She wished she hadn't left the safety of the school bus. They'd be getting off at the glittering white rock and her mother would ask why she wasn't with them.

Dirt smudged her hands and her knees bled where the hard ground and twigs had left scrapes. She crawled a few feet, then rose. The going was easier on the north side. She rushed behind magnolias and oaks to reach the cypress slough. On the other side stood the twined trees with the big opening in the middle, where she and Frances had played.

Pidge limped. Her right knee had taken a hard lick. The slough was misty and cool. There were plenty of

165

dry places if she watched for them. She expertly wound her way among the cypress and red oaks.

Reaching the double tree was disappointing. No sign of Frances. Several pieces of sycamore bark were stacked under the overhang niche, with a length of magnolia limb rubbed to a round point on the end.

Pidge picked up a flat piece of bark. Nothing on it. *What did I think, that Frances would write out an explanation for me on this piece of bark? I am losing my ever-lovin' mind.*

Several candy wrappers lay on the ground, and a pile of twigs where someone had tried and failed to make a fire.

Pidge looked for footprints. Several deer prints and a few wild hog prints, and what looked like Luke's sneaker patterns marked the ground, but nothing that even resembled a shoe print the size of her own, or what Frances might have made.

Disappointed, Pidge retraced her steps around the north and west fence rows, staying clear of the electric fence. Some of the plums were turning yellow. They weren't ripe yet, but she put down her books, picked a few, and filled the front pockets of her jeans.

She crossed the road to the trail along Limestone Creek. She pulled off her shoes and waded in it. It was quiet and cool. She could hear a cardinal call, "cheer, cheer, cheer," and a bluejay threatening a blackbird. Maybe she should just stay on the creek trail. How far west would it take her?

As she came up behind the church in the crabapple patch, she could hear Preacher Willy's wife Linda in the back yard of the parsonage, talking to her pig.

"Sweet little Wiggly." Linda took the pig up and hugged it. "You're a darlin'."

"Best not get attached to that pig, honey." Rev. Willy took Wiggly from Linda and put it back in the pen. "It's a garbage pig. It'll go to the butcher in the fall."

"I know. But it's so cute."

Rev. Willy nuzzled his wife's neck. "You need to do something about those puppies, we can't keep them either."

Pidge stood for a moment listening, picking and eating crab apples which were just turning pink. They tasted as sour as the yellow plums. *I'd better stop this. These green things will give me a bellyache. What'll I tell Mom and Dad about being so late getting home?* She sighed.

Luke watched for her at the gas pumps. "Sounds like Mom's about ready to send you off to Siberia. Said Lena wants to know about history homework." He clapped her on the shoulder. "Whatever happened to you? Roly Poly beat you up?"

"No. I fell over an electric fence at the edge of Mr. Cook's field on my way to the double tree to look for Frances. Didn't find her."

"I'll distract Mom and you get into some clothes that are not splattered with mud." He walked to the door just as Pidge ran around the store.

At his "Hey, Mom," Pidge ran to her room and jumped into the shower.

When she walked into the kitchen, Rose asked. "Why'd you change clothes? Never mind, call Lena, and watch the store. Julie's walking Jasmine around the house five times."

"Why?"

"Jasmine needs the exercise. Eating food and sleeping won't cut it."

Pidge heard the store's front doorbell jingle.

"Did I see you coming in from the creek just now?" Linda, Preacher Willy's wife, had a box in her arms and a bag hanging from one hand. She was tall, blonde with a beehive hairdo and luminous eyes. She smiled most of the time, told people it was her job to smile and be friendly, in order to help her husband be a better minister. She believed that if you smiled at people, they'd smile back, and the world would be a kinder place.

"You did. I had been helping Roland with his homework." *There goes another lie.* Pidge was stacking them up. When will this stop? she wondered.

"I've got some stuff for the Free Box," Linda stood at the door. "Do you think somebody would want a puppy?"

Rose had stepped to the desk in the back. "No! Don't you dare put a puppy in the Free Box, Linda! We've got enough trouble here as it is. We don't have enough people to look after a puppy."

"Just asking." Linda turned around. She forced a smile. "I'll take the puppy back. My black mammy dog had two and this one is just so adorable."

Pidge walked around the counter and looked in the box. "Aaw, what a sweet little doggie."

Luke came in from the gas pumps and stuck his finger in the box. The coal black lab-mix pup grabbed his finger and sucked on it.

Rose walked to the front. "Get out of here with that dog, Linda. We cannot take on a puppy. A young girl about to have a baby is trouble enough. Take the puppy away."

"But—" Linda hesitated.

"No if, ands, and buts. Get that little dog out of here. It's cute but won't last a day with all the cars coming in and out around the store."

Linda handed the box to Luke who walked outside, petting the puppy.

"You might be right. I forgot about all the traffic here lately. One of those hippies scratched off in front of the church this morning. I told Willy we'll have to work on that hole he dug in the grass. Right under the sign."

"The hippies are supposed to be on their way to Georgia." Rose ripped open envelopes and stacked bills and shipping orders. "But it looks like too many of them are still hunkering down right here."

Linda nodded, poking a finger under her blonde beehive. "I can understand you wanting to help the young couple expecting a baby. And I don't want to speak evil of anybody, but the others are getting more and more bothersome."

"I wish Jasmine and Aaron would stay. We need a mechanic down here. It's hard to get a vehicle repaired way up in town." Rose continued to open envelopes.

"Guess I'll ask Birdie if she needs a puppy."

Rose laughed. "Birdie needs a brain. Maybe she'll settle for a puppy."

Linda patted her hair. "I'll put this bag with toilet tissue and sunscreen in the free box."

"I'm sure those will be appreciated by the young people," Rose told her. "Did you buy those from us?"

"No, I got a bargain in town." Linda turned to leave. "I would like to get a cold drink, though." She dug change out of her pocket.

"Those big grocery stores in town sell their loss-leaders cheaper that we can get them from our suppliers," Rose grumbled as she walked over and dug out a strawberry milk from the drink cooler.

Linda took a pull on her Nehi orange drink. "Freezes my brain." She rubbed her temple with a cold, wet hand. A serious look came into her eyes. "Rose, what are we gonna do?"

Rose shook her head. "Just keep going; do the best we can. Life changes every day."

"Willy says he's never seen anything like it. There are so many angry men in the neighborhood." Linda sipped her drink. "Mr. Dauber is organizing them for some kind of outrage. Threatening to organize a White Sheets march. He's got a petition and you'd be surprised how many are signing up with him. Richard has told Fiona to not even speak to me."

"That's another problem. Richard has also forbidden Fiona to help me with Jasmine's birthing. I need a helper. She suggested Granny Blue Sky, but she lives down in the swamps. When labor begins, we may not have time to collect Granny Blue Sky. It's Jasmine's first pregnancy—no telling how long it'll take."

"Richard is basically a good man, but he can be testy at times."

"So everybody says. Could you help me with the birthing, Linda?"

"I don't know. I had a class in college. But at the time I thought midwifing was out and hospitals were in. Why don't you all just run her up to the hospital and call Doc Collins?"

"She and Aaron don't have the money and the people there are hostile toward them because they think they brought the horde of war protesters."

"They'd probably rather do it the natural way anyhow." Linda rolled the last of her cold drink on her tongue. "I'll be with you, Rose. Don't know how much help I can give."

"Handing me clean towels and pads and washing up is not too hard at all," Rose told her. "You can't faint at the sight of blood."

"Oh, you don't have to worry about that. I was raised on a farm and saw plenty of calves being born. I watched; didn't help. I'll do the best I can."

"Thank God." Rose stood up. "You really are a blessing, Linda. Come on and I'll show you the birthing bag here. We've got one at the campground too, just in case."

"There is one other thing, Rose." Linda hesitated. "Mr. Dauber and his bunch will get hoppin' mad if the minister's wife offers to help with the delivery of a hippie baby. I won't be making friends and attracting people to attend church where my husband is the minister. I do want to help him."

"You'll be helping Jesus, Linda. Think about it. The haters won't feel good about anything until they get the young people out of here. I feel sure Rev. Willy will want you to act as a good Samaritan."

"You might be right." Linda told her. "With all that's going on, I wonder if anybody'll even come to church on Sunday."

Pidge walked out to the pumps and helped Luke pet the puppy. The church was the center of the community. What would happen if people stopped going to church? Her mom said that without churches there'd be no civilization. From the looks of it, everything around New Hope was on a downhill slide. She'd forgotten to give Linda a flyer about Frances.

Pidge

Chapter Eighteen

Pidge stretched luxuriously. Saturday, best day in the week for sleeping in. She rolled over and closed her eyes.

"Wake up!" Julie called from her bedroom door.

Pidge rolled back. "Why?"

"Mom needs you to work the front." Julie pulled off the bed covers.

"But nobody comes here on Saturday morning. They go to town and grocery shop in the big stores, then stop here on their way home to pick up what they forgot."

"I know that and you know that, but the hippies don't know from nothing. They're crowding the store and the auto shop right now."

Pidge reluctantly stood and stretched again. "Wonder why they're called hippies."

"Maybe it's because the girls have hair down to their hips." Julie poked her on the shoulder.

"Seems like it has something to do with music." Pidge pulled on a pair of culottes and a tee shirt.

"Couldn't Julie wait on customers?" Pidge asked Jasmine as she filled her breakfast plate.

Jasmine swallowed. "She's supposed to help me walk. I'm eating all this food Doc Collins and Rose prescribed and I'm getting shaky on my feet."

Pidge looked at Jasmine's stomach poked out to the table. "That baby looks like it wants to get out of there and grab a sausage for itself."

"I am so looking forward to having this childbirth over with."

"Bad, huh?" Pidge picked up Jasmine's plate and washed it along with her dishes.

"You have no idea." Jasmine stood up. "Thanks."

Julie appeared as if by magic and Pidge went into the store.

"Wow! Look at that picture Jasmine did of Little Indian Spring!"

Rose pushed up from the chair behind the desk. "Gives some class to this old store, doesn't it?"

Pidge touched the sketch. "That girl can really draw pictures. All it needs is a frame."

"I'll tell your dad to bring one from town."

"What can I do, Mom?"

"Go help people at the counter." Rose pulled a pile of shipping orders and bills toward herself at the desk.

After that, for what seemed like hours, work was constant. People put purchases on the counter, Pidge punched cash register keys, filled paper bags, said a quick thanks, and turned to the next customer.

"The very last Irish potato just walked out the door," Pidge told her mother.

"I'll call Mr. Cook. His potatoes are usually ready for digging about now. He may have early English peas, too."

Grant spoke from the door. "I'm going to see Mr. Cook. I'd be glad to pick up those things for you."

"That's great. I'll write him a note. He'll give you a bill for me." She looked up. "Uh, Grant, I'd put on a long-sleeved shirt if I were you. Mr. Cook has an aversion to tee shirts. It's kind of unnerving when that snake looks right at a person with its beady little eyes."

A grin flashed across the young man's face. "I've got a long-sleeved shirt."

Rose handed him the note for Mr. Cook. "You are a nice young man, Grant. Someday, when you are old enough to really see that snake tattoo, you'll have to pay someone lots of money to get it off."

"I know, Rose." He reached out and touched her on the arm. "Thanks for reminding me."

Rose shook her head and reached for another piece of mail.

Grant put the note to Mr. Cook in his pocket and walked to the counter. His serpent tattoo glistened with sweat. That thing looked so real, thought Pidge.

"What can you do for me?" asked Pidge, making a joke.

"Huh? Oh, I need some smaller change."

Most of the young people, so intent on stopping the war in Vietnam, never seemed to catch a joke. Pidge wondered if it was automatic that they lost the joy in living and laughter when they joined up with the anti-war protesters. The war was serious, but it might help a person's disposition to lighten up sometimes.

Pidge opened the change drawer. Grant handed her a fifty.

"Two twenties and a ten, or two fives?"

"Either," Grant told her. "I have no idea how much Mr. Cook will want for his yearling and I want to be ready with small bills. Surely it won't be more than fifty dollars, do you think?"

"You're buying a yearling from Mr. Cook?" Pidge pulled out change from the cash register.

Grant shifted from one foot to the other. "Somebody from the camp stole a yearling from Mr. Cook. I want to try to make amends."

"Stole a big calf?"

"Yes, I was told the yearling was taken from the pasture."

174

"They know how to kill and butcher a young cow?" Pidge was sure the snake winked at her as Grant waved his arm.

"The way I heard it, several of the guys tied a rope around the animal's neck, pulled him over the electric fence and hauled him on a truck to the butcher pen across the river." Grant shrugged his shoulders. "They grilled and ate the yearling. Now I've been elected to deal with Mr. Cook, since I carry the donations for gasoline, travel money, and food."

"That enough change?"

"I have no idea."

"Hey, Mom," Pidge called out. "How much would a live yearling be worth?"

"How much is somebody asking for it?"

Pidge and Grant grinned at the same time.

"Better give me some more fives and ones," he said. "Nothing to do but offer my young self over to the enemy. If I don't come back, remember me, okay?"

"I'll certainly remember your tattoo. It keeps winking at me. Be careful with Mr. Cook. On second thought, look for my dad out at the auto repair shop. He might go with you."

Grant mock-wiped sweat from his brow. "That's a great idea."

Maybe there was a little humor in this one anyway, thought Pidge.

The phone rang. It was Mr. Cook. "Have you got sweet potatoes, Pidge?"

She looked at the hamper. "Sure," she said. "Not a lot, about half a hamper full."

"Good," he said. "The hippies have trapped a possum near my barn and I was telling them how to bake it with sweet potatoes, then realized I don't have any left."

"Send them here. You show them how to butcher the possum?" Pidge grinned in spite of herself. Mr. Cook was having a time dealing with the hippies.

"I did. It's not too different from butchering a gopher tortoise."

"They're eating the gopher turtles?"

"On the line between my field and your dad's is an old gopher turtle hole. They found one and brought it to me, wanted to know how it got from the Gulf of Mexico to our field." Mr. Cook was enjoying himself. "I explained the difference between a sea turtle and land gopher tortoise, then showed them how to cook it."

"Hope they don't eat all our gopher turtles."

"They eat everything they can get from the river and around the camp," Mr. Cook told her. "They smoke enough marijuana to keep them from straying too far away. I see a car pulling up. Thanks, Pidge." He hung up.

Julie poked her head in the door from the kitchen. "Mom, we've finished walking and Jasmine is lying down to rest. Could I go to Mandy's?"

Rose looked up and swiped a tendril of hair out of her face. "Her dad may still be mad with us. Call her."

Rose saw the look on Julie's face when she hung up the phone. "Don't worry about it, Jules, there's always boxes to open, groceries to price and shelve," she said.

Josh walked in from the kitchen. "Don't worry about what?" he asked, as he bit into a tomato sandwich.

"Mandy's dad told me I couldn't play with Mandy; that I couldn't go to their house anymore." Tears sprang to Julie's eyes.

Anger flashed in Rose's face. "You need to talk to Richard," she told her husband. "This is ridiculous to involve children in grown-up animosities. Julie and Mandy are ten years old, for Pete's sake."

Josh chewed and swallowed. "You're right. That's a good point to bring up at the meeting tonight."

176

"I'm nervous about the meeting." Rose stood. "How come no women are invited to talk about the young people on our land? We're getting them out as fast as we can in a civilized manner. What's with Dauber and his followers?"

"I don't know," Josh told her. "I'm with you on the whole mess. In the first place I don't believe protests can stop the war in Vietnam. In the second place, I think these young people will grow up along the way to speaking their minds. Why couldn't our country's leaders hear them out, maybe have some debates?"

"I suppose that would be too adult and civilized." Rose shrugged her shoulders. "I'm going to check on Jasmine. I have a gut feeling we won't have long to wait on that baby."

Luke stuck his head in at the front door. "Doc Collins' car is pulling up at the auto shop," he called out, then closed the door.

"Speaking of checking and babies," said Josh. He headed out the front as Rose went out the back to bring Jasmine.

For the first time, the store was empty. Pidge and Julie opened boxes of corned beef and stamped prices on them. "Here's a bent one," Julie said. "I'll take it to the Free Box." She stopped. "Why don't we eat the bent-can stuff?"

"Mom told me that people who put up their food in jars don't trust the cans, say the bent place might let in air and spoil the food. Make people sick."

"Oh." Julie peered suspiciously at the can of beans. "If it might make somebody sick, how come we give them to people?"

Pidge put her hands on her hips. "Seems there's a law, or something. People around here won't buy them."

Julie shook her head. "But they eat them from the Free Box?"

177

"Yep, go figure," Pidge answered. "You want a Nehi? I'm getting one."

"Grape soda," Julie said. She went to the door and called out to Luke. "You want a soft drink?"

"Sure, orange, if you'll bring it to me." He pulled out a gas nozzle. "Doc told me to drive his car over to the shop for Aaron to check. Said it makes a yuk, yuk sound." The delight at being invited to drive the doctor's late-model Buick, even a short distance, was evident in the fourteen-year-old's voice.

In the kitchen Doc Collins set his bag on the table. "Meet my prettiest patient ever, Mavis," he told his wife who hugged Jasmine around the shoulders.

"You certainly didn't exaggerate," she told him. "You're a brave young lady, Jasmine."

"I don't know about brave," Jasmine told her. "But I sure am grateful to the doctor, and to Rose for their help."

Doc Collins checked Jasmine's blood pressure, listened to her heart, and pinched her ankles to see about swelling. "You are ready," he told her. "But the baby's time will be up to it."

"I know," said Jasmine. "I'll be so glad when it decides." She walked into the store just as the soft drinks were pulled from the ice water. "Strawberry punch for me," she told Pidge.

Pidge pointed to the bulletin board. "That sketch you made of Mom. Could you make one for me?"

"Sure. Stand still, I'll draw you right there."

"No, not me." Pidge's face turned crimson. "I want one of Grant, without the snake, of course."

"I think I can do a draft of him from memory." Jasmine pulled the sketch pad closer. "I didn't know you were sweet on Grant, Pidge."

"I'm not, uh, sweet on him." Pidge rolled her drink around and around in her hand. "I, uh, just think he might be good-looking, without the snake tattoo."

Doc Collins and Mavis followed Rose to the motel room prepared for the birthing.

"We've got everything ready, here and at the campground," Rose told them. "I am sort of nervous. Fiona's husband won't let her help, so I asked Preacher Willy's wife Linda to fill in, even though she's never been at an actual baby birthing."

"I'm sure she'll do fine," said Doc Collins.

She and Mavis shared glances, then smiles. After all, he was a man, a spectator to the mysteries of childbirth. Both sexes shared in the creation, but the actual birthing of a child was a female miracle. They walked down the hall shoulder to shoulder.

"I'll come too when my husband gets the call," Mavis told Rose. "Maybe I can help."

When the women walked into the grocery store, Pidge and Julie were unpacking, stamping, shelving and sipping their sodas.

"I could carry some of these cans to the Free Box." Mavis picked up a couple of cans of pineapple that had bent in shipping. "Isn't it strange that so recently food was preserved in glass jars. Now it's put in cans. And we're warned to check out bent ones, that they might be spoiled. Have you ever opened a can and found spoiled food in it?"

"I haven't," Rose said. "You may be onto something, Mavis. Write a letter to the Agriculture Department."

Mavis went out the door and Rose reached to the top shelf for the cutter to open cardboard boxes. "It's sort of nice to be free of the crowds for awhile, though the customers' money is welcome."

179

At her words a scream split the air. Rose, Pidge, and Julie crowded through the door. Jasmine struggled to get out of the office chair, then gave up. Mavis was sprawled out on the ground beside the Free Box. Luke lifted her head. He looked up at his mother. "She fainted."

Doc Collins, Josh, Aaron, and David hurried over from the auto shop. Doc Collins dropped to his knees. "Get my bag off the kitchen table," he told Pidge, who ran for it.

Minutes later Doc Collins roused his wife from her faint. As he reached to help her up, she had one hand locked around the handle of a small suitcase.

"I'll take that," Rose told her and pulled on the light blue leather suitcase. Mavis wouldn't turn loose.

"Let Rose take the suitcase." Doc Collins' hand covered his wife's. Josh grasped Mavis under the arms from behind and pulled her to her feet. Doc Collins tried to pry his wife's fingers from the handle

"No," cried Mavis. "Don't take the suitcase. It's mine."

"It's been sitting beside the Free Box for several days," said Rose.

Grant drove up, the back seat of his convertible filled with boxes and crates of new Irish potatoes and freshly-picked English peas. "I should have taken a truck," he said, then noticed the group huddled around Mavis. He poked Luke. "What did I miss?"

"Ms. Mavis fainted," Luke whispered. "She says that old suitcase is hers."

Mavis overheard the whisper. "It is mine," she said, her face pale. "See?" she turned the small suitcase and pointed to the initials under the rusty handle. "M.A.C., Mavis Anne Crowder. That's me."

Understanding dawned on the faces of those around her. "Let's take it inside," Doc Collins told her. "And look at it more closely."

"Let me help," David told them. He gently lifted Mavis and the suitcase.

"I'll bring a chair from the kitchen." Luke left and came back with a chair he set before the counter.

With the suitcase on the counter, Doc Collins pried her fingers from the handle. Rose struggled with the rusted hinges.

"Here." Josh handed her a small bottle of oil and a rag. "Try this." They rubbed at the rust until the clasp popped loose.

Mavis looked in the suitcase, empty, elastic sprung on the side pockets. Her hands rooted about the soiled interior. She found holes in what once had been shiny, thin rayon fabric.

"I loaned this suitcase to my sister Claudia, five years ago when she went off to Stanford for a master's degree. I lost track of her. I wrote to her and called but got no answer. They said she dropped out after two months. I haven't heard from her since."

As she rummaged around inside the case, she cried out. "There's something," and held up a gold earring with amber baubles hanging from it. "I gave her these earrings for her birthday."

As the others watched, Mavis kissed the earing and looked again. "That's all there is here of my sister—one earring."

Grant cleared his throat. "I saw some clothes in there, tees and shorts, I think."

"Orion said they might fit Arthur's mom. I gave those to him," offered Pidge. "We could see if she still has them."

"How long did you say the suitcase has been here?" asked Doc Collins.

"Maybe close to a week." Luke scratched his head and looked at Pidge. "Since the day Linda tried to give us the puppy."

"You mentioned it to me right after I replaced the gas pump on that red camper-trailer," said Aaron. "There were two girls when I towed it from the camp, then a pretty black-haired girl came and got it. I remember she paid for it mostly with one-dollar bills."

"My sister has black hair." Mavis was excited. She pointed her nose at Aaron like a bird dog that's picked up a scent.

"I'll look in my receipt book," said Aaron.

"I'll go with you." Mavis followed him, clutching the suitcase handle. "Maybe Claudia is still at the campground. Let's go," she called out to her husband.

"This place is constantly astir with drama," said Rose. She helped Jasmine from the office chair.

"Julie get off the phone and go in the kitchen and you and Jasmine shell peas." Rose was in her element, spitting out orders and organizing workers.

"Pidge help Grant bring in the produce. Put a box of potatoes and a hamper of peas in the kitchen. We'll have new potatoes and early English peas, with a big pan of cornbread for supper. Hooray." She raised clasped hands in the air.

"I see a gas customer." Luke went out the door.

Josh followed the Collinses, Aaron, and David, to the auto shop.

"Won't it be wonderful if Ms. Mavis finds her sister?" Pidge carried a hamper of English peas into the kitchen, plunked them down and returned to the car.

"I hope she does find her," said Grant. "But it's not likely. More and more of the people are leaving. There's no telling where that red camper is by now. Maybe near Atlanta already."

"A man who wears a snake on his arm that winks at people doesn't believe in the possible?" said Pidge.

"I am basically positive," said Grant. "But lately I've come up against more negatives than I like."

"You can say that again."

"How old are you, Pidge?" Grant handed her a box of potatoes.

"Twelve. I'll soon be thirteen. Why do you ask?"

"You look older than twelve." Grant grinned. "I thought I saw you winking at Arthur."

"That was your snake you saw wink at Arthur. I'm not interested in Arthur, except as a friend."

"Aha." Grant hefted a box of potatoes. "You're only twelve. You haven't got your woman shape yet. In a couple of years you'll be a teenager and you'll grow curves. Then you'll like boys. Every day's a change. There's no way to stop it."

Pidge chucked Grant on the arm.

Arthur, the gas customer, asked, "What's happening?"

"You're going to get in trouble for driving your dad's truck," Luke teased him.

"I don't know about that." Arthur hefted a hamper of peas from the back of Grant's convertible. "Mr. Josh told me he got a license when he was twelve."

Grant spoke up. "Back then there weren't as many cars on the road either."

Luke filled the tank on Arthur's dad's truck. "Did you give those shorts and tees from the blue suitcase to your mother?"

"I did," answered Arthur. He struggled to drag a box of potatoes up the steps. "She said they might be too small for her, though."

"Doc Collins and his wife, along with Aaron, David, and my dad are on their way to the campground with the suitcase. Ms. Collins says it's hers. They'll be looking for your mother by now."

183

Arthur dropped the box on the top step. "I saw your dad's truck and a Buick scratch off. I'd better go see if I can help."

Pidge felt a pang of conscience watching Arthur drive toward the river field. *I should have asked to go with them and look for Frances,* she told herself.

A somber group returned from the campgrounds. Aaron's list of people included two names attached to the red camper, but it had already left. Information on the legal pad included the names with the camper tag number. The date recorded showed the women had left for Georgia three days ago. Neither of the names matched Mavis' sister. Aaron promised to call his uncle and ask him to locate the women and the red camper. Others had promised to keep a lookout at the campgrounds in the event the women came back.

Mavis didn't recognize any of the shorts and tee shirts. Her sister *had* been missing five years.

Aaron and David returned to the auto shop. Josh and Doc Collins waited at the door of the grocery store.

Rose patted Mavis' shoulder. "I hope your sister can be located."

"We could make flyers like these for my friend Frances." Pidge tried to comfort the doctor's wife, whose tears streamed through the remains of her makeup.

"I would like that," said Mavis quietly. She held tight to the handle of the ragged-looking suitcase. "I'll go home and find a picture." The Collinses left, promising to return soon.

Pidge went to work in the kitchen. Josh and Rose stood at the front door and watched them go.

"I expected some problems, but none like this." Josh folded Rose in his arms. The store was quiet for a change. No customers present and the only sounds, happy chatter, came from the kitchen where Pidge, Julie, and Jasmine shelled peas and put new potatoes on to boil.

"I'm just tired," Rose told her husband. "We've never done this much business in food and snacks. It's exhausting. I know we're trying to get them to move on, but I've grown fond of some of them. There are many nice young people among them. Some are grunges, but Jasmine and Aaron, David and Doris, Jeremiah and Cindy, Grant, Arthur, and Orion, I'll be sorry to see go."

"I know," Josh agreed. "That big question out there about the war, the zeal the young people have, the energy, the purpose, is here now in our neighborhood. And it's not just us, Rose. The travelers are meeting people like us over this entire country as they make their voices heard."

Rose sighed. "We've got to help them, Josh. They are being treated terribly in some places. I'm almost afraid of newspaper and television news. Instead of the love and peace they talk about, these young people are facing hatred. In the meeting tonight, try to get the supposed leaders of this community to give the youngsters a little slack."

Their embrace was long and solemn. "I'll do my best," Josh promised.

Josh

Chapter Nineteen

Pidge stood behind the counter watching local men gather in the store to go to the community meeting. She couldn't get the campground out of her mind. If Frances were hiding, she'd surely be drawn to the camp at supper time. Hunger, if not fear of the darkness among the oaks, magnolias, and cypress, would surely bring her in from the woods to seek people.

Rev. Willy was the first to arrive. He made a V peace sign to Pidge, then sat down in the office chair.

Grant came in from the campground with the donations bucket. "Somebody took the money out," he told Pidge.

"Who on earth would do a thing like that?"

"You'd be surprised." Grant handed large bills from his pocket, which he and Pidge broke down for the change bucket. "You try to help some people and they take you for a sucker." He left for the campground.

Aaron and David came in from the auto shop. Josh was in the kitchen.

Usually talkative, Rev. Willy was quiet. He smiled, but his eyes reflected frustration, gloom. Aaron went to find Jasmine, who would stay with Rose, Pidge, Luke, and Julie.

Tony the surveyor, and Bradley the contractor who had furnished portable toilets, came in and reached into the soft-drink cooler box, sloshed ice and water around until they found drinks, then gulped down the cold liquid.

"Can't beat a cold, creamy strawberry punch," said Tony.

Jeremiah and Arthur's father came in. "We hated to leave the juveniles unattended, but we left Doris in charge. She's better than us with the quarrels and disturbances. We'd like to be at the meeting, if you think it's all right."

"We can ask Josh and Aaron." David dipped his head in greeting. "They have more of a feel for these things than I do. You're right about Doris. She is one strong woman, I am proud to say. Legally, it's all right for us to be at the meeting, since they are rumored to be discussing us, but it might be easier for Josh to deal with them if we're not there."

"Where?" The Collinses came in the door. Mavis handed a wallet-sized picture of her sister to Pidge.

"The men of the community have called a meeting to discuss the camp, and those in it." David shook hands with Doc Collins.

"Josh told them the young people are moving on as regular as we can move them." David leaned against the banana-pod post.

Josh walked in. "Did I hear my name?"

"I was telling them what you told Mr. Dauber." David said.

Doc Collins reached out his hand and Josh shook it.

"I don't think he took it into his pea brain." Josh stepped toward the front door. "Guess we better go tell him again."

David turned as Aaron came in, wiping his hands on a grease rag. He handed the rag to Pidge, who dropped it into a tin can under the counter.

"Rather be early than late, let's go," Josh reached for the doorknob.

"Us too?" David asked. "It might be better if the protesters stayed away, since they're meeting about how to get rid of us."

"It's essential we bring as many as we can to speak up for the young people," Josh reminded him, with a questioning look at Aaron. "What do you think?"

"We're all needed, especially David." Aaron surveyed the group. "Everybody wearing shoes?" He grinned.

"We are," David told him. "And regular shirts. No tees with slogans. Except for the long hair, we look like regular people, kinda."

"Pidge, you got any extra hair ties?" Josh asked his daughter.

"Sure do, and rubber bands." She counted out what was needed, then clapped as each of the young men subdued their long hair in ponytails. "Wish I had film in my camera."

"That's better." Josh stifled a grin.

"I'm coming with you," said Doc Collins. "Mavis can stay here, if that's okay."

"Sure Doc," Josh told him. "I hope we don't require your services, but you are certainly welcome."

"Dad." Luke came in from the gas pumps. "Could I go with you?"

"I'd rather you didn't," Josh told him. "There may be some language not suited to your young ears."

"But, I'm fourteen. If twelve is the age of responsibility, then I've been almost a grownup two years. I've heard plenty of bad language."

Josh poked Luke on the shoulder. "You're growing up fast, son. We don't need to rush the process. Besides, your mother and Pidge need you at the store."

"Uncle Jim could watch the front."

188

"He'll be at the meeting, more than likely. Maybe next time."

Luke walked out the door and leaned against a gas pump, then stood up straight when a small car turned in. "Somebody pulled your car before it got ripe," he told the pretty girl behind the wheel.

A group of men had gathered beside the big limestone rock when a green pickup drove in. John Walters, editor of the *Holmes County Advertiser* newspaper, got out, a Canon camera with a big lens draped about his neck.

"May I park here and walk to the meeting?"

"Sure," Josh told him. "Some are walking, some are driving."

Across Highway 2, just past the graveyard, a television van went around the group of walkers. At the old school building which housed the community meeting room on the main floor and the Masonic Hall upstairs, Sheriff Clark pulled his official car up to the steps.

"I hope we won't need his services either." Josh nudged Doc Collins and pointed.

Two more Sheriff's cars filled with deputies pulled in between the Clark's vehicle and the television van.

"I don't know if I feel safe." Doc Collins nodded toward a deputy known for shooting himself in the foot.

"At least it was his own foot, not somebody else's."

People milled about inside. Some were angry men of the community, and some were younger ones with sour expressions who had been forced by their fathers to attend. Josh poked Doc Collins with his elbow, then pointed to his hair. The men around Josh's age and older had short buzz cuts. Some of the younger ones had bangs like those originally worn by members of the popular

Beatles band from England. No longhairs among the locals, yet.

Six-thirty and they were right on time. Aaron pointed to empty chairs along the south wall of the large room. A table there held cables and TV equipment; another table stood empty, except for Uncle Jim, natty in his plaid shirt and red bow tie. As Josh moved with the others to seat themselves around the table, Joe Dauber noticed them and snorted in anger.

"You hippies and hippie-lovers get out of here," he yelled, filmed, of course, by the TV camera.

Josh stood and clapped his hands. Most of the men gathered began to settle into chairs.

"I was invited to a meeting to begin at six-thirty to discuss something of importance to this community," Josh said. Dauber sputtered as Jim Warell and Claude Shipper moved menacingly toward Josh. Shipper dragged Fiona's husband Richard by the arm.

At a nod from Sheriff Clark, several deputies walked to the front and Dauber's sinister-looking supporters returned to their seats.

Rev. Willy stood beside Josh.

"These war protesters are an abomination," yelled Joe Dauber, with his voice aimed at the audience, his good side now turned toward the camera. "That camp beside the river is a festering sore of evil." He waved his arms about as he jumped up and down. "The Bible says to purge them from our midst."

"The Bible says no such thing," called out Rev. Willy, drowning out Dauber as he opened his mouth to yell. The television and newspaper cameras swung to Rev. Willy.

"The first commandment is to love God; the second is to love our neighbor as ourselves."

"Amen to that." Josh spoke up. "These young people, however temporary, are our neighbors, and we should treat them as we would hope others in this country would treat our own children."

"Look what they've done to Mr. Cook: stole his chickens, his calves, tromped over his fields. Speak up, Mr. Cook." Dauber pointed to Mr. Cook, who stood.

"I think you are aware, Dauber, that they paid me for what was destroyed. Some of them are working for me now, digging new potatoes and picking English peas. I can get along with most of these young people. They are far from home, speaking out for a cause. I remind myself daily that they are somebody's children."

"Our own children would not travel in a group across the country in support of war protests," yelled Dauber. The youths with Beatle haircuts glowered at him as the TV camera zoomed in on Josh and Rev. Willy.

"Kindness is the key word here, not hatred." Rev. Willy raised his voice to match Dauber's but modulated to a lower key. "I refer you to Hebrews 13:2. In case you forgot, it tells us to entertain strangers, that they might be angels."

"That's blasphemy," yelled Dauber. "They are a bunch of dirty hippies, practicing free love down by the river."

"I would refer you to Jesus Christ, who said 'I was hungry and you gave me food, I was thirsty and you gave me drink, I was a stranger and you invited me in.' Matthew 25:35." Rev. Willy's voice rose above the noise. "When have you done any of this for anybody, Joe Dauber? Much less these young people protesting an unpopular war."

"This is my community and I say what goes on around here," Dauber yelled, his eyes dilated as engorged veins popped out on his neck.

Rev. Willy held his ground. "These young people wound up here because they took a wrong turn on their way to Atlanta to march for peace. We are helping them leave in an orderly manner. They will be gone within the next few days."

"They will be gone before daylight tomorrow, or bear the consequences," Dauber danced around, waving his arms, and screaming.

Rev. Willy stepped back. "I would like to introduce the leaders of the group camped on Josh Reed's land." He waved his hand for Aaron and the others to stand.

Dauber jumped in front of the camera and reached to grab Rev. Willy by the shirt, but Josh's fingers wrapped around his wrist.

"Let him hit Rev. Willy and I'll throw his enraged carcass into my jail." Sheriff Clark took out a pair of handcuffs.

"No," Josh told Sheriff Clark. "We don't need to give this rabble rouser that kind of publicity." He turned to Dauber, "If you think you can sit behind the podium and call this meeting to order, I'll release your arm." Out of the corner of his eye, Josh saw Richard scurry out a side door.

"Can you do that and follow Robert's Rules of Order?" Sheriff Clark asked Dauber, jangling the handcuffs before his face.

"I can." Dauber waved his other hand to signal the TV camera away.

As Dauber moved to the podium, he saw Jim Warrell and Claude Shipper leave the building. Dauber looked astonished at his main lieutenants, realized they had left him high and dry, then called the meeting to order.

"Before we get to the other business at hand, which is deciding how to chase these dirty longhairs out of our community, I wish to make a note for the record that Josh Reed will be reported to his commanding officer for harboring war protesters on his land."

Dauber gathered his notes, postured before the TV camera and turned to direct his remarks toward the newspaper editor. When he looked up, only those with Josh, Aaron, and David remained in the meeting room. Several shook Rev. Willy's hand, then exited the building.

Dauber stood, dumbfounded. He had no support team. Not one of his followers had remained. The TV cameramen rolled up cables and walked down the aisle and out. "This meeting is adjourned," he finally announced.

Rev. Willy replaced him at the podium. "I will be happy to welcome each and every one of you to church tomorrow," he said, then proceeded to shake hands with those in the building, including Sheriff Clark and his deputies.

"Be careful," Rev. Willy reminded them. "This is not over. Dauber is a troublemaker. He will not give up. The worst is yet to come."

"My men will be around the river field to keep order until every protester is safely gone from here," Sheriff Clark promised.

When Josh arrived home Daylight Grocery was closed and his family was asleep. He turned on the television with the sound low, but Pidge could hear it from her room.

"Hate meeting fizzles as Second Commandment quoted: Love your neighbor as yourself." When Dauber's diatribe came on the screen, Josh hit the off button and went to bed.

Pidge

Chapter Twenty

Pidge woke up early, trying to devise a way to get to the campground to search the Indian trail to reassure herself on where Frances might have gone. Daylight Grocery was closed 'til three o'clock on Sunday. The family attended church services and had family dinner. In the afternoon was Sunday baseball, just south of the church. Pidge had time to mimeograph more flyers about Ms. Mavis' sister and Frances and hand them out at the baseball game.

"Mom, could I sneak into the office and run off some flyers?"

"Sure," said Rose. "Keep a low profile. If somebody sees you, they'll want to buy something. Nothing draws customers like Sunday morning when we're closed. Like bees to honeysuckle."

Pidge and Lena walked to the wood-framed, white-painted Church cater-cornered from Daylight Grocery. Several boys pitched crab apples at one another from the bushes along Limestone Creek, shrieking when the hard-as-rocks fruit connected.

"Stop," yelled Pidge. She and Lena ran for safety behind the church. "Those are almost ripe. Leave them on the trees."

Luke, Arthur, and Orion, with two neighborhood boys their age, turned and pelted the girls with the fruit.

194

"We're telling!" The girls retreated to the front of the building.

Josh and Rose walked across the highway. "We did that when I was a young girl," said Rose. "I don't know how the neighborhood women gathered enough of the crab apples to make jelly."

"They're called mayhaws in Georgia. When I was growing up I stayed with my grandmother in the summer and we picked them from along creeks like this one. Mayhaw jelly was sold at produce stands along the road to Brunswick." Josh shook his head at Luke and the rough-housing stopped.

There were a lot more people than usual in the churchyard. Many of the long-skirted and tee-shirted young men and women from the campground stood in clumps at the side of the building. Josh and Rose joined Rev. Willy, his wife Linda, and Uncle Jim, to greet the strangers and invite them inside.

Handing out bulletins at the door, Pidge noted that they all wore shoes, mostly rope sandals and the Jesus sandals that she admired. She'd have to hand out more rubber bands for the long hair if they were still here next Sunday.

"All ye who are sore and heavy laden, come home," called out Rev. Willy.

Most of Pidge's family joined choir members gathered behind the preacher. Pidge and Lena, who were not in the choir, sat in the audience. They moved over when Mr. and Ms. Cook sat beside them on the pew.

"We made it just in time," muttered Ms. Cook. "No rest for the weary."

"You've been gathering stuff from the garden?"

"We left six hippies picking peas, digging potatoes and singing peace songs. Squash, cucumbers, and tomatoes will be next."

Rev. Willy made his usual invitation to join the choir to those familiar with the hymns listed in the bulletin.

"We're missing our best tenor today." Rev. Willy looked over the congregation. "Maybe he went to one of the other churches and took Fiona and Mandy with him."

"It's his loss," the choir director told him. "Anybody want to take his place? You don't have to sing tenor."

"I don't sing tenor, but I'd like to help." David, leaving the pew, leaned toward Pidge. "You girls don't sing?"

"We can't carry a tune in a paper bag, so we fake it by singing loud," Pidge told him.

A rustle of awareness moved around the church sanctuary when David's baritone rode strong, along with the rest of the choir's "God be With You 'Till We Meet Again."

"I'll be sorry to see David go," said Rev. Willy. "Is it all right if we add more songs to our music today?"

"Solo, solo," called out Uncle Jim. "David's got the voice of an angel."

"What's your favorite song, David?"

"In the Garden."

"I can play that," called out Veda Harris at the piano.

Music swelled from the modest white-painted church.

"What about 'Life is like a Mountain Railroad'?"

Music floated in and around the old church building. Time seemed to stand still. They sang from the latest hymnal and tunes from long ago. Singers, even those who weren't, but merely tried, made "a joyful noise unto the Lord."

As the ending words of "Come Home, Come Home," rang out, Rev. Willy pulled out a red bandana and dried his eyes.

"Such a wonderful, impromptu, concert," he said. "I can't begin to tell you how much it means to me." He looked at his watch and up at the congregation. "We have used all our time singing, to our betterment. The main gist of what I had intended to talk about is the second commandment: 'Love thy neighbor as thyself'."

"A synopsis of my sermon is in the bulletin. I add one thing: Turn to your neighbor and give him, or her, a hug. All who are able, come back next Sunday. 'Nuf said."

As the congregation filed past Rev. Willy, shaking his hand at the door, Pidge and Lena escaped outside.

Orion ran up to them. "What'd I miss?"

"The best Sunday singing ever." Pidge and Lena gave him a group hug.

"What's that for?"

"Rev. Willy said to hug your neighbor. Guess you're ours." Pidge and Lena turned him loose.

"I told my parents that you people around here have fun all the time." Orion "pulled a smile" all over his face and ran to join Luke and the other boys running bases on the baseball field between the church and Limestone Creek.

Back at home, Pidge dipped new potatoes and English peas from a big pot on the stove. Baked ham and potato salad made with some of the new potatoes were already on the table, plus hot biscuits, butter, relish, sweet potato casserole, and strawberry pound cake.

Josh filled his plate. "Three kinds of potatoes for Sunday dinner. Looks like an Irish table to me. Except for the English peas."

Rose filled Jasmine's plate, then her own. Aaron was in line behind Josh. Luke picked up a glass of sweet tea and raised his eyebrows.

"Unsweetened for me," said Aaron, "and water for Jasmine."

David grabbed a glass of ice water. "I need this after that singing marathon."

"Most beautiful music I ever heard." Rose turned to Josh. "If we'd had Richard's tenor along with David's baritone, we could rival any choir in Christendom."

Josh swiped his plate with his last bite of biscuit and pushed back from the table. "I can't understand why Richard is such a nice fellow most times, then can turn peevish on a dime. I'm going with Aaron and David down to the river field."

"I've got work at the shop," said Aaron. "You guys go on without me."

"No baseball game?" Rose gathered plates, raking the leftovers into a bucket for Linda's pig.

Josh wiped his hands on a dish towel. "I don't know. I've been so busy I didn't notice a sign. Richard usually puts a sign out by the white rock."

"Richard is mad, remember? He joined Dauber and Warrell, who want the protesters gone." Rose collected dishes from the table.

"Guess we better swing by the baseball field, then," Josh told David, slugging down the rest of his tea.

Rose dried her hands. "Pidge, it's your turn to wash. I've got bookkeeping to do before I open at three. Maybe nobody'll come in."

"I wouldn't count on that, Rose," David told her. "There was a whole slew of people down at the campgrounds packing up to get over to Georgia."

"C'mon Pidge. You wash. I'll dry," said Julie, "then we can check out the baseball field. If they're not playing, we'll wade in the creek."

"Could be nobody wants to play us." Pidge said.

"What about you?" Rose asked Jasmine. "You ready to go up front with me, or had you rather take a nap?"

"I think I'll try to eat some more food." Jasmine eyed her full plate. "If you need me though, I could go on up front with you."

"You're fine. Try to eat a little more if you can. If you're full wrap up your plate and put it in the fridge. I'll see you in a little while." Rose took off her apron and headed for her desk and bookkeeping tasks.

Just as Josh and David got outside, a big green delivery truck with pictures of tomatoes, bananas, celery and cauliflower pulled into the parking lot. The driver jumped out.

"Jonah," Josh called out. "Am I glad to see you!"

"Thought I'd get a head start on my route."

"Good idea We're out of just about everything, especially hoop cheese. These protesters eat so much cheese, they might start running around squeaking like mice."

"They use up rolling papers pretty fast too," Jonah laughed.

"We'll help you unload," Josh told the grocery truck driver. "This is David, one of our visitors at the river field."

Jonah shook David's outstretched hand. "So, you're on your way to Georgia?"

"Started out that way." David laughed and picked up a box. "Where do I put this?"

Josh opened the storage room door. "Bringing a load today is a smart idea," he said. "I never dreamed there'd be so many people buying so much."

"Me neither," answered Jonah. "I appreciate it though. I'm socking back all the overtime money I can get. Your grocery store selling all this stuff to the hippies is about to wear me slam out—in a good way." He wiped the sweat off his brow, pushing the moisture up with his hand to smooth the ever-expanding Afro encircling his handsome, dark-brown face.

"We're moving them on their way as fast as we can." Josh picked up one end of a large box of canned tomatoes. "You're right," he smiled, "the money is nice, though."

David grabbed the other end and they walked the box to the back door. "Still, it's a good day when we can get a caravan headed out."

Jonah pulled down a dolly and stacked boxes and cartons on it. "I been meaning to talk to you guys."

David turned to Jonah. "We're listening, man. Lay it on us."

Jonah straightened up. "You all need to be careful about that Mr. Dauber. He's evil as old Satan himself. When I was a little boy, he and a bunch of Klan people burned a cross at our church. The church didn't move, but lots of members were scared to go there for a long time. Some left home and settled up north."

"Joe Dauber is dangerous," Josh agreed. "It's scary the way he's riling up the neighbors against the hippies."

"You are right on spot with this, man," David added. "He mostly talks trash. There are some around here who are against his hate-filled garbage, though."

"Besides warning you all against Mr. Dauber, I wanted to see what you think about something."

"Okay," Josh told him, and picked up another carton.

David turned to Jonah. "No sweat. What is it?"

"I'm against this Vietnam War, all the way." Jonah paused and rubbed his hands against his pants leg.

"I tried to join up with the military, but they wouldn't take me because of a busted ear drum. I wanted to join the protesters after Martin Luther King Jr. and Robert Kennedy were shot to death, but I didn't. These boys," he nodded at David. "They got courage. They doin' something."

"We're giving it a try," David said.

Jonah looked thoughtful, then turned full-face to David. "Would you all let me go along with you?"

David stood up to his full height and clapped Jonah on the shoulder. "Yes," he said. "Be proud to have you."

"You a military man," Jonah turned to Josh. "Do you approve of the war 'way over there?" The two held opposite ends of a large carton of dill pickles. After they settled the box in place, Josh gave him a long, hard look.

"When you are in the military, you don't question why, Jonah. You just follow orders."

"Does that mean if you were sent over there, you'd fight?"

"I'd be obliged to. The military follows orders. Otherwise, we'd have anarchy."

"Something in my gut, in my heart, tells me I ought to be protesting this war."

"Then you follow your gut and your heart." David stacked cold drink cartons in front of the coolers.

"I'm troubled about it." Jonah turned to David. "I could keep furnishing food for people by delivering groceries to stores, and telling them I think the war is wrong, or I could follow you dudes to Georgia."

"We could sure use you in the marches and sit-downs. The main thing for you is to remember that we are Americans and we are free to voice our opinions. Right or wrong. It's called freedom. Fought for by our ancestors, yours and mine."

"Thanks, David. I'll think on it."

"Right idea."

"Get back with you, brother."

David gave Jonah the peace sign and Jonah returned it as he drove away.

"You guys through out there?" Rose called out. "It's getting close to time for opening the store and for the Sunday afternoon baseball game."

"We're outta here." Josh and David headed for the river field campground.

"You're still at the table." Rose entered the kitchen, ledger in hand and sat down across from where Jasmine stared at her piled-high plate.

"I gave you too much." Rose said.

"I'm full." Jasmine nodded.

"I'm sorry. I'm not paying close enough attention. I was worrying about the bookkeeping. Forgetting to check on you."

"It could be something's wrong," Jasmine told her. "I feel strange. The baby's kicking more than usual. Maybe it's on the way."

"If you get a hard pain, write down the time and how long it lasts. Lay down on the couch and try to take a nap. I'll check on you every once in awhile. Yell if you need me. I hate to, but I really need to get some more of that paperwork done before I open the store."

"I've got a bunch of pictures to sketch. Maybe I should stay near you. I'll be there in a few minutes."

"Good idea." Rose leaned over the table, picked up the ledger and pen. "Just keep up with the time between contractions."

Pidge

Chapter Twenty One

Pidge and Julie could hear the ruckus of boys and men getting set for the Sunday afternoon baseball game. They walked to the ball field, separated from the graveyard and the woods by a tall chicken-wire fence. The New Hope team, the Blue Jays, were already fitted out. They waved bats, called to one another, and ran around the bases with glee. Lids on the wooden gear boxes slapped up and down as mitts and balls were located and thrown out onto the field.

Rev. Willy called to Tony as the surveyor got out of his pickup. "Wonder why Sweet Gum Head hasn't shown up?"

"I called Rudolph. He said he can't scrounge up enough players. Most of the older ones are mad about the protesters and don't want anything to do with us; we're a bunch of hippie lovers."

"I heard that." Josh walked up, followed by David.

Pidge and Julie stood beside the gate. "Are we gonna have a game?"

"The umpire's here," Jimmy John had walked up from the creek road. "Don't see why we can't play ball. You girls go hold down the bleachers and cheer for us."

"Great!" Pidge and Julie ran down the field and waved as Arthur, Grant, and Orion pitched a ball back and forth with Luke and several neighborhood boys.

"Wonder if the hippies can play ball." Rev. Willy threw the catcher's chest protector and shin guards to Josh.

"I'd be willing to bet they can." Tony leaned against the tailgate. "It's a cultural thing, Rev. All guys play baseball, whether sandlot or Yankee Stadium."

Josh waved. "Here comes Sheriff Clark. Wonder what he's got up his sleeve."

The official sheriff's car circled past the cemetery and stopped at the ball field. Sheriff Clark leaned his head out the window. "When's the game start, boys?"

"Sweet Gum Head won't play us, because of the hippies." Josh and the others gathered around the car.

"Them boys just looking for something to get their noses out of joint. The protesters are mostly harmless. Hah! They want to make love not war." Sheriff Clark laughed and switched his cigar to the other side of his mouth.

"You got enough deputies for a team?" Jimmy John fanned himself with a head protector.

"No. And don't mention prisoners. My wife told me not to fill up the jail with them dirty hippies. She's the jailer and the cook besides. Says she's not equipped to fill her jail with them protesters."

"I don't blame her." Josh looked over the field. "We could cut down some on numbers, but we would need enough to cover the bases."

"I can manage and pitch," David suggested, "and Jimmy John could umpire for both sides." He turned to the Indian with a grin. "Think you could be fair?"

Jimmy John matched his grin. "I am always fair." He put his hand over his mouth and did a dance complete with a war whoop.

Sheriff Clark, always the politician, got out of his car and shook hands all around. "Might be I could go down to the river field and scare us up some players,"

204

Josh scratched his head. "You want to help the sheriff, Grant?"

"Sure." Grant waved his arm and the snake tattoo cut a grin. "I'll follow Sheriff Clark. Tony, bring your truck. We ought to be able to find enough to field a team. We've already got me, David, Orion and Arthur. What about Jeremiah? And maybe we could get Aaron to close up the car-fixing long enough for a game."

Pidge watched as the group drove off. I should have asked to go along, she told herself. I could have looked around for Frances.

She and Julie waved at Mandy running toward the ball field. "Is your dad going to play?" asked Julie.

Mandy stopped. "He's still mad. But my mom said he can't keep me from the most fun around on a Sunday afternoon." The two girls climbed to the top plank of the homemade bleachers.

Slowly the bleachers filled. Uncle Jim offered to umpire and was told he could sub if Jimmy John was hit by a stray ball.

"Can't do much running anymore."

"How about helping Rev. Willy keep score?" Josh reached to a high shelf in the dugout and handed Uncle Jim the book. "You can see who we've got here for our side."

He looked puzzled. "I usually just watch."

Pidge and Lena ran down the bleachers and sat beside him. "We could help you."

"Aw, I know how. Just didn't want to do it." Uncle Jim tousled Pidge's hair.

Twins Pete and Mike, who lived below the sand-bed curve, ran up to "late, late, slowky, poky," jeers. "Pete, get on first, Mike, you take second, I'll call first." Rev. Willy threw Josh the catcher's guards, helmet and face mask.

Mike, the home-run king, had the best snarl and pawed like an angry bull when up to bat.

"Luke, since Richard's not here, you're the pitcher. Tony's already oiled the glove." Luke dipped his head to hide his grin and skipped to the pitcher's mound, where he raked and pushed the red clay to suit himself.

While Rev. Willy named, pulled, and pointed player positions, more cars and trucks pulled up. Pete on first, Lena's dad "Boots" shortstop, Charles, Butch, and Louie infield.

The recruiters brought Jeremiah and George from the campground. Plus cheerleaders, including Doris and Cindy.

"Two baseballs and two mitts were all the gear we could find," David told Rev. Willy.

"We can share." Rev. Willy punched David on the shoulder. "We always have extra gear in the box. Some of the gloves don't look that great, but they're usable."

Josh pulled on the catcher's outfit for the home team and David took on the manager's job for the campground team.

"Good luck, guys." Sheriff Clark slapped each campground player on the shoulder, then sat on the bleachers beside Uncle Jim. Pidge and Lena moved to the south end of the bleachers, nearest the creek.

"This ought to be some kind of exciting." Sheriff Clark rubbed his hands together.

Uncle Jim fixed him with a level gaze. "Exciting? Baseball is always exciting."

"Every last one of the barefoots, with the exception of Aaron and a few others, are as stoned as goats." Sheriff Clark's cackle echoed off the woods along Limestone Creek.

"How about Grant, Arthur and Orion. That's almost a team without those stoned." Uncle Jim stood up.

"Aren't you supposed to arrest them for smoking marijuana?"

Sheriff Clark cackled again. "Why? My jail's not big enough to hold them. It's Sunday afternoon. Sit, Jim, and enjoy the game. They're up first."

A green truck screeched to a stop and a short man jumped out, carrying a speed-graphic camera. "Wait for me," John Walters called out. "I want pictures for the newspaper."

Rev. Willy made sitting room for the editor. Uncle Jim moved over.

Tony coached for the home team. Campground players had David as coach, Aaron as pitcher, Grant on first base, George on second, and Jeremiah on third. David added Arthur as shortstop, with Orion, Quincy, and Marvel in the outfield.

"Come on boys, line 'em up and move 'em out," David called, slapping his hands together.

By the time the positions were figured out, the bleachers were almost filled by locals and brightly clothed protesters wearing tie-dyed shirts, Jesus sandals, and barefoot girls with multi-colored toenail polish. Catcalls echoed against the tree line.

Pidge saw Mandy's dad Richard behind a magnolia tree. He'd promised the rabble rousers he'd not play, but he didn't tell them he wouldn't watch.

"By the way," David called out, "We're the Hippies, and our mascot is Two Toe Tom, the fire-breathing alligator."

"Yeah, yeah, we're the New Hope Blue Jays," called out Josh. "See our mascots flying around, policing the sky?"

At least a head taller than anyone on the field, David threw his perfect baritone voice into the air. "First up to bat is Grant, a strong, serious hitter." David's thick black hair swayed as he rocked back and forth.

Grant took position, spaced his legs, lifted his arms and swung his bat. "Come on Luke, put it right here."

Catcalls rang out over the baseball field: "Hey, hey, time to play," "batter, batter, batter," "come on, come on, hit it to me," "swing that bat, if you can," "don't worry, it's not that bad to lose."

The calls overlapped, blended into the singsong of baseball. The Blue Jays at first, second, third, and in the field, held a collective breath as Luke pulled up a leg, leaned back, then released the ball in a movement that looked slow and easy.

Like a gunshot, the bat collided with the ball. With a look of confidence born of the love of the game, Grant watched his ball soar high above the field, then hit the ground running. The ball tipped on the backdrop of chicken wire, raised high in the air, spun back and landed at Louie's feet. Catcalls rang out "Way to go," "Run Grant run," "You can make it," as Louie fumbled with the ball. "Come on, throw it to me, Louie." Mike on second jumped up and down as Grant slapped first, then slid easily onto second. The ball zipped into Mike's glove just as Grant settled in on second base.

Spectators went wild. By now the homemade bleachers were almost filled. Some of the teenage girls had formed cheering squads and leaped about, roaring. "Hot time in the old town tonight," they sang out. "Way to go Hippies."

Tightening up, the home team members leaned over as Arthur limbered up, then strolled jauntily to home plate, pulled back, eye on the ball, and swung.

"Streeeike," Jimmy John's hand came down.

"Don't wait too long to swing," a heckler called out.

Arthur flipped his head to get a swatch of red hair out of his eyes and pulled back his bat.

Luke postured, as pitchers do, then let loose.

"Swish," went the ball. "Streeeike," called out Josh.

Action at the plate held all eyes, except Bradley's as Grant hopped eagerly between second and third, then ran back to second.

Arthur stood still and watched Luke pull up his leg, swing his arm back and aim the ball. Arthur's bat nipped the edge of the ball just enough to flop it into the ground beside Bradley on third, who scooped it up and zipped it to second just as Grant slid in to third. Arthur made it safe to first.

Marvel was up next. "Watch his smoke," laughed Sheriff Clark as he stood and hitched up his pants, then sat back down.

"Two on." Rev. Willy slapped the post beside the bullpen.

For a pot smoker Marvel moved fast up to the plate. He took some time to inspect the bat, then gazed out at the field.

"Come on, Marvel, we ain't got all day," called out Luke as he went through his gyrations, winding up to pitch.

"What 'cha say, Luke?" Marvel leaned his head to one side, then shook it. "Ooookay. I'm ready."

He looked ready too, but when the ball zipped across home plate, he jumped back. "You don't have to hit me." Marvel scowled. He settled in on the plate and swung the bat back and forth. Only a high ball would connect.

Luke didn't pitch a high ball; he zipped it right across the plate.

"Streeeike." Jimmy John's voice echoed against the tree line.

"What do you mean strike?" Marvel turned a menacing look on Jimmy John.

"Hold your bat down some, it was a fair pitch."
Aaron's quiet voice soothed Marvel.

"I can do that." Marvel shifted his posture. When
the ball roared toward him, he squinted his eyes, and
connected. The ball rocketed up, then leveled out to land
just inside the chicken-wire wall, with Louie and Butch
bird-dogging it.

By the time the ball reached First, flew in to Third,
then reached Josh the catcher, Grant was home, Arthur on
third, and Marvel on second.

"No, no, this can't be happening," groaned Sheriff
Clark.

Uncle Jim patted him on the shoulder. "Baseball is
everybody's sport. From the time we're born we play
stickball, then baseball. What made you think these young
people were any different?"

"'Cause they smoke dope, don't take baths and
wear those tie-dyed shirts, bell bottom jeans, and mostly
no shoes."

"None of that has to do with baseball." Uncle Jim
chuckled, his eyes glued to the action around third base.

"I can bring them in, ask anybody." Orion argued
with Aaron and David. He looked around. "Well, not
anybody here, but back home they could tell you." For a
second Orion, a head shorter than Aaron, who wasn't tall
himself, looked homesick, then determination spread over
his face.

"See that muscle?" He flexed his arm. "That's
tough as steel."

"Okay." David rolled his eyes.

With short, firm steps Orion took his place,
rocking the bat back and forth. "Any day now," he called
out to Luke.

"Streeeike."

David rolled his eyes as Orion examined the plate,
rubbed a handful of dried red clay on his hands, changed

his stance, looked over at the church steeple, then shifted into position.

There was no mistaking the power as the bat collided with the ball, which sailed up, up, up and over the chicken-wire fence. "Sounded like it hit Limestone Creek," muttered Sheriff Clark. "How old did you say that boy was?"

Uncle Jim hitched up his suspenders. His voice climbed high over the medley of cheers. "That's a gone ball. Run, Orion, run."

When the noise died down from four runs, Scorekeeper Rev. Willy shook his head. "Four to zero." His words dripped humiliation. He looked at Luke. "No outs yet."

Tony the coach and Luke held a confab. "I don't know why I thought they couldn't play ball." Luke swung his arm around and around.

"Never assume," Coach Tony told him. "These people are just like you and me, except they are on a quest that rivals Jason's search for the golden fleece. Most everybody plays baseball. We just have to do it better."

A new cast came into Luke's eye as he faced George, who had come with one of the early groups at the river field. He didn't know what George could do, so he'd not give him a chance. Luke wound his ball, slipped his middle finger forward, and threw the ball like a fastball, but spinning from the opposite direction so that it broke before it reached the hitter.

"Streeeike."

There was a long moment before the sound wave broke over the field. "Curve ball George, watch out," was the strongest cry, followed by "Hey buddy, buddy, Hit it to me, Gimme a chance, Long way home."

George eyed Luke. He turned. "Try a lefty. See what you get."

A slight hesitation, an adjustment of fingers and stance and Luke let fly.

"Streeeike."

"Another curve from the opposite side," yelled Sheriff Clark. "Way to go, Luke."

George and Luke stared at one another. No expression on either side. George turned the bat over to right-hand control. Luke launched the ball. George swung, just an instant too late.

"Streeeike."

The crowd went crazy.

"One out, nobody on." Rev. Willy danced, swinging the score book.

Using the same delivery style Luke struck out John and Carl.

"Now we'll see what you locals can do," David called.

Dauber, leader of the enemy troop, drove up. He had forbidden his followers to play ball, yet he came with soft drinks to sell. "I see you behind that tree, Richard. Come help me with these." The two men set up a folding table and soon emptied the washtub of everything but ice, which the players started eating and throwing at one another.

"One, two, three, what do you see,

"The Blue Jays ball's goin' over that tree," sang the home team cheering squad. Pidge and Lena jumped up to join them.

"Hippies, hippies, sitting on the fence,

"Couldn't tell a dollar from fifteen cents."

"What does that mean?" Sheriff Clark asked Uncle Jim.

"Doesn't have to mean anything." Uncle Jim stood and clapped.

"Blackbird, blackbird, what do you know?

"That hippie team is all just show."

212

Doris and Cindy led the hippie team cheerleaders in a whirling dance.

"Campground boys gonna' win this fight
Even if it takes us stayin' here all night."

"This is great," Uncle Jim told Sheriff Clark.

"Watch them Blue Jays, hippie boys
All they do is make a lotta noise."

"Score is still four to none," called out Rev. Willy as he fiddled with knobs on the loudspeaker.

"Won't be long," called out Sheriff Clark. "Let's see how the Blue Jays do."

Rev. Willy got the loudspeaker tuned just right. He cleared his throat. "This is a great baseball game. Wish I could get this many people to church on Sunday morning."

"Way to go Rev." called out Aaron. A few whistles echoed over the field.

"I know a lot of you are heading out for Georgia. I may not see some of you much longer, and the rest of you ever again. I just want you all to know that God loves you, and I love you too." He walked up to home plate and bellowed out: "It's time for cheers for the visitors."

Calls from the crowded baseball field filled the churchyard, the tree-covered backdrop of Limestone Creek, the two-story old school building, and the graveyard filled with generations of ancestors.

"And now applause for the home team." Rev. Willy was in his element. Locals and hippies rocked the air around the homemade baseball field with roars that faded into catcalls.

"Now," called out Rev. Willy, "Let's play some more ball."

Lineup for the home team started off with Mike, who gave his trademark snarl and pawed the red clay.

"Woo, woo, look at that. Bet he can't hit worth a hoot." Aaron pulled back, twisted his body and let loose.

The ball skimmed over home plate, Mike swung at exactly the right instant, the ball silhouetted against low-hanging clouds, then dropped straight down to land in the outfield at Quincy's feet.

The hippie, his brain stoned to a pudding consistency, stared at the ball as it landed and rolled up to his right big toe. "Hey," he called out to no one in particular. "There's a ball. Is it ours?"

Arthur, Orion, and Marvel yelled at once, "Pick up the ball, Quincy. Get it. Throw it home."

Arthur and Orion collided as Mike rounded to first, second, third. They yelled as Marvel picked up the ball, examining it carefully, before he handed it to Quincy.

"It's yours. Throw it to Aaron. Throw it home. Throw it. Throw it."

But Quincy wouldn't take the ball. Mike line-danced his way from third to home.

The field went wild. David and Aaron shook their heads. Josh doubled over laughing.

Sheriff Clark jumped up and down, pounding Uncle Jim on the back. "I told you. I told you it'd be a show."

"They're still three ahead of us." Uncle Jim was not impressed.

Pidge and Lena forgot to cheer. Their screams mixed in with the cacophony of catcalls and laughter. "Calm down. Calm down." Rev. Willy's loudspeaker carried his voice above the others.

Back at their places on the bottom bleacher, Pidge glanced over at the magnolia tree where Richard had hidden earlier. Somebody peeked from behind the tree. It couldn't be, but was it? Frances? Lena saw her too and grabbed Pidge's arm.

"Turn loose," Pidge told her. "You stay. I'll catch her." Her feet moved and at that instant Frances saw her and ran onto the trail beside Limestone Creek. Pidge put one foot in front of the other, mechanically, like pistons. Frances tried zig-zagging, but Pidge stayed right behind her, steady, bent on the chase.

Just before the intersection of the river trail Pidge gave that extra push and landed square on Frances. The tackle was swift and sure. Frances lay under her with wrists pinned to the ground. She tried to wriggle out from under Pidge but failed. Finally, she stopped her struggles.

"Turn me loose. I won't run," she wheezed out.

"Not until you tell me why you have been dashing away from me, and from Luke. I've been worried crazy about you. Where are your parents? Have you been kidnapped?"

"Let me up and I'll tell you how it is."

Pidge moved aside but did not slack her hold on Frances' wrists. "Tell me."

"Let me go."

"Not until I get some answers. Why did you run from us?"

"I didn't want you involved."

"Involved in what? Who are the people you are with?" Pidge pulled Frances' arms behind her back. She wished she had some twine. She held on tight.

"Sam and Betty were our neighbors. My parents had our truck loaded and they made room for me in their back seat. Just about everything we owned, and theirs too, was in the truck and their car." Frances took several gulps of air. She shook her head.

"I was riding with them and at first we caravaned fine. We stopped at the same places, ate together, stayed in motels. We were all headed to Georgia. Sam and Betty changed the route along the Old Spanish Trail. They didn't go up through Mississippi and across Alabama, they came on to Florida."

"Why?" Pidge was relaxing her hold on Frances' wrists.

"Some people at a gas station told them they could get to Atlanta quicker this way; that these people had a farm to go to."

"What about your parents?"

"They told me that the people they talked to would tell my parents which direction to take and that they'd catch up with us. You can turn me loose. I've wanted to talk to you, to tell you this, but they told me they'd kill me and tell my parents I ran away, if I let on to anybody."

"Luke said they seemed worried; they said they had searched for you, that they were afraid they'd be blamed if you weren't found."

"I heard the lies they told Luke. I was hiding behind a huckleberry bush. They told me I'd never see my parents again."

"So, you *were* kidnapped." Pidge rubbed her hips. Her legs hurt. "Why didn't you tell me? Sheriff Clark can put them in jail."

"They'd say the same things they said to Luke. Who'd believe me over two grownups who claimed they were taking me to meet up with my folks?"

Pidge looked her steadily in the eyes. "You can come home with me. My parents will protect you."

"I was afraid to get anyone here involved, especially you. What if they kidnapped you too?"

"But you can't live out here in the woods."

"You have to cross your heart you'll not tell anyone, but I have found a place where I'm safe. Those people will leave. And when they do, I'll come find you."

Pidge crossed her heart, crossing her fingers on the other hand behind her to even it out. "Geeze, Frances, you're taller than me."

"Yeah. I thought I could outrun you too."

"Mr. Whittle will be glad you're okay."

"Mr. Whittle? Why?"

"He said you're the best forward he's ever had on the basketball team."

Frances grinned. "Did he say that?"

"He said to get you back in school as soon as possible." Pidge brushed twigs and leaves from her jeans and shirt.

"Wish I could." Frances' face clouded. "They'll miss you at the ball game. When you get back, don't tell nobody you saw me."

"That is going to be hard."

"You crossed your heart. Not even Luke." Frances turned and like a rabbit down the south river trail.

Pidge let her go. What Frances had said made sense. *That trail goes to the Indians' home beside Dead River.* If Frances was with Granny Blue Sky and Jimmy John, she'd be all right. Pidge turned back on the trail beside the creek and came out of the woods at the crabapple patch.

"I couldn't catch her," she told Lena. "What's the score?"

"Tied. Those hippies can play ball. Except for Quincy and Marvel. They finally took Quincy out."

Pidge looked at the bull pen and saw Quincy seated on the bench, leaned up against the wall, his mouth open, snoring peacefully.

They watched as Arthur walked to the plate, swinging the bat like a cudgel. After two strikes, he sent a low drive to the left and made it to first, his short legs working like pistons.

Pidge felt hollow inside. She almost wished she hadn't caught Frances.

"I don't feel so good," Pidge told Lena. "I think I'll go home."

"I can fill you in on the way to school." Lena gave her a quick hug. "See you in the morning.

Pidge

Chapter Twenty Two

For the first time in a week, Pidge had no trouble falling asleep. Frances was safe, the protesters would leave, Frances' parents would be found, and if they agreed her friend could finish out the school year here. She still had plenty of questions but had heard from Frances' own mouth that she was all right.

Yet when she awoke, Pidge felt awful. Happiness had masked the terrible truth. She would have to pretend, to keep handing out flyers, to fake despair, to look sad, to put on a phony smile. Two words, dejected and despondent, described how she would have to appear to the others.

Worse, on the school bus, Mr. Bob was cheerful, pleasant, hopeful.

"Everybody to the north side of the bus," he called out. "We're not giving up on Frances."

Even Roly Poly was quiet. Not a derisive remark to Pidge when he got on the bus.

"Good morning, Roland." Mr. Bob patted him on the shoulder.

"Morning," Pidge echoed.

Roland's "G'morning" answer was subdued. He fingered the bandage on his nose and stepped directly to a seat.

Pidge felt nervous. It was hard to look out the window and search for someone who looked like Frances when she knew her friend was in hiding and had assured her that she felt safe. Inside she rejoiced, but she pulled a long face for the benefit of her friends. She searched instead for Sam and Betty's tent. She wished she knew what they looked like. Luke had said sort of like Frances' parents, only a little younger.

Pidge nudged Luke's shoulder. "Do you see the tent she's supposed to be living in, or the people?"

"I can't see them from here, and I can't get out now. I'll look this afternoon."

"Ain't that the fuzzy-haired . . . . . . that delivers groceries out there?" a voice yelled out.

"We don't use racial slurs on this bus, young man." Mr. Bob looked up at the mirror and pointed his finger. "That's disrespectful. I will write you up if I ever hear that again."

The kid slumped down in his seat, muttering to his seatmate. "I don't care what he says. I'm telling my Uncle Joe Dauber."

Pidge whispered to Lena. "Old Dirt Dauber's nephew. No wonder."

Mr. Bob stood up. "We are supposed to be looking for Frances."

The students stared. "I don't see anyone that looks like her," Pidge called out.

After a time Mr. Bob started the bus. "We won't stop hoping," he promised.

"So, tell me, what happened at the ball game after I went home?" Pidge asked Lena.

Lena chuckled and so did Julie and Mandy. "That was the craziest ball game I ever saw. Quincy didn't wake up for the rest of it. Marvel made everybody laugh when he balanced the bat on his nose. Mostly they all played good ball. We weren't better than the hippies. They kept up with the Blue Jays all the way. We won by only one point. Best ballgame I ever saw."

"How did Arthur and Orion do?" Pidge shifted her books on her lap.

"Great. You wouldn't believe how they held their own. Arthur slid into third one time and left red clay plastered up one whole side of his clothes. I don't know how he'll get that clay out."

Pidge wished she had been there, instead of gathering a secret that aimed to bust out so bad that she had to hold her hand over her mouth.

"What's wrong with you?" Lena peered into her face. "You sure are strange today."

"I don't know exactly," Pidge told her. "But I now have a good feeling about Frances. I believe she'll be all right."

"That's wonderful." Lena walked ahead of her out from bus and across the school yard. "Coach Whittle ought to get our school team and the hippies to play on the baseball field here."

"That'd be a sight to see." Pidge's happiness about Frances showed on her face under different colors.

At school Pidge felt a strange sense of foreboding. Students seemed to be running and screaming less between classes. Pidge noticed a crowd gathered in the teachers' lounge and in the front office. Adults carried transistor radios, holding them to their ears. She couldn't think of reasons for that many meetings, but then where teachers were concerned, a person could never tell.

Study hall was quieter than usual. "Teacher will return soon" was written on the blackboard. She actually finished her book report. She wondered why no one had informed her of any more punishment for the fracas with Roland.

"What's going on around here?" she asked Lena whose nose was buried in her book.

"You haven't heard?"

"Heard what?"

"Earlier today the Ohio National Guard opened fire on student protesters at Kent State University."

She sounded to Pidge like an announcement on television. "Were any of them killed?

"Four. Put a bunch more in the hospital. It's all over radio and television. That's why all the people are in the teachers' lounge."

Images swirled in Pidge's head. People shot for being hippies, for having long hair, dressing funny, for going barefoot. Demonstrating for peace. "I don't understand why anyone would shoot students."

Tears flowed from Lena's eyes and dripped off her chin. "Me neither. You don't just kill a person for being against a war. Do you?"

"I wouldn't think so." Pidge hugged her notebook. "Soldiers go to Vietnam to fight the communists for our victory. Or, that's what I thought they did."

Lena stood and gathered her books. "I don't understand this Mockingbird stuff either," Lena muttered. "This is the hardest book report I've ever been faced with."

They walked by the office on the way to the bus. Her anger and attack on Roly Poly now seemed silly. *How childish of me, when people are shot because they're against the war, killed for standing up for what they believe in.*

"What is happening to our country?" Pidge stopped in the step well of the bus.

"Huh?" Mr. Bob taped a flyer about the missing Frances on the front window. His shoulders slumped with grief. "It feels like I been kicked in the gut. Our country isn't safe for college students anymore. If I speak out about the war will somebody shoot me? Soldiers don't kill their own people." He turned and seated himself, then wiped his face with a red handkerchief.

Pidge made her way to her seat. "What can we do?" she asked Luke.

"I don't think we can do anything. I think this bus crowd is in shock. The usual random chatter is missing."

"Everybody is sad." Pidge sat beside Lena. "You still working on that book report?"

Lena opened her notebook. "Don't rub it in. I know you finished yours first. You always do. What's a comma splice?"

"When you have two sentences and put a comma between them instead of a period." Pidge sucked on her pencil. "What's that got to do with anything?"

"It's here on the instructions. 'Watch out for a comma splice.'"

Mr. Bob called out, "I'm not stopping today." The bus reached the bridge, then slowed so Luke could leap out at the gallberry bushes.

Pidge lowered her window. The lack of noise was reflected from the campground. It appeared smaller, as if more campers had left for Georgia.

At his stop, Roland got off without a word. Pidge sort of missed his mocking remarks. In a good way, though, she reminded herself.

Even the Daylight Grocery was quieter than usual. Uncle Jim stood idle beside a gas pump. Few customers were in the store, but Aaron seemed to have a large number of vehicles parked around the auto repair shop. Looked like he was helping the hippies get ready to leave.

Julie and Mandy stopped at the glittering white rock to talk as the other youngsters moved on off toward their respective homes.

Inside the store, Rose and a miserable looking Jasmine moved slowly around. The bank book lay open where Rose had worked on it and Jasmine's sketchpad was on the stool beside the banana pod post, a picture of Grant half-finished.

Pidge picked a ripe banana and peeled it, looking a question at her mother.

"I'm walking Jasmine and counting," Rose told her. "She's having contractions. I think they're false labor, but we're checking the time between them anyway."

"How far apart?"

"Fifteen minutes, but they vary too much to be constant."

"Did you call Doc Collins?"

"Not yet. We want to be certain what we're dealing with."

"Wow." Pidge took a big bite of banana.

Julie came in. "Want me to walk Jasmine?" she asked.

"Not now," Rose told her. "Do your homework. I'll call you if I need you. As it is, we're not sure what's happening with this baby. It has a mind of its own."

"The baby might be on its way," Pidge called out the door to Uncle Jim.

"Hooray," he answered without lifting his head.

She was ready with her excuse about Luke having a project at school, but nobody mentioned him. They were too distracted. *The shooting. What a horrible thing to happen.* She snagged a sausage and biscuit in the kitchen and went back to the store's counter.

Undisturbed by the few customers, Pidge stamped prices and put up canned goods, flour, and salt.

"Is that everything?" she asked a girl from the protester's camp approaching the counter. Then she looked up to see tears rolling down the girl's face.

Pidge put a flyer about Frances and the one about Ms. Collins' sister into the young woman's grocery bag. "It is a terrible tragedy," she said.

"I just can't understand why anyone would shoot college students. Now everything about the protests against the war has blown up in our faces. Killing those young people is just wrong. It puts a new face on all our lives." The girl grabbed her bag of groceries and ran for the door. She almost collided with Rev. Willy.

"Hey," he said, as he held the door open for her. "I'm so sorry."

"Somebody made a stupid decision. Opened fire on the students." Rev. Willy pointed to a sign posted earlier on the banana pod post. "Prayer meeting for families of Kent State shooting victims. Baptist Church. Six-thirty tonight, May 4, 1970." He wiped his face with his hands and turned to Pidge. "Tell everyone you see."

"I will," she whispered.

Grant came in with the donations bucket. "I need change." He looked grim.

"I still can't believe the shootings," Pidge told him. "It is just plain crazy."

"It couldn't be worse." Grant wiped his face in his hands. "The government wouldn't stop the war in Vietnam; now it's *here*. Too much war. Too many dead people."

"Will the protesters go to Kent State now, instead of Georgia?"

"It's hard to tell. They were already leaving for Atlanta. Now some are heading straight to Washington, D. C. to demonstrate against the war and against sending troops into Cambodia. Some are going back home. Some are afraid to go anywhere. It seems safer here to me until this all unravels." He looked up. "If you see Rev. Willy, tell him he'll have a bunch of us at the church tonight."

"He left a pile of flyers about the prayer meeting. You want some to put up at the campgrounds?"

"That's a great idea, Pidge. You've got some brains up there in your noggin." He tapped her on the head. "Thanks a lot."

Pidge peeked into the living room. The TV was dark and quiet. Rose washed Jasmine's hot face with a cool cloth and held her steady as they walked circles in the living room and kitchen. "It's probably a false alarm," she told Jasmine in a soothing tone. "We can practice what to do when the real birthing pains start."

Pidge left through the front door, to find Uncle Jim gone. Luke leaned on a pump, fanning with a sunhat generally kept on a hook on a post for that purpose.

"Did you talk with Sam and Betty again?"

"They were gone. No sign of them or their tent. Neighbors said they cleared out right after the Kent State news. Don't worry, Frances wasn't with them. She may not be safe, but she's safe from those yahoos."

"I'm not supposed to tell you, but I caught Frances at the baseball game. She said she's fine, then she ran south on the trail toward Dead River, toward Granny Blue Sky and Jimmy John."

Relief flooded over Luke's face. "I've had a feeling about that all along."

Pidge looked across the road toward the baseball field. "Killing someone for protesting the war is the most awful thing I can imagine."

"Me too. Why on earth would soldiers shoot college students?" Luke wiped the pump handle with a paper towel.

"They must have been doing something really terrible." Pidge tried for a moment to imagine anything bad enough for that. She couldn't dredge up an image.

Josh came from around the building. "From what I've learned, the student war protesters got angry at President Nixon's announcement of the invasion of Cambodia, although he ran for office on the promise of getting out of Vietnam. The ROTC building was on fire, the governor called in the National Guard, a planned protest meeting at noon today was prohibited. Some students were throwing rocks and yelling, so the Guardsmen opened fire. Four students are dead and nine wounded."

"Because some were against the war?" Pidge still couldn't understand the tragedy.

"Because a few were violent, they ruined it for the mostly peaceful protesters. They scared the governor and the head of the National Guard." Tears gathered in Josh's eyes. He reached for his children and pulled them to his chest. "This is a sad day."

"They'll close the university." Luke stepped back to the gas pump to service a pickup truck loaded with a tent and household goods.

"We're leaving." The young man said. "Fill 'er up."

As he held the nozzle, Luke watched the girl in the truck. She held her face in her hands and wiped her tears with the hem of her tie-dyed skirt.

"Are you going to Georgia?"

"No." She lifted her head. "We're going back home. Protesting the war is not worth getting killed for."

Pidge stood beside Luke, watching the truck drive off and a large camper take its place.

"You going home?" she asked.

"No," answered the driver. "I'm headed for Georgia, to protest in Atlanta, then on to Washington, D. C. Today they declared war on us, man. All of us."

Pidge went inside where Rose and Jasmine circled the living room. In the kitchen, Julie smeared mayonnaise on a slice of bread. Pidge picked up a slice and plastered it with plum jelly—homemade last spring—added peanut butter to another slice, slapped them together, and headed back to the store counter.

Most of their customers seemed stunned. They chose their purchases, put them on the counter, paid Pidge, and left without a word. After the first "Have a nice afternoon," and the blank look she received in return, she stopped saying anything. She wondered about Frances' parents. Had they gone on to Georgia, searching for their daughter? Pidge yearned to go to the river field, to see where Sam and Betty's tent had been. She felt a connection with the hippies, even if most of them were older than herself. After what had happened today, she realized time had turned a page; she was either a part of whatever was new, or she was not. Frances had sworn she was safe, but was that still true? Pidge wanted to go to the camp, to be among the protesters.

Just before six-thirty, Rose led Jasmine to the desk chair, and turned to Pidge. "Is it all right if Jasmine and Julie stay with you and Luke while your dad and I go with Aaron to the prayer meeting?"

Surprise! Rose asking instead of telling. Pidge could feel that the tragedy had left an indelible mark on her mother, on everyone. The world, her world, had turned on its axis. Life would never be simple again. If you disagreed with the government, you could be shot dead.

"Sure," Pidge nodded. She patted Jasmine's shoulder.

"I'm all right now," Jasmine said from the cushioned chair. "Rose said the pains were false labor." She sat very still. "Well, I am not exactly all right."

"Me neither." Pidge walked behind the counter. She looked at Jasmine, who stared straight ahead, wringing her hands, wailing softly.

"None of us are." Pidge punched buttons on the cash register.

"Don't think we'll ever be again," observed her customer, who picked up her grocery bag and walked out the door.

Pidge stood with Luke in the parking lot and watched the large crowd of locals and self-styled war protesters file into the church across the road. The parking area was filled with cars, trucks, all sorts of vehicles. Some looked packed and ready to travel. Several young people sat on tombstones near the edge of the cemetery. A breeze fluttered through the stand of pines and magnolias just beyond the baseball field.

Uncle Jim walked up, bright red bow-tie and suspenders identifying him as of an age long past. "I came to help you two but looks like the action is at the church."

"You can go on over. We're okay," Luke assured him.

"You can clue us in later on what happens." Pidge went back into the store.

"We can add our prayers," said Jasmine, holding tight to the chair edge.

At seven, when they decided Rev. Willy would have begun the prayer vigil, Luke came into the store.

Jasmine swiveled around in the desk chair and raised her voice to gather the others (who had become like younger siblings to her). "Hey you guys, come here. Let's hold hands and say a prayer."

Luke and Pidge and Julie came close to her. Pidge and Julie each took one of Jasmine's outstretched hands, and one of their brothers'. Jasmine stayed seated as they stood around her, forming a small circle.

"We can take turns praying, " Jasmine said. "I'll be last. Who wants to go first?"

"I will," Pidge said.

They bowed their heads and closed their eyes.

"Dear God, please help our country, especially the friends and families of Kent State students who got killed . . ." Pidge went silent, choking back tears.

"We pray for the wounded too," Luke said, "and for those who already died. We hope they are in heaven," he said, then paused.

"Help us not to feel so mad and so . . . scared," Julie blurted out suddenly, starting to cry.

Jasmine squeezed the little one's hand, then took her turn. "Dear God, please help everyone involved in this terrible crisis, especially the ones who were there . . . Even the National Guardsmen who were following orders. Please help the leaders of our country to stop perpetuating violence. Help all of the people of the world to learn how to love and respect each other . . . so my baby can live in a peaceful world." Jasmine stared to cry and took her hand out of Pidge's, placing it on her own pregnant belly.

"Amen," Pidge said, reaching to hug Jasmine.

Luke and Julie joined them, for a group hug. Then they all let go to wipe their eyes. Jasmine reached for a box of tissues on the desk, taking one and extending the container. They all took turns grabbing tissues and blowing their noses.

After that, few customers remained at the Daylight Grocery. Pidge stood outside with Luke, listening to the rise and fall of voices from across the cemetery. Occasionally Josh's voice rose above the others. David's robust baritone joined with the powerful voice of Rev. Willy.

"I think I heard old Mr. Dirtdauber yelling." Luke cupped his hand behind his ear.

"Me too, but Rev. Willy is matching him breath for breath." Pidge walked back to the door and straightened items in the Free Box. "Hey, Luke, here's a skateboard."

"I saw it. Here comes a rattle-trap from the campground." Luke said, as a vehicle pulled up before the gas pump.

"Need a skateboard, Orion?" Luke pointed to the Free Box.

"Nah, I've got one." Orion followed Pidge inside.

"My dad made me promise not to go to the church. I didn't promise not to come to the store. I thought you might have heard something."

"Nothing but loud talking and yelling. You guys staying or going?"

"We won't know until the meeting's over. My mom is acting crazy. She wants my dad to get his rifle and for us to head out."

"I'll be sad to see you go," Pidge rang up his soft drinks and chips.

"My mom and I like it here, but my dad's ready to go somewhere and fight. He's mad. At President Nixon and anybody else who has anything to do with our government."

At Pidge's expression, he added, "Especially the National Guard. He says your dad should resign from the Guard."

Luke stuck his head in the door. "Add two dollars for Orion's gas. Looks like the meeting's about to break up. I see people getting into cars."

Orion handed two dollars to Pidge. "I'd better get back to the campground." He jumped into the truck and rattled off.

Remnants of the meeting swarmed into the store. Josh's face was red. Rose was right behind him. Aaron went to Jasmine and held her close. David, Rev. Willy, Tony, and Bradley came in together. Uncle Jim trailed in with several other men, then announced he was heading home.

"The nerve of that Dauber," was the first comment out of David's mouth. "We can't all simply evacuate the campground in one night."

Aaron's anger boiled over. "We're getting people out of here as fast as we can. Sheriff Clark is helping. We've got up signs warning away new campers."

Rev. Willy clearly saw his role as that of peacemaker on a downhill slide. "I can't get that man Dauber, or his followers, to listen to me."

The voices and arguments sounded like more of the same, over and over. Some of the men went into the living room and turned on the television. "I wish my children didn't have to be in the middle of these protests," said Josh.

"Aw, Dad, I want to be in it, I want to hear it all." Luke hung up the "Closed" signs and turned off the gasoline pumps.

Pidge eased over to her mother. "Can I go for a walk? Julie and Jasmine are in the kitchen."

"I don't see why not." Rose was upset. She didn't even mention the river field, much less warn Pidge not to go there.

Pidge could see on her mom's face the distress about the tragedy, the vile language among the men, the divisions forming between people who were neighbors that had once been friends.

Pidge slipped out the kitchen door and ran, loping at first, then going faster and faster. She hurried along the creek trail, sounds of night creatures blending with her deep breathing as her feet slapped the uneven ground.

Up ahead at the river field camp, many tents were gone, but a large number still spread over the open area, with even more bordering the river under the ancient trees. The lights near the road were muted and most of the campers had gathered around a big campfire in the middle of the field. Flames rose, and people huddled together, fewer than yesterday.

She saw Jonah, the grocery delivery man. He must have quit his job and joined up with the protesters, thought Pidge. He was dressed like the hippies, with an arm around the shoulder of a skinny guy with a bigger Afro than his, and another wearing a dashiki.

Fear, from the news of the killings at Kent State, was like an angry fog, swirling through the campgrounds. Many were packing belongings into cars and trucks, but more just sat, reflecting dread, like bile in their throats, and staring into the flames.

Pidge walked to the edge of the highway, and turned, to watch people move, slow and wavy, around the fire. Barefoot men stood around the edges, passing fat cigarettes around, inhaling deep breaths, then exhaling the smoke, slow and easy.

Dogs barked, and one came up, smelled her feet, and sauntered away. She stood still and looked back the way she had come. The highway was empty. The trail was empty and she grew frightened. She could see Arthur and the reflection of the flames seemed to dance on his face.

Slowly she turned toward home, down the dark trail beside the whispering water, listening to sleepy bird sounds, scurrying feet of rabbits, squirrels, and raccoons. The walk seemed to take longer than usual, but Pidge was in no hurry to arrive at a scene of conflict, or friction over a horrible tragedy which had happened far, far away. She wanted her life as it had been before the arrival of the protesters. Yet she liked many of the hippies. She had met new people, seen a slice of a kind of life she had never even imagined. She could feel a difference within herself, but there was no way to change what had happened, and what would likely happen next.

She came out of the woods at the crabapple trees and walked slowly across the cemetery, running her fingers over the tall headstone of her grandfather. It was quiet and peaceful. When she passed the big white rock she saw that the store and house were dark. Inside they were all in bed. She was the only one still up.

Pidge

Chapter Twenty Three

When Pidge awoke, she wondered if school would be closed, and whether any hippies were still camped at the river field. Old Dirt-Dauber and other neighbors wanted them gone. Some protesters would consider the attack at Kent State as a warning and return to their homes. Others, the more angry ones, would head straight into even more danger. She rubbed her eyes, splashed water over her face. In the kitchen she heard her dad on the telephone.

"Okay." He hung up. "School as usual." He sighed, his face drawn, his eyes sunken. What a toll the Kent State shootings had already taken on Pidge's father.

"Will you go to work at the Armory?"

"I have no choice. I took off last week. I have to work, to keep things running as near to normal as I can."

Rose walked up. "Good luck," she said, in a wry tone. "Jasmine wants to go to the camp site, to help Aaron's crew try to calm the young people. I told them to go ahead. I'll put a closed sign on the auto repair shop."

"You could close the store," Josh told her. "Put up the black ribbon, the way you do for funerals."

"I'll feel better out there busy with the groceries. I'd best keep to my routine."

Pidge worried about Frances. *Some of the others could have grabbed her and taken her to Georgia with them.* But she's with the Indians, she argued to herself.

233

She waited for the bus at the big white rock with the other neighborhood children.

"You said Frances had stayed at the double tree," Pidge told Luke. "When I caught her at the baseball field she ran away from me down the south trail. I couldn't follow her because it was too dark by then. It's hard for me to get it into my head that she's safe. She said she was, then ran down that trail toward Dead River."

Luke agreed. "It makes sense she would follow the Choctawhatchee trail to Granny Blue Sky and Jimmy John's house in the swamps."

"But Jimmy John brought frog legs and he played baseball yesterday. If she's living with him and Granny Blue Sky, why didn't he mention Frances."

"Why would he?" asked Luke. "He's not much of a talker. When Frances ran south, she would naturally come to their house. It's just off the trail."

In spite of what Frances had told her, and Luke's reassurance, Pidge still held on to the fear for her friend. Maybe she'd worried so long, it had become a habit. The gnawing uneasiness wouldn't go away.

Nobody said much on the way to school, not even Roland. Mr. Bob stopped the school bus and he and the students stared at the campground. People worked loading vehicles. At some tents, hippies tamped down breakfast fires and others were making the trek to the spring for water. The music group's bus was no longer parked beside the highway.

Pidge could see Aaron and Jasmine in front of their tent, talking with people. David's great head rose above the rest. Tony stood with them, marking off names of people getting ready to leave. Jeremiah helped Arthur's father check over his truck. Grant stood nearby with the donations bucket.

Pidge would sorely miss Jasmine and Aaron, Grant with his snake tattoo, and Arthur and Orion. Especially David with the wonderful voice. He had fit right in with the church choir.

"Anybody see Frances?"

Nobody spoke up. Pidge shook her head.

Mr. Bob speeded up the bus and they set out for school.

"Almost there?" Pidge opened her notebook.

"Oh, no," Lena grabbed her copy of *To Kill a Mockingbird*. "I'm not near being through. How come you always finish your book report ahead of me?"

"I read faster than you?" Pidge grinned and bumped shoulders with her friend. Then dropped the smile. "Seriously, don't you think Mr. Whittle should have closed the school? It doesn't make sense to just go on with our lives as if nothing's happened, when those protesters were shot dead."

"Maybe they're trying to act normal, stick to a routine." Lena held her book open. "After all Ohio and Kent State are a long way from here."

At school Pidge and Lena noticed groups of teachers gathered in the lounge, eyes aimed at the television set.

Pidge waved at Ms. Wren as she passed the office, but the secretary didn't respond.

Lena stopped. "What about the protesters against the war who are here in our community? We have lots of them at the river field. We could cry here at school. Why don't the teachers explain what's happening, so we can understand?"

Pidge's first class was English. "The deadline for book reports is Monday," the English teacher announced. She seemed to be trying to hold back tears.

"See why I got my book report in early," Pidge whispered to Lena.

"Your book wasn't as hard as *To Kill a Mockingbird*," Lena whispered back. "I like the book, but it gives you too much stuff to think about."

"If it makes you think, it should be easy to write about. Just put your thoughts into words, like you just did."

Lined up at the cafeteria, Pidge couldn't get over the strange quietness. People whispered, even the students and food-line workers.

There was very little pushing and shoving. "Why can't we talk about it?" Pidge asked Lena, who kept her nose in her book as they munched on ham sandwiches.

When lunch was over, Pidge felt as if the air had thickened, that she had walked through a cloud of sadness to study hall. She finished her few assignments and put her head down on her desk.

"You asleep?" asked Lena.

"No. Just sad." Pidge kept her head on the desk. "Nothing seems right anymore. The grief. It's sort of noiseless."

"I know." Lena moved her chair-desk nearer to Pidge and opened her book.

Pidge looked around the room. Students stared out the windows. She could hear the television in the teachers' lounge down the hall. Black ribbons decorated classrooms. A subdued John Walters from the newspaper walked around the building asking teachers and students for their reactions to the shootings.

One of the teachers came in and sat down, shifting papers, wiping tears from her cheeks. "I don't understand it. Four war protesters shot to death by National Guard soldiers in Ohio and we still have school. Don't these people even care?"

"I'm sorry." Pidge stood beside the teacher.

The young woman looked up. "Me too. On television they said schools and colleges were closed. But not here. It doesn't make sense. I wish the people we elected could run this country without violence." She turned back to her papers.

A sorrowful group of students formed a line when Mr. Bob came with the school bus.

"What's happening here?" Mr. Bob tried a fake-sounding chortle. "We always have to wait for slowpokes. Anybody missing?"

"They made us go to school because they don't care about the dead hippies," one of the older boys spoke up. "The National Guard blames the killing on the protesters. The president told us to go ahead with our lives, that the students shouldn't have burned a building. But on TV the leaders of the protesters said they didn't set fire to the building."

"Hard to believe this is taking place in our country." The bus driver took a long look at the students. He shook his head.

"Believe it, Mr. Bob. It's happening." Luke took his seat and opened a school book.

Along the bus route, Pidge saw honeysuckle buds, thick, ready to burst into sweet smelling flowers. Farmers made wavy trails as they ran tractors over the fields, marking rows or dropping seeds and covering them up, harrowing grass from beside baby plants. Mr. Bob drove the bus along the winding route, stopping to let students off, looking both ways at crossings and railroad tracks.

"Hardly ever see a train along here, but you can't be too careful." Mr. Bob switched gears and stared down the deserted track.

"He sure is being slow," Pidge told Lena. "Maybe he's afraid to go home to look at his TV for the latest on what happened at Kent State. I believe he's worried there will be more shootings, all over the country."

She realized she felt the same; she didn't really want to know what had happened that day. Students killed and a large number of wounded in the hospital. What if her friends among the protesters here had been at Kent State? What if they went on to Atlanta to protest the war and wound up dead like the students?

"You okay?" Lena looked up.

"Sure." Pidge pulled her eyes from the scenes outside the window: the fields, peanuts blooming, baby corn tassels, soybean bunches like little bouquets, a dark green tractor circling a garden plot.

"Sounded like you groaned." Lena went back to her book.

At the bridge over the Choctawhatchee River, Mr. Bob slowed the bus. "You can move to the north side if you wish," he said. The students obeyed, moved over, and stared. Pidge could hardly focus. She thought she saw Arthur and Orion pitching a baseball back and forth, but she couldn't be sure. No one called out.

Mr. Bob's questioning look at Luke went unanswered.

"We are all so shocked by the Kent State shootings, we can't hold our attention on anything else." Mr. Bob sighed.

Pidge walked to the front. She attempted to whisper to Mr. Bob. "Luke and I believe Frances went down to Dead River where Granny Blue Sky and Jimmy John live."

"Yes!" Mr. Bob looked at Pidge and almost swerved off the bridge. "That would be the right thing to do. I understand the people who tried to hold her hostage have already left the campground. She'll be safe."

"I hope so." Pidge was surprised to feel that the words released something in her that had been tensed like a bow string. She felt lighter. The sun seemed brighter, the air more clear, her place in the world more secure. She stood in the exit well until the bus reached the stop beside the glittering white rock.

Off the bus, Pidge ran for the kitchen. Dead students! She still couldn't wrap her mind around it. She could see the activity inside the Daylight Grocery store and vehicles lined up at the gasoline pumps. She made a quick ham sandwich and stepped into the store.

"I'm here to help, Mom," she told Rose.

Rose wiped her hands on her apron. "Thank goodness, I'm about ready to collapse. Mavis Collins called and said she heard from her sister, that she is safe in the Georgia camp." Rose sat down at the desk. "Not dead like those students."

Pidge walked behind the counter. "Luke's here. He didn't have to work on his project." It made her head hurt, but she wouldn't have to lie anymore.

"What about Frances?"

"I think she's with Jimmy John and Granny Blue Sky."

"Good. Safe with the Indians." Rose's voice sounded automatic. She was already deep at work on bills and orders.

Pidge rang up purchases as customers came in, bought beef hash, sardines, crackers, drinks and chips.

"I join you in your grief," Pidge told Grant, as she helped him with change for the donations bucket.

"I hope Aaron can open the auto repair shop tomorrow." Grant separated money and checked off names from his list of requests. "Lots of people are leaving and need work on their trucks and cars."

The preacher's wife Linda stuck her head in the door. "We've got to run errands in town," she called out. "We won't be long."

"Okay. Keep in touch. No telling when I'll need you." Rose turned back to her work.

"Have you ever noticed, Mom, that Ms. Linda looks like Lily Tomlin in her telephone operator comedy routine when she pushes a pencil under that big teased hairdo?"

Rose looked out the window toward the church. "Now that you mention it, she does, but the difference is that Lily Tomlin is funny."

The two chuckled in spite of themselves.

At a lull in store business, Pidge walked out to the gas pumps. Arthur drove up in his father's rackety truck.

Luke grabbed the gas nozzle. "Come to say good-bye? Wish y'all would stay here."

"Everybody's shocked about the shootings. Getting ready, just in case."

Pidge walked with him into the store. "I'll miss you guys," she told him. "Guess Orion'll be heading out for Georgia too."

"I think so." Arthur piled chewing gum and candy on the counter. "If we do leave, let's you and me keep in touch."

"Yeah. There's the phone, and mail."

"Could be we'd come back this way some time too." Arthur rummaged in his pockets for change.

Pidge wrote her name on a Daylight Grocery business card. "Keep this. It's got the information."

"Don't forget me." He tucked the card in his billfold. "Friends forever."

"I saw an old saying in a book." Pidge cocked her head to remember. " 'Till the sun grows cold, the stars are old, and leaves of the Judgment Book unfold'."

240

She didn't notice that his face was bright red as he nodded and left the store.

"Hey, Sis," Luke called from the door. "Come look."

Pidge walked outside. "At what?"

"All those cars gathering at the old school building."

"Huh. You're right. They're probably holding a meeting in the upstairs Masonic Hall."

"On Tuesday evening?"

Josh walked around the building. "What's on Tuesday evening?"

"Looks like the Masons are gathering." Luke pointed.

"Probably Dauber and his bunch." Josh shrugged. "They like to have meetings and say bad stuff about people."

Inside the store, Josh leaned down to kiss Rose. "How's it going?"

"I can't tell. All you get on television is blaming and shaming. Same old stuff, over and over. I turned it off."

"I meant around here." Josh reached for the doorknob.

"We're all right. Many of the young people are leaving. Some heading to Georgia, some going back home." Rose stood up. "Aaron and Jasmine are at the campground, grieving with their friends."

"I hope this is not too much on Jasmine."

"Me too." Rose followed him into the kitchen.

Pidge waited on a few customers before going outside again. She and Luke watched as cars and trucks came and went at the old school building.

Uncle Jim walked up. "I came back to offer help, but it looks quiet around here."

"The store's quiet, but the old schoolhouse looks busy." Luke scratched his head. "It's got us puzzled."

"Me too." Uncle Jim stared. "I'm a Mason and nobody invited me to a meeting." He walked off. "I'll check on this."

"Dad said it's probably Mr. Dauber and his rabble rousers, that it looks like they're in the meeting room." Luke followed him to the highway, then returned to the gas tanks.

"The old school building's lights are on upstairs and downstairs." Pidge went back into the grocery store.

"I miss Jasmine," Julie told her. "I've finished my homework. We're usually walking ourselves ragged all over the place to keep her healthy."

"You can help me cut some more hoop cheese," Pidge told her.

The sun was balanced on the treetops along the creek when Uncle Jim rushed into the store, dirt on his pants legs, his bow tie askew. "Where's your dad?"

"In the kitchen I think," Pidge told him. "Are you okay?"

"I don't know," he answered as he hurried through the door.

Josh, Uncle Jim, and Rose came into the store. "You've got to be kidding," said Josh. "What is Dauber thinking? That guy could mess up a one-man parade."

"He's serious, Josh. And he's got his followers. I tried to reason with him, but he shoved me off the porch." Uncle Jim sucked in a deep breath.

Stride for stride, Rose matched the men headed across the graveyard. "It won't do any good for you to talk to him, Josh. We ought to call Sheriff Clark."

Pidge, Luke, and Julie stood at the big rock. Voices escalated, Josh and Mr. Dauber the loudest. They could hear Rose yell: "Are you people crazy?"

Rev. Willy ran from the parsonage. "What's going on?" his voice climbed above the others. Answers echoed from the old school building across the baseball field, church, graveyard.

"I'm calling Sheriff Clark." Luke ran to the telephone, then came back outside. "He's on his way."

"It takes twenty minutes from the Sheriff's office. They'll have somebody killed by that time." Pidge stood on her tiptoes.

"The dispatcher said they have squad cars at the campground." As Luke spoke they could hear sirens coming from the east.

"I'm going inside." Julie turned. "I don't want to get shot like the protesters at Kent State."

"Me neither." Pidge followed her but stood at the door of the store.

"Git! Git!" she could hear Sheriff Clark's voice rise above the rest. "Git away from here. Go on home. There is no meeting." After he had been ignored several minutes, he held his arm high in the air and fired a shot. Immediate silence.

"The hippies are getting out of here as fast as they can." He climbed upon the hood of his official sheriff's car and spoke through a bull horn. "We are doing all we can to keep the situation defused. They are not a threat to any of you. Dauber if you say another word, you're going straight to jail."

Cars and trucks cranked up. Men yelled, cursed, and muttered, but they left.

Pidge stood beside Luke at the white rock straining to hear what was said. It was only after every person and vehicle had left the parking area around the old school building, church, and baseball field that Rose and Josh came back to the store. They were followed by the sheriff, preacher, and several others.

Uncle Jim was still agitated. "That reprobate Dauber shoved me to the ground," he complained. "I'd like to shoot him right between the eyes."

With sudden relief, the others burst into laughter. "Uncle Jim," said Sheriff Clark. "That don't sound like you. I'd like to get ahold of him too. But that kind of thing is what led up to the Kent State shootings."

Rev. Willy leaned against a post. "I'm supposed to be a peacemaker, but right now I feel more like socking that rabble rouser and his buddies in each individual jaw."

"The sad thing is that scenes like this are playing out all over this country." Josh rubbed a knuckle against his jaw. "We may feel isolated, but we aren't."

"You're right." Tony walked to stand beside Josh. "We are a microcosm of every community in this 'land of the free and home of the brave'."

"I don't feel very brave right now." David came in the door, eyes flashing and black hair waving. "I have to get back to the campground. Jeremiah may need help with security."

"We've got coffee." Rose brought the pot and Pidge helped with cups and creamer. "Take some with you," she told David. The smell and taste of coffee helped. Smiles replaced frowns and tensions ebbed.

"Hey," called out Rev. Willy. "Times like these, we need a prayer."

As heads dipped and eyes closed, Rev. Willy turned his face toward the ceiling. "Heal us, Lord," he said. "Heal this nation. Help every one of us to remember who we are. Stop the violence. Amen."

With the "Closed" signs up, Rose, Josh and Pidge went into the kitchen. Luke and Julie had prepared a platter of bacon and a pitcher of pancake mix.

"I didn't remember if we had any supper or not," Julie said.

244

"Just what we need." Rose poured up bacon grease and drizzled Mickey Mouse pancakes in the iron skillet.

"Make mine a harvest moon." Pidge pulled syrups from the pantry: Ribbon cane, strawberry, chocolate, and plum jelly that hadn't jelled enough. Julie slathered butter between each pancake.

Halfway through her pile of pancakes, Julie looked up. "I miss walking with Jasmine."

Rose jumped up. "Oh, heck. She went with Aaron to defuse the fright among the campers. Wonder if she came back and slipped into bed."

"I'll look." Julie ran from the room and came right back. "She's not there."

"Finish your food, clean up, and go to bed." Rose washed her hands. "Your dad and I will check on her."

Footsteps sounded outside, then Grant rushed in. "Rose." His voice sounded shaky and he looked frightened. "Jasmine's water's broke."

"When?"

"Just now."

"Call Doc," Rose told Josh as he ran to the telephone. "Call Fiona and if she can't come, call Linda."

Rose ran to Jasmine's room with Grant behind her. "Get the duffel bag off the chair."

Grant grabbed the bag. "Anything else?"

"Pidge, come with us."

"Me?" Suddenly Pidge's knees felt week.

"Yes. If none of the women show up, you're my helper." Rose smiled. "I've told you what to do. Birth is a natural thing. Nothing to be scared about."

Josh called out. "Doc Collins is on the other side of the county delivering the Johnson baby. Mavis said she'll get him and come as quick as they can."

245

He dialed again. "I told Fiona, but Richard jerked the phone away. Nobody's answering at the parsonage. I called Jimmy John's number, but nobody answered."

"Go get Granny Blue Sky. We'll ride to the campground with Grant."

Josh's truck sped away.

Rose got in the front seat of Grant's convertible and threw her equipment in the back with Pidge.

"You're my designated helper," Rose told her. "I have to depend on you."

The duffel bag took up most of the back seat of the convertible. With the top up, Pidge could hardly see out the window. "I thought you already took a bag filled with birthing supplies to the campground."

"Gad. I forgot." Rose turned around. "That's all right. Can't have too many old sheets, towels, and waterproof pads."

Panic surged through Pidge. Her face felt fiery. "What if it's born when we get there?"

"We'll just clean it up, and Jasmine too," Rose was in mid-wife mode, her mind running a mile a minute.

"It usually takes a while, sometimes many hours, after the water breaks. We may be sitting around waiting when daylight comes."

"Why are we rushing, then?" Pidge felt confused.

"Because you never can tell about baby-birthing. That baby will come when it takes a notion."

Grant punched hard on the gas pedal. The little car zoomed up to the entryway of the campground and parked. He grabbed the duffel bag and, with Rose and Pidge behind him, ran to Aaron and Jasmine's tent. It was easy to find; groans flew above the ordinary sounds of people cooking, talking, grumbling, complaining and packing. Music came from the tents of guitar players.

The inside of the tent looked pleasant and comfortable to Pidge. Rose and Jasmine had filled a bookcase with baby items. It stood close beside the single bed where Jasmine lay on her back. Shelves were jam-packed with towels, old sheets, plastic squares for waterproofing, piles of blankets, diapers, undershirts, newborn and onesies in yellow and green, good for either a boy or girl. Colorful muumuus for Jasmine. The dirt floor was covered with woven mats made from bamboo stalks. *So the hippies found Jimmy John's bamboo fishing pole forest.*

Jasmine looked gratefully at Rose and made an effort to smile.

Aaron jumped up. "I am so glad you're here."

"How close are the contractions?"

"Just over five minutes." He held a stopwatch.

"Calm down, we've got time." Spitting out orders, Rose examined Jasmine. "Check the water drum. It should be kept full. Build a fire. Put on a big pot to boil water."

"We can do that." Aaron grabbed the biggest pot and hung it over the fire pit outside the front door. David added kindling to the fire and Grant dipped buckets of water from the drum.

Doris and Cindy came in. "What can we do?"

"Get a musician to sit outside and play soft, mood music. That'll help Jasmine to be more calm," Rose told them. "Right now, I need a bucket of warm water."

Doris, David's wife, set a bucket half filled with warm water on the bamboo mat beside Rose. From the bookcase, Pidge pulled a bath cloth and container of mild soap and put it in the bucket. Rose worked beside the single bed already covered with a waterproof mattress. With several layers of old sheets spread out over the bottom half of the bed, she gently bathed Jasmine.

"How do you feel, except for the labor pains?"

"Just tired in between. Does it have to hurt, Rose?"

247

"I'm sorry, honey, but I've only heard of one woman in my life who didn't have labor pains. My Aunt Ina Mae. She spit babies out like persimmon seeds."

Suddenly Jasmine screamed. "I want my mama." The pains were back.

"Pidge, hold her hand and wipe her face with a wet cloth. Aaron hold the other hand and talk sweet."

Aaron murmured over and over, "I love you, Jasmine. We're going to be parents."

"Nobody told me it would hurt this bad," yelled Jasmine.

Rose rubbed Jasmine's legs and put warm towels on her hips. "We could use a little more light," she said, and Jeremiah's wife Cindy hung another lantern on the pole in the middle of the tent.

"Five minutes on that one." Aaron held the stopwatch in one hand.

"She's dilated, but not enough. It'll start to move faster now." Rose looked composed and confident.

Suddenly Pidge felt as if her legs had turned to rubber. She sat on the floor.

Without missing a beat, Rose took the wet cloth from Pidge and handed it to Cindy. "Wash the sweat from her face and arms as well as you can. Aaron give the stopwatch to David. Pidge go outside and take deep breaths."

"I'm all right," Pidge protested.

"Don't need you fainting on us. Go outside." When Rose used that tone of voice, Pidge fled.

Fiona ran up, holding her side. "I left Mandy with Julie and Luke. Richard went to another of Dauber's infernal meetings and I had to walk."

"You can't know how happy I am to have you here." Rose handed Fiona a pair of plastic gloves. "That baby is about ready to come out into the world."

Josh

Chapter Twenty Four

His foot grinding the gas pedal, Josh drove as fast as he could down Dead River road to Jimmy John and Granny Blue Sky's house. At the edge of the clearing he jumped from the truck and ran to the front stoop. The small unpainted log house appeared to be empty. Jimmy John's truck was gone.

Josh stood in the moonlit clearing surrounded by live oaks decorated with fishing poles and Spanish moss. Glassy deep green leaves of a magnolia tree reflected the moonlight. As his eyes adjusted he saw Granny Blue Sky sitting on a log beside a cypress tree, her head bowed.

"Praying, Granny?" he asked.

A wide smile appeared, rearranging the deep wrinkles on the old Indian's face. "Josh! I was in a trance. Jimmy John went to Dothan to deliver fishing poles. But we're ready," she said, and stood. "Come on out Frances."

Frances came hesitantly from the house and into the clearing, looking fearfully at Josh. "I'm scared to go to the campground."

"I know that, child." Granny Blue Sky gave her a hug. "We can leave you with whoever is at the store while I help Rose with the birthing."

"Don't worry Frances," Josh said. "Luke, Julie, and Mandy are there. Uncle Jim too. You'll be all right."

"Where's Pidge?"

"She's with the others, helping Jasmine."

Granny Blue Sky settled in the car's front seat, Frances in the back.

"It calms me to connect with the spirits." Granny Blue Sky patted Josh on the shoulder.

As Josh circled around potholes and ridges on the dirt trail he glanced sideways at Granny Blue Sky. "It calms me to know you'll be there when the baby comes."

Granny Blue Sky smiled.

They were silent until he drove onto the paved road near the old school building. It was surrounded by vehicles—cars, trucks, four-wheelers.

Granny Blue Sky grabbed at her chest. "Something is wrong."

Oh, no, thought Josh. Is she having a heart attack or something? Then he realized what had disturbed her. "I guess Dauber's had another meeting," he said aloud.

Daylight Grocery was closed. Frances jumped out and ran to the house.

Josh turned east on the highway and headed toward the river. "The men are marching down the road toward the field where the hippies are," the old woman said slowly. "It's the White Sheets. I hear footsteps tramping."

"Lord have mercy." Josh saw nothing unusual at first. He turned off the headlights. The moon didn't seem as bright as it had in the swamp. Then he realized that the road was filled with shimmering white ghosts, row after row, covering the highway, wearing the recognizable garb of the Ku Klux Klan.

"I didn't think Dauber would go this far," he said slowly. Then anger filled him, overflowed. He speeded up the truck. As the front of his truck reached the Klansmen, he raced the motor, but the men didn't move out of the way.

"I'm tempted to run straight through them," he muttered.

"No. Don't do that, Josh. There is too much violence already." Granny Blue Sky's voice was low, tranquil.

"You're right," he told her, as he pulled the truck to the side of the road. "We can walk to the camp. Hope the baby hasn't arrived already."

He parked on an incline, near a fence beside the highway. They trotted to the camp. Josh took Granny Blue Sky's hand and they went to the north edge of the grassy right-of-way. Just as they reached the campground entrance, the two were almost even with the men who carried a huge cross made from two-by-fours.

"Don't look at them, Josh," Granny Blue Sky cautioned. "It will only make you more angry. It is best we remain calm."

"Easier said than done," Josh whispered back.

At that instant one of the men lunged toward Josh and shoved him backward into the ditch. His head hit the edge of a fence post and he crumpled into a heap.

"No," screamed Granny Blue Sky. "God help us." She crawled into the ditch and cradled Josh's head in her lap, tears falling. With her wide apron, she wiped the bleeding wound on the side of his head, opened her mouth and sent a high-pitched keen flying into the air. Granny Blue Sky watched as the Klansmen marched past the ditch into the campground. "Help," she called several times, but nobody answered. The Klansmen held their shoulders straight, their eyes aimed straight ahead. Their feet tramped up and down, like soldiers marching to their own beat.

"Someone will come," she promised Josh. She pinched the skin around his wound and held it tight with her fingers.

Staring at the men tromping past, she began to recognize their shoes. "How can this be that *these men*? Most of them I taught to fish in the Dead River and

Canady Lake. How can they wear sheets and hoods and hurt people?" She wiped perspiration from Josh's face. He twisted in her lap and groaned.

"Somebody will come to help us, Josh. Hold on." The old woman shook her head. "My goodness, Josh, most of these men are our neighbors. We live among people and believe we know them. Must we be reminded in this way of how precious is life, to search ourselves and live the day as if it were our last?"

Many shoes she didn't recognize. That annoying Joe Dauber had brought in men from other places. *The hate spreads. Why can't love?* She thought of individual grownup men she had known as children, all raised much the same. School and work. Play and church. Some were smarter than others in book learning, but some who hadn't fit the schoolbook mold had common sense and could repair machines, raise bigger and better crops. Jake, who won ribbons for his excellent corn at every county fair, hadn't liked school. He read books and studied planting and growing seasons. He was an excellent farmer. She searched for Jake's old brogans but saw mostly farm work-boots, ankle boots, cowboy boots and Sunday dress-up wingtips on the feet tramping past.

Josh stirred again. "Shhh," she told him. "Doc Collins will be here soon." She crooned an old Indian song about the earth, wind, and sky, and held Josh's head. He was breathing fine. The wound didn't look so bad now that the bleeding had stopped.

Pidge

Chapter Twenty Five

Outside the tent Pidge sat on a wooden box, put her head between her knees, breathed deep, and counted to ten.

"You okay?" Arthur handed her a wet cloth.

She sat up and wiped her face. "Thanks, the tension in there about did me in."

"I understand." He handed her a glass of water.

She drank it and stood up. "I'd better get back. Sounds like the baby hurricane is revving up again." She returned to the tent.

"Almost time." Rose gave her a glance. "Contractions getting closer and dilation larger."

Rose pulled white pants and smock over her clothing and slipped plastic gloves on her hands. Her hair was covered by a net and tied with a cloth.

"I hear sounds outside," Rose told Pidge. "It could be Doc Collins." Pidge stepped out of the tent.

Before her stood men wearing white sheets and Ku Klux Klan head gear. They marched in place, chanting. The lead Klansman held a noose, with a length of rope dragging behind him.

"Run," yelled Arthur as he sent out the low-pitched danger-warning whistle Pidge had taught him.

He grabbed at Pidge, but she jerked away and skittered back into the tent. "Mom, there's a crowd of Ku

Klux Klan people right in front of the tent, chanting something and planting a big wooden cross."

"What!" Rose rushed outside. Before her, men hacked at a hole in the dirt, hoisting a huge cross. "You people crazy?" She swatted at the nearest man, grabbed his Klan hat and pitched it to the ground.

"We don't need white sheets parading around here, we need kindness and civility. A baby is being born. Get away from here."

The Klansman holding the noose chanted "Aaron, Aaron," with other voices behind him following his lead, chanting louder and louder, moving their feet up and down, marching in place.

"Rose," yelled Fiona from inside the tent. "The baby's moving down, fast!"

"Git! Git!" Rose screamed and grabbed the noose as she shoved the Klansman to the ground.

"I see the head," Aaron called out.

A Klansmen grabbed at Rose, one stepped on the rope and sprawled in the dirt as Rose jerked it away. Still holding the noose, Rose pushed other Klansmen aside and ran back into the tent, dropping the noose in front of David, who snatched it up and ran to the front of the tent.

Rose grabbed a fresh pair of rubber gloves. "Hold on Jasmine. Hold on. The baby is coming out."

Aaron's knees gave way. He knelt beside Jasmine. "Wipe her face," Rose told Aaron. "Oh, no," she saw the baby had turned and was coming out backward. "A breach birth." Reaching her hands inside the birth canal, she turned the baby, guiding its head forward.

"Doris, wipe Aaron's face. Fiona, I saw your husband out there."

"No!" Fiona ran outside and gazed in amazement at the chanting Klansmen in a row before her. "How could you men do something like this while a baby is being born into the world? Are you stark raving mad?" Her voice rose high in the air. "Go home! Stop this nonsense."

Then she saw him. "Richard? Is that you?" Fiona snatched her husband's headgear off and grabbed the sheet, jerking it over his head. "You're wearing the pink sheet Linda put in the Free Box," she screamed.

"He's color blind," a voice offered from the crowd.

"Aaron, Aaron," the Klansmen chanted as their feet moved up and down in cadence. Several held the cross, trying to set it afire. A slosh of kerosene missed the wood and landed on David's foot. He leaned over and pitched the noose into the flames under the bucket of boiling water hanging over the firepit.

"Hold fast," Jeremiah told the others, who had formed a circle of protection around the tent where the baby was being born.

Fiona grabbed her husband by the arm and jerked him inside. "You've done some stupid things, but this takes the cake. People could die tonight, and it would be your fault."

"I can explain." Richard stammered.

Fiona pushed him aside. "There is no explanation to this. I'll see to you later. Stand there and watch while we catch the baby."

Rose held out her arms and guided the baby toward her. "What a beautiful head."

"Is it a boy or girl?" Aaron held tightly to Jasmine.

Rose wiped the membrane from the baby's body while Fiona tied off the umbilical cord. As the hands were cleared the baby flipped and pulled upward on Jasmine's body with both hands, its mouth opening and closing, head swinging from side to side, searching for the breast. Rose laughed.

"The breast crawl. It's a girl. A beautiful little girl, with a head of coal black hair."

As the baby clamped its mouth on the nipple, Jasmine gave a squeal, then a sigh of relief, of happiness. "Look at our baby, Aaron."

The new father gazed at his wife and child. "Is it over, Rose?"

"Not yet. We have the afterbirth coming. It won't feel as bad as the baby being born, but it will hurt."

As the women cleaned up Jasmine and the birthing site, Pidge bagged up soiled sheets and rags.

Rose noticed Richard standing as if in shock at the side of the tent. "You've seen a baby born before, haven't you?"

"No," he said. "Mandy was born in a hospital. I sat in the lobby."

"Now you know what happens when women bear children. Huh?" She chucked him on the shoulder with her elbow, holding bloody sheathed hands high.

Richard gave a frightened smile.

Pidge's eyes were round. What an amazing thing. She felt shock at the pain and the sight of so much blood, but proud to be a girl, a woman someday. Birth was no longer a secret thing, whispered about among her friends. She was now a part of that spiritual, mystical, and creative universe. *A human being just came from another person's body. That's how life begins.*

"Isn't this the most beautiful baby you've ever seen?" exclaimed Fiona.

"I'll never look at a baby the same way again." Pidge's knees felt shaky. "Now that I've seen where a newborn person comes from."

Rose collected the afterbirth and smoothed the sack-like object. "I heard some women eat the placenta. It's supposed to be filled with vitamins and minerals to get the body back on track."

"I'll take your word for it." Jasmine shifted under the suckling baby girl.

"While you're cleaning up, I'll pitch this in the barrel," Rose told Fiona.

"No, keep it for me." Jasmine's face rose above the baby's head. "I want to sketch it, so I can show it to her."

"Sure." Fiona took the afterbirth and smoothed it, then placed it in on a shelf. "It looks like a leather handbag."

Rose stepped outside, holding the bucket filled with bloody water.

Before her stood the angry Dauber. "You low-life, helping a hippie give birth," he snarled, raised his hand and slapped her across the face.

Rose almost lost her footing. A hard flash of anger washed over her. She looked at the man before her, his eyes filled with hate, and slung the contents of the bucket into his face.

Dauber staggered backwards, yelling curses as he swiped at gobs of blood and membrane dripping onto his Klan costume. "Grab her," he yelled to the white-sheet garbed men around him. Eyes were wide with surprise, but not a man moved to follow his instructions.

When Granny Blue Sky, who was still in the ditch with Josh, heard angry screaming she had recognized the voice. Rose seemed to be attacking the Ku Klux Klan. Granny Blue Sky raised her head and she could see men protesters circling the tent, like watchmen, holding chunks of kindling wood.

Sirens wailed. Granny Blue Sky wished Josh was awake to see the next wonderful sight: Sheriff Clark's patrol cars flashing across the bridge.

At that moment the lines of marching Klansmen broke ranks and many skittered down the embankment, running past where Granny Blue Sky still huddled over Josh. They ran through the ditch, across the highway, and into the woods, dropping sheets and Klan headpieces as they went.

"A bunch of scared jackrabbits," muttered Granny Blue Sky. "Wake up, Josh." Suddenly the low whistle Josh's family used echoed across the campground. One whistle after the other. The hippies called the warning. At the sound, Josh's head snapped up. He rose from his waist.

"Something's wrong with my legs," he told Granny Blue Sky.

"You'll be all right, Josh. You fell." She tugged at one of his arms. "Hang on. Sheriff Clark and his posse have arrived."

Revolving lights atop the sheriff's vehicles gave a surreal cast to the campgrounds. At that instant a baby's cry overreached all other sounds. "Boy or girl?" Sheriff Clark called out.

"Girl," answered Rose.

"Sheriff Clark and his deputies are cleaning up the chaos out there," said Rose. "Wonder what happened to Josh and Doc Collins. Linda and Rev. Willy for that matter." She opened her arms and hugged Pidge and Fiona, then Doris and Cindy. "We did all right without them, didn't we?"

"Speak for yourself," Fiona told her. "I'm a wreck."

"I don't know what I am, but it was a sight to see." Pidge took a deep breath and pulled herself up to her full height. "I won't ever forget I watched a baby being born."

Sheriff Clark wasn't missing a beat, bellowing orders to deputies from a bullhorn. "When you fill the cars, cuff the rest and put them into the old school bus. I

258

want every sorry one of them booked on everything from endangering lives and disturbing the peace, to trespassing, threatening, and anything else you can think of."

The patrol cars filled with Klan members, minus sheets and headpieces. The protesters sawed the two-by-fours of the Klan cross to feed a giant bonfire. Every shred of the noose and rope had burned.

When Granny Blue Sky stood to tug at Josh, a light flashed into the ditch and Doc Collins ran toward them, his wife beside him.

"Is he hurt?" The doctor plopped beside Josh and opened his bag.

"I'm going to the tent, to see about the baby." Mavis ran.

"Stay by my side," Doc called out. But she was already gone.

The doctor put gauze over Josh's head wound, while Josh pushed at the ground, trying to stand.

"I think my left ankle's broken or sprained." Josh turned paste-white and sat back in the ditch.

John Walters, the short, wiry newspaper editor, ran from the highway, waving his Speed-graphic camera. "What did I miss?"

"Josh is injured. Sheriff Clark's men are collecting the Klan members for jail." Doc Collins put both hands under Josh's arm. "Get his other side."

As the men lifted Josh to his feet, Granny Blue Sky jumped up and ran to Sheriff Clark.

"Help," she called as loud as she could. It came out a croak.

Sheriff Clark looked down at Granny Blue Sky. "Are you okay?"

"I am, but Josh isn't." She led Sheriff Clark to the ditch. A shaky Josh stood, balanced on his right leg. Walters let go and snapped a picture. Sheriff Clark took

Josh's arm. He and the doctor helped him onto the front seat of Doc Collins' car.

"Is my ankle broken?"

"I don't think so. Just sprained. It will need x-rays. Sit here," Doc Collins told him. "I'll check on the baby and be back."

David's voice boomed over the campground. He held one of Sheriff Clark's bullhorns. "Gather every sheet, headgear, anything that looks like the Ku Klux Klan, and throw it on the bonfire."

Pidge stood before the tent, gazing at the scene.

"Look at me," Orion called out. "I'm a miniature Klansman."

"Sure you are." Pidge grabbed at the sheet he had wrapped around himself. "You're a doofus."

Grant dragged a bundle of sheets toward the fire. "You two help pick up Klan stuff for the bonfire."

Pidge and Orion gathered Klan costumes from the sides of tents, off guy wires, against car fronts and truck tires. Plus they got sheets and headpieces deputies had snatched from the men as they had clicked on handcuffs.

"We ought to count them," Grant said as he took an armful from Pidge.

"What does it matter?" Orion asked. "The deputies will count the yahoos when they book them into the jail."

Mavis Collins burst into the tent. "Rose!" she called out. I'm too late for the birthing, aren't I?"

"You're just in time to see Jasmine and Aaron's new baby girl."

"We missed you." Fiona hugged Mavis. "Pidge, Doris and Cindy helped."

Rose held out a spray bottle and rag. "There's always cleaning up to do."

The women stood in awe as the baby nursed. "Birth," said Mavis reverently. "It's an awesome thing."

Doc Collins poked his head in at the door. "Am I at the right tent?"

"About time you got here." Rose grinned as she piled pillows behind Jasmine's back.

"You did fine without me, didn't you?"

"We managed. But we missed you."

"It's a girl." Aaron held out the baby.

"Aaahh, what a beauty. Got all her toes and fingers." As Doc Collins unwrapped the baby, she suddenly opened her mouth and bellowed. He rewrapped her and smiled. "Great lungs, too."

The bellowing stopped as quickly as it had begun when Aaron rocked her back and forth. "Oooh, my sweet baby girl," he cooed.

Doc Collins patted his shoulder. "It's amazing how fatherhood turns men into simpering clowns."

"I know," said Aaron. "It's the coolest."

Doc held out his finger, and the baby latched on to it. "I agree, Aaron," he said and turned to Jasmine.

"How do you feel?" He lifted her arm to check her pulse.

"Exhausted." She gave him a wan smile. "But happy."

"You rest, and sleep. You may be tired, but you're beaming like the sun. Your baby appears healthy and ready for whatever life has to offer."

"I weighed her," Rose told him. "She's eight pounds, six ounces, if we can believe the hand-held scale. She measured out at 20 inches." She pulled out her pad and pen to finish recording the birth.

Doc Collins took the pen and signed the birth record. "What are you naming her?"

"Rose for, uh, Rose, and Ann, for my mother."
She looked a question at Aaron.

Aaron wiped a hand across his flushed face.
"That's a beautiful name."

"Fine baby," Doc Collins said. "Let's not move
Jasmine for the night. She'll be okay here. Looks like the
boys and Sheriff Clark have everything under control. We
can do a complete check tomorrow at my office."

"Right on, man." Aaron, the new father, reverted
to hippie talk. "It was far out."

Doc Collins turned to Rose. "You need to get a
good night's rest, so you can bring this family to my
office in the morning. Come on, I'll take you home." Doc
Collins picked up his satchel.

"I'm fine with that." Rose shrugged out of her
bloody clothes, rolled them in a ball, tugged the handle of
her birthing bag over her shoulder.

"Fiona, could you stay with them? And Mavis, in
case there are any complications?"

"Sure." Fiona wiped her hot face with a wet cloth.

Mavis threw her husband a kiss and turned back to
cleaning the area with disinfectant.

Rose headed for the door of the tent. "Sheriff
Clark said his wife wouldn't let him fill up the jail with
hippies. Wonder where he's putting the Klan members."

"The armory in Bonifay?" Doc looked at Richard
on the tent floor, his head hanging on his chest, fast
asleep. "What about him?"

"Let's leave him be," answered Fiona. "If he goes
outside, he might wind up in a paddy wagon."

When Pidge saw the doctor come out of the tent,
with her mother close behind, she dropped her armful of
white sheets and ran to them.

"I'm ready," Rose told the doctor.

"Mom, you going home?"

"Yes. Come with us."

"I could stay and go with Dad later," Pidge said. "Where is he?"

"I don't know. He was to bring Granny Blue Sky, but they never showed up."

"They're fine," Doc Collins told her. "Josh has a busted head and a turned ankle. Granny Blue Sky is out there with him."

"Where?" Pidge asked.

"Just past the campground entrance. In my car."

My dad's hurt. Granny Blue Sky's with him.

"Thanks, Doc." Pidge ran, her feet moving like pistons, past the bonfire, around people, through scattered sheets, to the ditch, and to Doc Collins' car. She could see a leg sticking out the door and another folded on its knee.

"Dad!" she screamed. Then there he was. He reached out. She jumped into his arms. Half on his lap, trying to avoid his injured leg.

Granny Blue Sky eased out of the back seat. Pidge threw one arm around her dad's neck and another around the old midwife.

"Frances?"

"We left her at the store with Luke, Uncle Jim, and the girls." Josh pulled loose and Pidge stood up.

A smile spread across Granny Blue Sky's wrinkled face. "You helped your mother with the birthing?"

"I don't know how much help I was. But, what I saw," Pidge started, then broke into tears, "was a person come right out of the body of another person."

Her father enclosed her small hand in his big one. "I know how it feels. I was there when you were born."

Granny Blue Sky patted Pidge on the back. "I am so proud of you, Pidge. You shared in the miracle of birth. What you saw will be a part of yourself, always. It's a privilege you won't soon forget.

Epilogue

Rose's fight with the Klan did not go unnoticed. John Walters called her courageous in the newspaper. Sheriff Clark asked about charges against Joe Dauber for slapping her. She laughed. "Dousing him with blood from the baby's birth is enough satisfaction for me."

Dauber was punished by the law. The other Klansmen caught in the raid were fined $500 each and given warnings, but the Judge sentenced Dauber to the prison at Lake Butler for a year and a day and fined him $1,000. Sarah Mae Dauber apologized to Josh and Rose for the trouble her husband had caused in the community. "He wasn't always so cruel. He changed. He became so filled with hate, one day I realized I was a captive in my own home. He'll come out of prison a different man, or he won't live here, at least not with me."

Pidge's punishment for socking Roland was two weeks in-school study-hall detention where she would help him with his homework. They became friends, and he made all A's for his first time ever. Frances stayed with Granny Blue Sky and Jimmy John, and finished out the school year, excelling in basketball, much to Coach Whittle's delight. Her parents came to visit, then returned to California, promising a longer visit next time.

Josh rode in the passenger's seat and the young family in the back seat as Rose took them to see Dr. Collins. Rose Ann and Jasmine were declared healthy.

Josh received twenty-three stitches on his scalp, a bandage around his sprained ankle, and a pair of crutches.

Both sets of grandparents arrived soon after Rose Ann's birth. Aaron and Jasmine decided to stay in New Hope for awhile. Aaron would repair vehicles until all the protesters were gone, then help Josh plow and plant peas, butterbeans, okra, and crooked neck squash at the river field.

Historical Note

Some of the protesters went back the way they had come, but most of them continued their plans to gather in the Georgia field and be ready to join in an Atlanta march. Jonah was among them, along with several of his friends, including Wilbur who had chosen to follow a pretty girl. From there, the activists joined 100,000 others at a May 9, 1970, protest in Washington, D.C., making their voices heard in objection to the war in Vietnam and the invasion of Cambodia.

Eleven days after the four Kent State students were shot to death on May 4, 1970, two students were killed at Jackson State College in Jackson, MS, on May 15, 1970.

Over the country, demonstrators marched, made speeches and held sit-ins. Many went to Canada to escape the military draft. Anti-war protesters burned draft cards. Violence escalated over the United States after the Pentagon Papers, leaked to the press in 1971, revealed that President Richard Nixon and military leaders appeared to have no intentions of closing down the unpopular war in Vietnam.

The rebel look started entering mainstream fashion. Hair became extremely important. Young men and boys often grew their hair to the shoulders and longer. Some wore ponytails. Big, bushy Afros were popular. Girls and women wore long, straight hair and wild curly manes. It was all about the natural look, even with makeup.

Girls wore colorful mini-skirts, long flowing skirts, peasant blouses, vintage clothes, and bright headbands. Boys and girls wore tie-dyed tee shirts, bell-bottom jeans, cutoffs, Jesus sandals, and rope sandals.

Many radio stations refused to play anti-war songs in protest of the Vietnam War, which had started out Nov.

1, 1955 as the Second Indochina War. The U. S. had joined to offer military assistance as South Vietnam was "trying to restrict Communist domination." The "assistance" had escalated when in March, 1965, the U. S. landed 3,500 Marines in South Vietnam. By 1968, more than 500,000 U. S. troops were in the country. That 10-year leg of the war was filled with protest marches, outcries, flag-burning and sit-ins. The draft ended in 1973. The end of the war was announced on April 30, 1975. The attitude of youth, especially college students, had been one of rage, alienation, and insolence, throughout the late fifties, sixties and early seventies.

Protest songs fanned the anti-war movement, including Pete Seeger's "Turn! Turn! Turn!" (1959), "Bring 'em Home," (1966), Arlo Guthrie's satirical "Alice's Restaurant" (1967) and John Lennon's "Give Peace a Chance" (1969). Cat Stevens introduced "Peace Train" in a 1970s concert and it became popular with young people over the country long before being released in an album in 1971.

Among war protest songs buried in haunting melodies and plaintive words (in order to pass scrutiny by radio and television) was Peter Paul and Mary's 1963 rendition of "Blowin' in the Wind," written by Bob Dylan. It points to President Richard Nixon with the words, "How many deaths will it take 'till he knows / That too many people have died?"

The '70s geared up the protests in songs like the poignant, heartbreaking lyrics by Crosby, Stills, Nash, and Young (1970) with "Tin soldiers and Nixon coming / we're finally on our own / This summer I hear the drumming / Four dead in Ohio." Another song, "What About Me?" by Quicksilver Messenger Service (1970) declared "I can't get behind your wars." One called "War," by Edwin Starr (1970) went "What is it Good For? Absolutely nothing, Good God Why Y'all?" Marvin

Gaye's "What's Going On" (1971) "Far too many of you dying" was number 4 on *Rolling Stone* magazine's list of top 500 songs of all time.

John Lennon's "Imagine" with moving lyrics, "Imagine all the people/ Living Life in Peace," remained a radio staple for many decades after it was recorded in 1971.

Over time alternative songs and albums came to be known as Classic Rock music.

After the war Army fatigue jackets also became standard teenager attire, along with faded jeans, loose tops, tie-dyed tunics, caftans, ponchos, and native-American style jackets with leather fringe.

~ ~ ~

Included are some Protester-Hippie language still common in the 2020s. These are mostly from my memory, and certainly not all inclusive. There are probably many more. Add the words you remember that are now a part of our language. Many have been added to dictionaries.

Bad scene = terrible
Bag = belief, preference
Bookin' = headin' on
Bread = money
Brother = close friend or acquaintance
Bug out, or bug off = get out of here
Bummer = bad thing
Burn rubber = scratch off in a car
Burned out = exhausted
Catch some rays = get in the sun

Catch some z's = take a nap
Chill out = stay calm
Cool = even tempered, progressive,
          acceptable-to-awesome
Cool cat = awesome person
Crash = go to sleep
Crocked = drunk or stoned
Cut out = leave
Dibs = first choice
Dig it = understand or agree
Dough = money
Downer = not so good
Down with = in agreement with
Dude = male
Fakin' = lying
Far out = incredible, stellar
Flee the scene = leave
Flower child = term for protester
Freak out = get excited; go weird
Funny money = counterfeit
Fuzz = police
Get down = to the nitty-gritty (basics)
Gimme some skin = shake hands
Go ape = weird out
Groovy = very good, fun
Hang it up = to quit
Hang loose = stay relaxed
Hang out = stay around
Hip = fashionably cool
Hustle = fake off, or lie to
Jive = talking nonsense
Laid back = calm, cool and collected
Lay it on me = tell it straight
Let it all hang out = be open and free
Make tracks = leave, fast
Man = exclamation

Mess = problem
Mop top = Beatle haircut
No problem = don't sweat over it
No sweat = stay calm
Outta sight = great
Pad = Place to crash
Pits = low down
Rad = radical
Right on = Agree
Righteous = fantastic
Rockin' out = great fun
Soak up some rays = get some sun
Sock it to me = Tell the truth
Spaced out = stoned
Split = Leave
Stoned = High on pot or drugs
Swappin' spit = kissing
Talkin' trash = lies or garbage
Threads = clothes
Toke = take a puff on a joint
The man = Number one guy
Turn off = disgust, bore
We're tight = friends
What's your bag? = what are you into?
Way out = far out
Wig out = go wild

ACKNOWLEGEMENTS

As a journalist during protests against the war in Vietnam, I was exposed to stories in the news every day (some widely reported, some overlooked). I saw young people swarming to marches and sit-ins who became stranded in small communities. They often faced confrontations, sometimes with the Ku Klux Klan.

For comic relief I added to the mix an old myth about a fire-eating dragon/alligator which ambled down from Alabama into West Florida. According to the tales I heard, he settled not far from where I grew up on the Choctawhatchee River. The enduring legend is that his tracks can be seen at Sand Hammock Pond near Esto, where a Two Toe Tom festival is held each year.

I may not have finished *White Sheets*, or my first novel if it hadn't been for lots of heavy-duty nudging. "That's good. crank out another one," Mary Putman told me after reading *Louette's Wake*.

My daughter Alda Thomas, who also writes, praised the book, made suggestions, and assisted with the final draft. Grandson Daniel Thomas (a poet and published author) did an early read and offered helpful advice. Granddaughter Merri Rose Fink (who has a degree in graphic design and has worked on other books) fine-tuned the covers. The whimsical artwork is by another granddaughter who cheered me toward the finish line.

Brenda Ameter insisted that I had fiction-writing abilities; Dawn Radford and Adrian Fogelin edited and plotted, trimmed and critiqued; Persis Granger, with the Fiction Among Friends writing retreat, served up fun and writing companions. Nancy Campbell and Anita Smith never gave up on me. These, and many other lifelong friends, keep me aware that I should continue my efforts to wrap hard truths in words of humor and hope.

AUTHOR with laptop, leaning against a large
pecan tree at Mims Hill near Geneva, AL.

Photo by Debra Brackin

Sue Riddle Cronkite spent her early years in the
Wiregrass, attended New Hope elementary school
and Ponce de Leon high school, both in Florida, and
began her newspaper career in Geneva, Alabama, and
other Wiregrass towns. She worked with the *Birmingham*
(AL) *News* and returned to the area as executive editor of
Wiregrass TODAY. She was a correspondent for *Life
Magazine* and was honored by *USA TODAY* newspaper
as one of the top 100 university scholars in the country
in 1995. She has had many short stories published and
a novel, *Louette's Wake*.

Made in the USA
Columbia, SC
23 June 2021